DEATH
AND THE
OLIVE GROVE

D0842083

Also by Marco Vichi

Death in August

About the author

Marco Vichi was born in Florence in 1957. The author of eleven novels and two collections of short stories, he has also edited crime anthologies, written screenplays, music lyrics and for radio, written for Italian newspapers and magazines, and collaborated on and directed various projects for humanitarian causes.

There are four novels and two short stories featuring Inspector Bordelli. The latest novel, *Death in Florence* (*Morte a Firenze*), won the Scerbanenco, Rieti, Camaiore and Azzeccagarbugli prizes in Italy. Marco Vichi lives in the Chianti region of Tuscany.

You can find out more at www.marcovichi.it.

About the translator

Stephen Sartarelli is an award-winning translator. He is also the author of three books of poetry. He lives in France.

MARCO VICHI

DEATH AND THE OLIVE GROVE

AN
INSPECTOR BORDELLI
NOVEL

Originally published in Italian as *Una Brutta Faccenda*
Translated by Stephen Sartarelli

HODDER &
STOUGHTON

First published in Great Britain in 2012 by Hodder & Stoughton
An Hachette UK company

I

Copyright © Ugo Guanda Editore, S.p.A., Parma 2003
Translation copyright © Stephen Sartarelli 2012

The right of Marco Vichi to be identified as the Author
of the Work has been asserted by him in accordance with
the Copyright, Designs and Patents Act 1988.

All rights reserved. No part of this publication may be
reproduced, stored in a retrieval system, or transmitted, in any form
or by any means without the prior written permission of the publisher,
nor be otherwise circulated in any form of binding or cover
other than that in which it is published and without a similar condition
being imposed on the subsequent purchaser.

All characters in this publication are fictitious and any resemblance
to real persons, living or dead is purely coincidental.

A CIP catalogue record for this title is available
from the British Library

Hardback ISBN 978 1 444 71223 0
Trade Paperback ISBN 978 1 444 71363 3

Typeset in Plantin Light by Palimpsest Book Production Limited,
Falkirk, Stirlingshire
Printed and bound by Clays Ltd, St Ives plc

Hodder & Stoughton policy is to use papers that are natural, renewable and
recyclable products and made from wood grown in sustainable forests. The
logging and manufacturing processes are expected to conform to the
environmental regulations of the country of origin.

Hodder & Stoughton Ltd
338 Euston Road
London NW1 3BH

www.hodder.co.uk

for Franco, my father

Our every act of knowledge begins with a feeling

Leonardo

To the vain, time turns all remedies into water

Anonymous, 21st century

Florence, April 1964

At nine o'clock in the evening a tiny little man no taller than a child came through the front door of the police station, out of breath. He pressed up against the windowpane of the guard's booth, yelling politely that he wanted to speak with the inspector. Mugnai, inside, told him to calm down and asked him which inspector he was referring to. The dwarf squashed a dirty hand against the glass and yelled:

'Inspector Bordelli!' as if Bordelli were the only inspector in the place.

'What if he's not here?' asked Mugnai.

'I saw his Beetle outside,' said the little man. In the end he was let in. Mugnai gestured to his colleague Taddei, a burly sort with bovine eyes who was new on the job. Taddei got up with effort from his chair and, with the dwarf following behind, started climbing the stairs. At the end of a long corridor on the first floor, he stopped in front of Inspector Bordelli's door.

'Wait here,' he said, glancing at the tiny stranger's shabby shoes, which were still smeared with mud after a cursory cleaning. Then he knocked, disappeared behind the door, and came back out a few seconds later.

'Go on in,' he said.

The little man hurriedly slipped inside and Taddei heard Bordelli say:

'Casimiro, what on earth are you doing here?' Then the door suddenly closed. Unsure, Taddei scratched his head and knocked again. He stuck his head respectfully inside.

'Need anything, Inspector?'

'No, thanks. You can go now.'

Casimiro, repeatedly swallowing, waited silently for the ox to shut the door. He declined a cigarette from the inspector and remained standing in front of the desk.

'What's wrong, Casimiro? You seem agitated.'

'I've just seen something, Inspector, up Fiesole way . . . I was walking through a field and—'

'If you don't want to smoke, have a beer at least,' said Bordelli, pointing towards the bottom drawer of a filing cabinet on the other side of the office. 'I'll have one too, please,' he added.

Casimiro dashed over and got the bottles, setting them down nervously on the desk. He was anxious to speak. Bordelli calmly opened the beers, flipping off the bottle-caps with his house keys, and passed one to Casimiro. The little man drank half of it in a single draught, grew a bit calmer, and finally sat down. The inspector avidly took two swigs, splashing his shirt, then set the bottle down on some of the papers strewn all across his desk. Hanging on the wall behind him was a dusty photo of the President of the Republic, with a horseshoe appended from the same nail. The air in the office always smelled of rotten cardboard and mushrooms, Bordelli thought.

Casimiro was squirming in his chair. He was wearing a child's jacket that was actually too big for him. Bordelli studied the dwarf's face, which was small and narrow, as if it had been crushed in a closing door. He'd known him since the end of the war, and the little man had always had the same tragic, nervous look about him. One rarely saw him laugh. At most he might make a bad joke about his physical condition and then snigger. Bordelli in his way was fond of him and had even, on occasion, invented phoney jobs for him as an informer, so he could give him a little money without making him feel too embarrassed.

'I was passing that way by chance, Inspector . . . If I hadn't seen it with my own eyes—'

'Sorry to interrupt, Casimiro, but the second of the month was my birthday.'

'Happy birthday . . .'

'Is that all?'

'What do you want me to say, Inspector?'

Bordelli felt like chatting that evening, perhaps because he was very tired . . . He could only imagine what sort of rubbish Casimiro had to tell him.

'Aren't you going to ask me how old I am?' he said.

'How old are you?'

'Fifty-four, Casimiro, and I have no desire to grow old. Fifty-four, and still, when I go home, I have no one to kiss me on the lips.'

'Why don't you get a dog, Inspector?' the dwarf said in all seriousness. Bordelli smiled and slowly crushed his cigarette butt in the already full ashtray. Picking up his beer, he leaned back in his chair. The bottle had left a damp ring on a report.

'Just think, Casimiro, maybe, at this very moment, in some part of the world, the woman I have always been looking for has just been born. But if she was born today, by the time she's twenty I'll be a dotty old bed-wetter. And even if she was born forty years ago, it was probably in Algeria, Poland or Australia . . . Fat chance I'll ever run into her . . . Do you ever think about such things?'

'Inspector, can I tell you what I saw?'

'Of course, forgive me,' said Bordelli, resigned.

Casimiro set his beer down on the desk and stood up, growing agitated again.

'I was walking through a field and almost tripped over a dead body,' he said in a single breath, for fear the inspector might interrupt him again.

'Are you sure?' asked Bordelli.

'Of course I'm sure. He was dead, Inspector. Blood was dripping from his mouth.'

'Where was this?'

'Just past Fiesole,' Casimiro said darkly.

Bordelli stood up and, with one hand, grabbed his cigarettes and matches and, with the other, took his jacket from the back of his chair.

'What were you doing up there at this hour, Casimiro?'

'I was just passing through,' the dwarf said with lying eyes.

'Let's go and have a look at this corpse,' said Bordelli, walking out of the office.

'But what about my bicycle?' Casimiro asked, trotting beside him.

'We'll load it into my car.'

Reaching the end of the Viale Volga, they turned on to the road that led up to Fiesole. Past San Domenico they began to see the city below, a great dark blot dotted with points of light. A pile of cow shit with little candles on top, thought Bordelli.

Casimiro's short legs were stretched over the seat, his worn-out shoes barely reaching the edge. He was quiet and fiddling with a good-luck charm, a little plastic skeleton barely an inch long, with two tiny pieces of red glass in the eye sockets. He'd been carrying it with him for years, and Bordelli had stopped ribbing him about it some time ago.

Past the piazza at Fiesole, the little man said to turn down the Via del Bargellino, and a few hundred yards on, he began to look around nervously.

'Stop here, Inspector,' he said suddenly, jumping to his feet on the car seat. Bordelli parked the Beetle in an unpaved clearing and got out. Casimiro hopped down, more agitated than ever.

'I'll lead the way, Inspector.' He climbed up the small, dilapidated retaining wall beside the road and began to penetrate the low, dense vegetation. Bordelli followed behind him, looking around with care. High in the sky, a big bright moon cast a lugubrious glow on the countryside, but in compensation made it easy to see. To the right was a large, untilled field with a few now withered vines and several ivy-smothered trees. It seemed a shame to see a field reduced to such a state.

'You said you were passing this way by chance?' Bordelli asked, laughing.

'Sort of,' said Casimiro, continuing hurriedly through the brush.

'Meaning?'

'I haven't got a lira in my pocket, Inspector, what am I supposed to do?'

'What do you mean?'

'Well, now and then I have to go out and look for vegetables.'

'Around this time there should be some beans.'

'It's still a bit early for that. For the moment, there's only cabbage . . . Come, let's turn here.'

'It's probably full of toads,' Bordelli said in disgust, hoping not to step on any. The grass was tall and damp and he could already feel his shoes getting wet. It had rained all week, and every so often he stepped in a mud puddle. The air felt almost cold. Spring couldn't make up its mind to arrive.

'Is it much farther?'

'It's down there,' Casimiro said softly, his little feet practically running. After passing through a muddy thicket they came out into a rather well-tended olive grove. The ground was densely carpeted with a short grassy weed. After all the mud, it was a pleasure to walk on. The light of the moon was so bright that their shadows were sharply outlined on the ground. And everything in shadow was all the darker.

'We're almost there,' the little man whispered, slowing his pace. Farther ahead, towering above them, was an eighteenth-century villa, a massive structure built on a steep embankment. The garden loomed sheer over the field, supported by a high, curved wall reinforced by great buttresses covered with ivy. The stone balustrade that ran along the top of the wall was the boundary between two worlds. The shutters on the villa's windows were all closed, and no light could be seen filtering through. Casimiro stopped a few yards from the wall, in front of a gigantic olive tree, and looked around in disbelief.

'The dead man was here, Inspector . . . I swear he was here!'

Bordelli threw up his hands.

'Apparently he woke up,' he said, laughing. Casimiro still couldn't believe it and kept walking round the olive tree. At a certain point he bent down to pick something up.

'Look, Inspector,' he said, holding up a bottle. Bordelli grabbed it by the neck. It was made of colourless glass and rather small, and there was still a bit of dark liquid at the bottom. It was clean and could not have been outside for very long. He read the label: *Cognac de Maricourt, 1913*. He didn't know it. He pulled out the cork and sniffed it. It smelled like good cognac. He overcame the urge to have a sip and put the cork back in.

'The body was right here! I'm not crazy!' Casimiro insisted. 'Maybe he was only drunk.' The inspector put the bottle in his jacket pocket and, with the little man following behind him, approached the buttresses. They were huge and well constructed. Seen from there, the stone wall seemed even higher.

'What did this dead man look like?' Bordelli asked wearily.

'I didn't get a good look at him . . . I was walking and, suddenly, there he was in front of me, and I ran away . . . All I saw was that he had blood around his—'

'Quiet!' said Bordelli, pricking up his ears. All at once they heard the sound of hurried footsteps and panting, and on the moon-whitened turf appeared the silhouette of a short-haired dog running towards them. The most visible part of it was its teeth, which shone like wet marble. The inspector barely had time to pull out his Beretta and shoot the animal square in the mouth. The Doberman yelped and its feet gave out from under it, but in the momentum of its charge it rolled forward into Bordelli's legs, knocking him to the ground. It cried out again, kicking its feet in the air for a few seconds, then drew its legs in and stopped moving.

'Shit . . .' said Bordelli.

'We're lucky you're a good shot,' said Casimiro, voice quavering slightly.

'Where the hell are you?' said Bordelli, unable to see him.

'Up here, Inspector.' Casimiro had climbed up an olive tree and was already coming down. Bordelli put his pistol away and got up. He looked around. Half his jacket was wet and his trousers were spattered with blood. He cleaned himself as best he could with a handkerchief, then knelt forward to have a better look at the Doberman. Its muzzle was a bloody pulp, and it had no collar.

'You know, Casimiro, I don't like the look of this one bit,' said Bordelli, looking up, but the little man was no longer there. He glanced around and saw him running through the olive trees towards the woods. He decided to let him go. He took a few steps back to get a full view of the villa. It was still all dark. The gunshot apparently hadn't woken anyone up. The house was either uninhabited, he thought, or whoever lived there was a heavy sleeper. He lit a cigarette and headed towards the woods. When he reached the car, he found the dwarf sitting on the bonnet, arms folded round his legs, eyes still flashing with fear.

'What got into you, Casimiro?'

'If I'd been alone he would have torn me to pieces,' the little man replied, shuddering.

'Do you come this way often?' asked Bordelli, cleaning his shoes against the wall's rocks.

'Now and then,' said Casimiro, hopping down from the bonnet and looking around with a tense expression on his face.

They got into the Beetle and headed back towards town. Casimiro sat there stiff and silent, the little skeleton between his fingers. They were already at the Regresso bend when Bordelli abruptly stopped the car.

'What are you doing, Inspector?'

'I'm going back up there.'

'Why?'

'I don't know,' said Bordelli. He made a U-turn and headed back up towards Fiesole, stepping on the accelerator. The Beetle's vibrations came straight up into their backbones. A short distance later he turned again on to the Via del Bargellino and parked in the same spot. He opened the car door and put one foot outside.

'You're not coming?' he asked Casimiro, seeing that he hadn't moved.

'I'd rather wait here,' the little man said gloomily.

'Suit yourself.' Bordelli got out of the car and, retracing the same route, rushed back to the olive grove. The moon was beginning to light up the walls of the villa, which made it look even more abandoned. He approached the buttresses, gun drawn, and saw at once that the Doberman's carcass was gone. All that remained was a bit of blood on the grass. He checked the immediate surroundings, but the carpet of compact grass showed no footprints. He shook his head, thinking he'd acted stupidly. If only he hadn't left the scene . . .

All at once he heard a sound of crunching gravel that seemed to come from the villa's garden. He crouched instinctively behind a buttress, hiding in the shadow. Looking up, he saw a man's head peer out over the balustrade at the top of the wall. He was able to get a good look at him in the moonlight. The man had very white hair and a long black mark on his neck. He stood there for a few seconds, scanning the olive grove with his eyes, then disappeared.

There was deep silence. The only sound was the wind rustling the leaves of the olive trees. In the distance a dog began to bark angrily, every so often howling like a wolf. The inspector waited a few more minutes, holding his breath and looking up until the coast seemed clear. He stepped out of the shadow but hugged the wall, to lessen the risk of being seen from the villa. When he found a more shielded path, he headed back towards the woods, turning round repeatedly to look at the house, but seeing no sign of life. He hurried back to the car and found Casimiro standing on the seat with his face against the window.

'The Doberman's gone, but I saw someone look out from the garden above,' said Bordelli, quietly closing the car door.

'That bloody dog . . .' Casimiro said with a tragic look in his eye, clutching his little skeleton.

Bordelli calmly lit a cigarette and blew the smoke against the windscreen.

'Any idea who lives in that house?' he asked the dwarf.

'Some foreigner who's never there.'

'How do you know?'

'Gossip.'

'Foreigner from where?'

'Dunno . . .'

'Where's the entrance to the villa?'

'Up above here, on the Bosconi road . . . Why?'

'Just curious.' The inspector started up the car, turned it round, and drove up to the top of the hill. That man with the black spot on his neck seemed familiar to him . . . He felt as if he had seen someone with a mark like that before . . . Or perhaps it was only his investigative imagination . . .

He turned on to Via Ferrucci, in the direction of the Bosconi. After rounding a few bends he stopped the Beetle in a spot where the shoulder broadened, not far from the villa's gate, which bore a plaque with indecipherable initials on it.

'You wait here,' he said to Casimiro, getting out of the car.

'Where are you going?'

'I just want to go and have a look.'

The road was feebly illuminated by a yellow street lamp. Bordelli arrived at the gate and tried to push it open, but it was locked. The garden was full of high-trunked trees and overgrown plants, which shielded the dark ground from the moonlight. Scattered everywhere were large, empty vases, terracotta jugs, and strange marble statues of varying size and shape. The villa was set back a good way from the road and surrounded by cedars that rose well above the roof. On that side, too, the shutters were closed tight, with no light visible behind them. The inspector pulled the chain of the doorbell and heard it ring solemnly inside the house. There was no reply. He rang it again, and again, then twice consecutively. In the end he saw some light filter out between the slats of one shutter. A small light came on over the stone moulding of the front door, which opened at once. A human silhouette appeared on the threshold.

'Who's there?' asked a woman's voice.

'Police. Could you please open the gate for me?' The woman went back inside, and the gate opened with a click. The inspector pushed the gate open with both hands, making it squeak on its rusted hinges. He entered the garden and headed down the gravel lane, through the shadows cast by the jugs and marble monsters. Wrapped in a black shawl, the woman waited for him on the threshold, in front of the great door, which she had pulled to. She didn't seem dressed in nightclothes and didn't look as if she had just woken up. The inspector stopped in front of her, pulled out his police badge, and bowed slightly.

'Inspector Bordelli's the name. Sorry to disturb you at this hour.'

The woman appeared to be about fifty. She was tall and slender and did not look Italian. She had a hard mouth. She stood there without moving, back erect, watching Bordelli from behind her glasses.

'Vhat can I do for you?' she asked in a strong German accent, pulling the shawl tightly around her. Her hair was all white and gathered into a perfect bun at the back of her head. Bordelli had the feeling that someone was spying on him from behind a shutter on the first floor, but he pretended not to notice.

'And you are Signora . . .?' he asked.

'I am baron's housekeeper,' the woman said icily.

'And his name is . . .?'

'Baron von Hauser.'

'And you are . . .'

'Miss Olga.'

'Is the baron at home?'

'No.'

'May I ask where he is?'

'Baron ist alvays travelink, he's not often at home.'

'Does anyone else live here?'

'No.'

'You live here alone?'

'*Ja.*'

'Year round?'

'I don't understant . . . Vhy all these qvestions?'

'I'm sorry, somebody called in and reported a shooting in this area.'

'I hear nothink, I go to sleep early.'

Bordelli threw his hands up and smiled.

'Well, that's all I have to ask. Sorry again for the disturbance. Goodnight,' he said.

'Goodnight,' the woman replied, poker faced.

Bordelli gave a slight bow of respect and headed back towards the gate, but after taking a few steps he stopped and turned round to face the woman again.

'One more question, Miss Olga . . . Have you got a Doberman in this house?'

'No.'

'Do you know by any chance if any neighbours—?'

'I don't know much about dogs,' the woman interrupted him, with a note of scorn in her voice.

'All right, then. Goodnight,' said Bordelli, and he headed back down the dark garden path. Closing the gate behind him, he noticed that the woman was still standing in the doorway. He walked back towards the Beetle without turning round, and moments later heard the sound of the great door closing.

In the car he found Casimiro asleep. The dwarf's head had fallen to one side, and he was snoring. The moment Bordelli started up the car, the little man raised his head abruptly and rubbed his eyes.

'I wasn't asleep,' he said.

'I'll take you home.'

'Did you discover anything, Inspector?'

'No, but there's something fishy about all this,' said Bordelli, staring into space. Then he turned the car round again and headed back towards town. During one straight stretch of road he pulled his wallet out of his jacket pocket, took out two thousand lire, and put the money in Casimiro's hand.

'You could use a little, no?' he said. The dwarf hesitated for a moment, as he always did, then took the money and put it in his shoe.

'Thank you, Inspector, I can't be too picky,' he said darkly.

'Cigarette?'

'No, thanks . . . If you want, I can try to find something out myself.'

'But you've already shat your pants once . . .' Bordelli said, laughing.

'I'm not afraid,' the little man said, slightly offended. He didn't like to be seen as a coward.

'Never mind, Casimiro, it might be dangerous,' Bordelli said in a serious tone.

'Why dangerous?'

'You never know.'

'I know what I'm doing,' said Casimiro, squeezing the little skeleton tightly in his hand.

'And what if you run into another puppy dog like the last one?'

'I'll bring a pistol this long . . .' said Casimiro, playing the tough guy. He seemed in the grip of a fit of pride.

'This isn't a cowboy movie, Casimiro . . . But I may have another little job for you in a few days,' Bordelli lied, already trying to think of something. Once he had even had the little guy tail Diotivede, telling him the doctor was a mafioso . . .

They rode for a few moments in silence. The Beetle descended slowly towards the city. At San Domenico, Bordelli turned to pass by way of the Badia Fiesolana for no reason in particular, perhaps only because he wanted to see one more time the steep descent he used to take in his toy wagon, always risking a broken neck.

'Have you got any news of Botta, Casimiro?' Bordelli hadn't seen Ennio Bottarini for quite a while. He wanted to arrange another dinner party at his place, with Botta at the cooker. The luckless thief wasn't a bad cook at all. He'd spent a number of years in jails across half of Europe and had learned from his various cellmates how to make the local dishes.

'He must be still in Greece,' said Casimiro.

'Free or in jail?'

'A few days ago I ran into a friend of his, who said Botta'd made a little money down there and is supposed to return soon.'

'You don't say . . .'

★　　★　　★

A few days later, a phone call came in to the station, and Bordelli set out in his VW, stepping hard on the accelerator. As usual, young Piras was with him. It was almost 7 p.m., and the sun had already set a while before.

There was a big crowd at the entrance of the Parco del Ventaglio, along with three police cars with their headlamps on. Bordelli parked the car beside the gate and got out, blood pounding in his brain. Piras walked beside him in silence. Ever since the tough, intelligent lad had joined the force, Bordelli had been bringing him along on every investigation, and to avoid always having a uniform at his side, he'd told him to dress in civvies. He got on well with Piras, just as he had got on well with Piras's father, Gavino, during the war.

The moon was covered by a thick blanket of cloud, and the park was as gloomy as the sky. To their left was a grassy slope, steep and dark, and at the top of the hill shone the glow of the police's floodlights, as a crowd of people gathered round. Bordelli and Piras began to climb. The soles of their shoes slipped on the wet grass, and the cuffs of their trousers were soaked after only a few steps. They heard a siren in the distance. When they got to the top of the hill, Bordelli started clearing a path through the crowd, advancing in long strides. Piras followed right behind him, stepping into the opening before it closed again. There were already some journalists scribbling in their notebooks, as well as a few photographers. The press were always the first to arrive on the scene, though it was never clear how they did it.

The inspector kept elbowing his way until he got to the police cordon. And suddenly he saw her: under the white light of the police lamps, the little girl looked like a bundle of rags thrown on the grass. She lay face up at the foot of a big tree, legs straight and arms open, like a tiny Christ. The inspector went up to her, with Piras still following, and they both bent down to look at her. She must have been about eight years old. Her mouth and eyes were open wide, and she had jet-black hair tied in a braid that was coming undone. She was so white in the light that she seemed unreal. And on her neck were some red marks. Her jumper was pulled up, and her belly bore the traces of a human bite. Bordelli looked at her a long time, as if to burn that image into his memory, then turned towards his Sardinian assistant. They looked at each other for a few seconds without saying anything.

Busybodies were falling over one another to get a look at the child, grimacing in horror and exhaling vapour from their mouths. A few women could be heard weeping and, farther away, someone was vomiting. But what most bothered Bordelli was all that commotion of legs and shadows around the little girl's dead body. He pressed his eyes hard with his fingers. He felt very tired, though perhaps it was only disgust for what lay before him.

The sound of the siren grew closer and closer, and the inspector wondered whether it was indeed coming towards the park, since, at this point, he thought, the blaring sirens were useless. The girl was dead, and nobody was to touch anything before Diotivede, the police pathologist, got there. Bordelli glanced at his watch. How bloody long was Diotivede going to take? He took one of the uniformed policemen by the arm.

'Rinaldi, do you know if anyone saw or heard anything?'

'No, Inspector, nobody saw or heard anything.'

'Then please send them all away.'

'Yes, sir.'

Suddenly a man's voice was heard above the crowd:

'So what are the police doing about this?'

Bordelli stiffened and started looking for the imbecile amid the herd of onlookers. He wanted to grab him by the collar and bash his head against a tree trunk. What were the police doing? Come forward, jackass! What do you want the police to do? Piras saw he was upset and squeezed his elbow.

'Forget about it, Inspector,' he said.

The ambulance entered the park, turning off its siren. Bordelli and Piras stared at the ground. Five men got out of the ambulance and started climbing the grassy incline, carrying a stretcher. Bordelli scratched his head.

'What are they doing?' he said to himself. He went up to

the doctor, a fat man climbing up the hill with a black bag in his hand.

'Nobody can touch anything before the medical examiner gets here,' Bordelli said. The fat man stopped in front of him, happy for the rest.

'And who are you?' he asked.

'Chief Inspector Bordelli. Tell your men not to touch the girl.'

'I'm sorry, but we're here for a woman.'

'A woman? What woman?'

'Somebody called us about a woman who collapsed. How do you do? I'm Dr Vallini.'

The inspector shook his hand and turned round to look at the stretcher-bearers, who were walking towards a small group of people. He saw them lay a woman down on the stretcher. Then they came back, and the doctor began at once to examine the woman. He felt her pulse, looked inside her mouth, then opened her eyes and shone a light into her pupils with a small pocket torch. Bordelli got close to have a better look at her. She seemed very young. Her face was pale, and rested on a cushion of black hair. A beautiful girl. Her mouth was half open, and she gently batted her eyelashes at regular intervals, about once per second. One of her arms slid slowly off the stretcher, and the doctor put it back at her side.

'It's nothing serious; she just fainted,' he said.

'Who is she?' Bordelli asked.

'The little girl's mother,' said one of the stretcher-bearers. The inspector bit his lip . . . The mother, of course. How could he not have thought of it? He leaned over her for a better look, and at once the young woman opened her eyes wide, found Bordelli's face right in front of hers and stared at it as if it were something amazing. Then she raised her arms and grabbed his hand. Ten small cold fingers wrapped around his own.

'Valentina . . . Valen . . .' she whispered, staring at him with empty eyes. Dr Vallini was already preparing an injection of sedative.

'Please be brave, signora. It's better if you sleep a little now,' said the doctor, and he stuck the needle in her arm and pressed the plunger down. The woman opened her mouth to speak, but it was too late. Her eyes rolled back into her head and her arms fell. The doctor gestured to the orderlies, and the group trudged off.

Bordelli pointed at the woman.

'Where are you taking her?' he asked.

'To Santa Maria Nova.'

'When could I talk to her?'

'Try phoning the hospital in two or three days, and ask for Dr Saggini.'

'All right. Thanks.'

'Goodbye, Inspector.' The doctor began his difficult descent down the slippery grassy slope, balancing his massive body with the help of his medical bag. Bordelli lit another cigarette and inhaled deeply. The white face of Valentina's mother, as delicate as that of her daughter, remained etched in his mind.

The siren of the Misericordia ambulance suddenly blared and just as suddenly stopped, as if it had been turned on by mistake. The vehicle then glided slowly and smoothly away into the darkness, engine whirring gently. Bordelli stood there watching it until it passed through the park's gate, then looked up over the roofs of the city, then down, lost in thought. Piras's voice shook him out of it.

'Inspector, can you hear me?'

Bordelli ran a hand over his eyes.

'What is it, Piras?'

'Dr Diotivede is here.'

Bordelli wasn't surprised he hadn't seen him arrive. Diotivede was as sly and silent as a beast of the forest.

'Come,' Bordelli said to Piras. They began to walk towards the doctor, whose almost phosphorescent shock of white hair was visible from a distance.

Diotivede was kneeling down over the little girl's body, his knees on a newspaper. He was studying her from very close up, touching her from time to time. His gestures were those of his profession, but he wore an offended expression on his face, as if he had just been slapped.

Bordelli and Piras stopped a few yards away so as not to disturb him. People were finally starting to leave, pushed away by the uniformed cops. The inspector smoked one cigarette after another, impatient to speak to Diotivede. A light wind was blowing, spreading a scent of dead leaves through the air. It was April, but it felt more like a nice November evening. The clouds were thinning out, and in the black sky a few stars were beginning to appear, along with a yellowish sliver of moon.

Bordelli kept an eye on the pathologist, trying to guess where he was in his examination, not daring to disturb him. He well knew that at such moments Diotivede didn't want anyone bothering him. One had no choice but to wait.

A few minutes later Diotivede had finished examining the corpse and, still kneeling, began to write in his black notebook, lips pouting like a schoolboy's. At last he rose and came towards the two policemen.

'Strangled. And she has a nasty bite on her belly, which probably happened after she died.'

The inspector tossed his fag-end far away.

'Nothing significant, in other words,' he said.

'For the moment, no. But I'll let you know after the post-mortem. You never know, something might turn up.'

'Let's hope so,' said Bordelli, disappointed. He went up to the girl's body again and lit his umpteenth cigarette of the day. He knelt forward and looked closely at that now grey little face spattered with mud. He saw an ant walking along the sharp edges of the little girl's lips and flicked it away with a finger, very briefly touching the dead flesh. She must have been a beautiful child. She looked a little like a woman he had once loved, many years before . . . He shook his head to banish the thought. Who knew why he thought of such things at moments like these? He took a last glance at the girl, her naked little feet looking as if they'd just sprouted from the ground – and then he turned towards the others. Diotivede was clutching his briefcase tightly against his stomach with both arms, ready to leave. Behind the thick lenses his eyes looked as if they were made of glass.

'I hate to say it, but this crime looks like the work of a maniac who may strike again,' he said.

'Unfortunately, I agree,' said Bordelli, tossing his cigarette to the ground.

'Unless it's a vendetta,' Piras mumbled, teeth clenched, thinking of the cruel feuds of his homeland.

'Need a lift, Doctor?' the inspector asked.

'Why not?'

The inspector gestured to Rinaldi to say that the body could now be taken away. Rinaldi raised a hand, and two policemen laid a cloth down beside the little girl, picked her up and laid her down on it.

'We can go now,' Bordelli said with a sigh, heading towards the park exit without waiting to see the body being taken away. The three descended the wet, grassy slope, taking care not to lose their balance. Piras was quiet, staring into space and looking sullen. He climbed into the back seat of the VW, letting Diotivede ride in front. Bordelli started up the car and drove off slowly, an unlit cigarette between his lips.

'Shall I take you home, or do you want to go back to the lab?' he asked, turning on to Via Volta.

'You can take me home, thanks,' said Diotivede. He remained silent the rest of the way. They dropped him off in Via dell'Erta Canina, in front of his little house and garden. Piras came and sat down in front like an automaton.

'What do you think of this murder, Piras?'

'What was that, Inspector?'

'Nothing.'

They returned to police headquarters and got down to work. Bordelli sent a few officers out to question people who lived in the neighbourhood of the Parco del Ventaglio. With a little luck they might find someone who had seen or heard something of interest, though he didn't have much hope of this. He drafted a communiqué for the television and radio to broadcast the following morning, to put the whole city on alert. And with Piras's help, he organised the shifts of plainclothes officers to patrol the city's parks, which were always full of mothers and children. But these were general measures that gave no assurance at all. The killer might strike again in another way and another place, as Bordelli well knew. In the meantime, however, there wasn't much more that could be done.

The in-house telephone rang. It was Mugnai.

'There are more journalists here, Inspector,' he said.

'Send them to Inzipone. I don't feel like talking to anyone.'

'Commissioner Inzipone told me to send them to you.'

'Then send them away. And the same goes for the next few days.'

'As you wish, Inspector.'

Bordelli hung up. He had nothing to say to the journalists. He massaged his eyes with his fingers. They burned as if he hadn't slept for three days.

To avoid being seen by anyone, he left headquarters through a side door that gave on to Via San Gallo. He got into his Beetle and, head full of thoughts, drove to the trattoria Da Cesare. Gesturing in greeting to the owner and the waiters, he slipped into Totò's kitchen, as he always did. He greeted the cook and plopped down on the stool that had been his place for years. He couldn't get the image of that little girl on the ground out of his head.

'What's the matter, Inspector? Y'oughta see your face . . .' said Totò, coming up to him with a wooden spoon in his hand.

'I'm just a little tired,' said Bordelli, knowing that the news of the little girl's murder hadn't yet spread.

'Just tell me how hungry you are.'

'Give me whatever you want, Totò. I don't feel like deciding.'

'Don't you worry, Inspector. I'll set you right,' said the cook, who went and started fiddling at the cooker. He soon returned with a steaming plate of fried chicken and artichokes, a speciality of his. Bordelli poured himself a glass of wine and set to his food. Totò was loquacious as usual and started talking about politics and love against a backdrop of sauté pans, never once losing the rhythm of his cooking. The uneducated cook knew how to get to the heart of things, even if his way of getting there was all his own.

'People getting married, people breaking up . . . I have this idea, Inspector . . . If a man and a woman want to work things out together, they can remake the world; but if they want to make war, then a plate of overdone spaghetti's enough to bring out the knives.'

Bordelli was gorging himself, washing it all down with wine and nodding in agreement with Totò. He had no desire what-soever to talk. He finished off his fried chicken and artichokes to the sound of the shrill, sharp voice of the cook, who talked about everything from the bloody vendettas of his home prov-ince to the recipe for pork with myrtle.

'Coffee, Inspector?' he said in the end.

'Make it nice and black, Totò. You've made me eat like a pig.'

'Then you'll need a little of this grappa I've got,' said the cook, looking on a shelf for the right bottle.

'You're shortening my life, Totò.'

'But making it better . . .'

'I can pick my poison . . .'

'No poison, Inspector – here, have a taste of this,' said Totò, filling his glass.

'Sit down with me a minute, Totò, you've been on your feet the whole time.'

Bordelli left the trattoria around eleven o'clock, feeling fatter and more tired, and swore he would not set foot in that kitchen again for at least a month. But he knew he would break his vow. After he got into his car, it started to rain, but in drops so tiny it wasn't worth the trouble of turning on the windscreen wipers. He drove slowly, smoking, and every so often a sigh escaped him. He stopped to have another coffee in Via San Gallo and went back to police headquarters. The rain was starting to fall harder as he ran inside. Entering his office, he collapsed in his chair, wishing he could go to bed. But the night was not over yet; there was one more ball-ache to attend to.

The round-up had been planned some weeks before and couldn't be postponed any longer. Bordelli hated this sort of thing, especially when he had a case as serious as the child murder on his hands. He had tried to talk Commissioner Inzipone out of it, even pulling out the excuse that, on top of everything else, it was pouring outside. But it had been no use.

'It's only sprinkling, Bordelli. Let's not have any tantrums. Every now and then these things have to be done. We have orders from the Ministry. Please don't make life difficult for me, the way you always do.'

Fine. If the round-up had to be carried out, Bordelli preferred to be there for it.

Shortly past midnight, a number of police cars and vans full of cops pulled up in Ponte di Mezzo. It was common knowledge that those low-rent blocks housed a clandestine gambling den for the poor and a couple of brothels of the lowest grade, and that a great many receivers and smugglers lived there alongside countless petty thieves who could open any door in the world. Ponte di Mezzo was one of the poorest quarters in town, reduced to rubble during the war and rebuilt mostly on hope, and full of disillusioned, pissed-off people. Bordelli often thought that in some respects the first twenty years of the Republic had done more harm to Italy than the Fascists and Nazis combined. Such districts were a necessary and even useful scourge of the great mechanism of a society so fashioned – badly, that is – and it was extremely unpleasant to go and give a bollocking to a whole army of people who scraped by to survive.

It was still raining hard. Bordelli, Piras and four uniformed officers ran through the downpour and slipped into a building in Via del Terzolle. Throughout the block there were underground tunnels and passages that in wartime had served several times to make fools of the Germans during round-ups. Bordelli and his men went into the basement and broke down a door. They entered a smoke-filled cellar where someone had managed to turn out the lights just in time. The policemen turned on their electric torches and put everyone up against the wall. The faces were the usual ones. Bordelli made gestures of greeting to a number of old acquaintances, then left the uniformed cops to check their papers, as he and Piras went up to the third floor of the building.

On the door was a tin sign that said: PENSIONE AURORA. They went in without knocking, dirtying the small pink rugs in the entrance with their wet shoes. Signorina Ortensia came running towards them with all her heft.

'Don't you wipe your feet before entering at home?' she screamed, the fat quivering under chin.

'Not so loud, Ortensia,' said Bordelli. The 'signorina' gestured crossly and two girls in dressing gowns ran upstairs with a giggle, slippers shuffling. A boa of red feathers was left behind on the threadbare carpet covering the stairs. The little drawing room was all light and shadow, with soft music playing in the background. There was an unbearable tang of sweat and cheap perfume in the air. A black silk stocking fluttered faintly on the back of a chair. It was one of the most squalid places Bordelli knew.

'For the love of God, why do you persecute me like this?!' Ortensia cried plaintively. She had massive thighs, and yet she danced on her feet as though she weighed ten stone less.

'It's just a routine check,' said Piras.

'And who the hell is this little boy?' said Ortensia, eyes popping, looking at him as if she'd just noticed him at that moment. Piras blushed and started biting his lips.

'Let's make this snappy,' said Bordelli, looking bored.

'A routine check . . . You call this a routine check! You're worse than the Germans!' the woman whined, pulling her flower-print dressing gown tightly around her. She started saying the usual things . . . That her boarding house was a respectable place, frequented by important people, high-ranking politicians, even an undersecretary . . .

'Bring the girls down,' said Bordelli, tired of all the chatter. He could still feel Totò's fried chicken churning in his stomach.

'If you shut me down you might as well shoot me!' the fat lady said, stamping her foot and making the floor shake.

'Go and get the girls, Ortensia. All of them. And if there are any clients up there, bring them down too,' said Bordelli, his patience wearing thin.

Ortensia looked at a crucifix on the wall and made the sign of the cross.

'You want to ruin me. If word gets round, nobody will come here any more!' she said in an angry whisper, forcing herself not to shout, so as not to alarm the clients.

'Never mind, we'll go and do it ourselves,' said Bordelli. He gestured to Piras, and they sidestepped the fat lady. Once upstairs, they started opening doors.

'Police. Everybody downstairs.'

Shouts and curses rang out, and in the semi-darkness they saw men pulling the covers over their heads. Bordelli and Piras went back downstairs to wait, ignoring Ortensia's protests. Nobody could escape. Bordelli knew there was only one exit. A few minutes later various girls and a few men came down.

'Are they all here, Ortensia? Because if I go up and find somebody hiding . . .'

'They're all here, General,' said Ortensia, eyeing him with hatred.

Bordelli gestured to Piras, and they lined them all up against the wall. The few clients huffed and smoked with an indignant air. Only one of them had the repellent look of guilt, eyes lowered and face sweaty. The girls all wore the same plush slippers with pompons. They sniggered and held their dressing gowns provocatively open to fluster Piras, who was casting surreptitious glances at them. Bordelli felt ridiculous concerning himself with such things when he still had young Valentina's dead body before his eyes. But he could do nothing about it.

They finished checking everyone's papers. There were no fugitives among them, and no underage girls.

'Ortensia, does the name Merlin mean anything to you?'[1] asked Bordelli, looking straight into her eyes, which were drowning in fat.

'It's all so easy for you, copper, but what am I supposed to do? Eh? Can you tell me what I'm supposed to do at sixty years of age?' asked Ortensia, swelling with hatred. She gave Piras a dirty look, as the Sardinian stared at her in disgust.

'Let's go, Piras,' said Bordelli, putting a cigarette in his mouth. They left the Pensione Aurora and came out on to the street. A few drops were still falling, but the worst was over. A number of people had been lined up against the wall outside, all men. It really did look like a German round-up, and it was hardly surprising that nobody liked it. Bordelli wished Inzipone could have been there to see the looks on all their faces.

Among them was Romeo, a poor wretch from the Case Minime[2] who kept pretty busy: robberies, receiving stolen goods, counterfeiting and other similar activities, though always very low-level. He often found his way into bigger circuits and regularly got a good thrashing. He had a moral code of his own, however: no blackmailing and no pimping. Everything else was fair game. He was short, skinny as a beanpole, with a round, shaggy head always tilted to one side, as if it weighed too much. He always wore a dirty bandana round his neck and coughed more and more each year. He made a pitiful sight, drenched in the rain like that.

'Ciao, Romeo. Are you clean or did they find something on you?' asked Bordelli, stopping in front of him. The little thief made a sad face.

'I was playing poker at the Mouse's place, and I was even losing.'

'Is that all?'

Romeo shrugged, embarrassed. A uniformed policeman came up to them.

'He had these banknotes on him, Inspector. They're counterfeit,' he said, handing him a few thousand-lira notes.

'Well, well . . .' said Bordelli, glancing over at a stony-faced Piras. Romeo took a step forward, pulled the inspector aside, and lowered his voice.

'Don't let them put me in again, Inspector . . . I've found a wonderful woman.'

'Are you trying to make me sorry for you?'

'It's true, Inspector . . . Look how pretty she is.' Romeo took a badly creased photograph out of his inside pocket, looked around to make sure nobody else could see it, then thrust it under Bordelli's nose. She was a chubby blonde with a pretty smile.

'Cute, Romeo, very cute. What's she doing with someone like you?'

'She's the most beautiful woman in the world,' said Romeo. He planted a kiss on the photograph and put it safely away again. Bordelli lit a cigarette and blew the smoke skywards.

'Get out of here, Romeo, and stay away from the phoney money. The stuff's not for you; there are some dangerous people in that circuit.'

'Don't worry, Inspector,' said the little thief, tapping Bordelli's elbow.

'Now get going.'

'Eh?'

'Get out of here . . .'

'All right, but . . . what about my money?'

Bordelli ran a hand over his eyes and heaved a sigh.

'By all means, Romeo . . . Actually, tell you what: I'll put them about myself, and we can split the proceeds . . . What do you say?'

'What was that, Inspector?'

'Make yourself scarce, Romeo. I'm about to change my mind.'

'No need to get angry . . .' said Romeo, starting to move away. Bordelli stood there and watched him walk hurriedly away on his toothpick legs. He had always felt sorry for Romeo.

The rain had stopped. The sky was beginning to clear, and a few stars were already coming out. Bordelli wiped his face with both hands and stopped in front of another old acquaintance.

'Look who we have here,' he said with a half-smile. The Saint was always well dressed and fragrant with cologne. He pulled everyone's leg with his claim of noble origins and always tried to speak with refinement, but his brutish face spoke much more clearly.

'Inspector, what a pleasure . . .' he said, giving a slight bow.

'Get a good look at this guy, Piras. He's the biggest liar you'll ever meet.'

'Why do you say that, Inspector?' asked the Saint, looking at Piras with an expression of innocence.

'You still robbing churches?' asked Bordelli.

'No, Inspector, I swear it. I deal in second-hand goods now.'

'You mean stolen property.'

'Never knowingly, Inspector, never.'

'Ever heard of unlawful acquisition?'

'Sounds like robbery, not my sort of thing.'

'I like you, Santo, but don't push your luck.'

'I promise, Inspector,' said the Saint, right hand on his heart. Whenever he didn't know what to say, he promised.

'Get out of here,' said Bordelli.

The Saint smiled faintly, nodded his head, and headed off serenely down the street, hands in his pockets, followed by Piras's amused gaze. It was the first time the youth was taking part in a round-up, and he now understood why Bordelli tried to avert them.

'I can't wait to be asleep,' the inspector said, dropping his cigarette butt into the rivulet of water flowing down the pavement. Looking at the poor bastards' faces he remembered that it was, in fact, during a round-up that he had first met Rosa, right after the war. At the time, three out of every ten women in the poorer quarters practised the profession. Rosa had stopped a few years later. Being one who knew how to economise, she was able to buy herself a nice flat in the centre of town . . .

Lost in thoughts of times past, the inspector gave a start when Officer Binazzi came up behind him.

'Inspector, we've found some weapons.'

'Oh, really? What kind of weapons?'

'Looks like stuff from the war.'

'In whose place?'

'In the flat of a certain Gaspare Mordacci, Inspector.'
Bordelli shrugged.

'I know him well,' he said. 'Those weapons are souvenirs of
his Partisan days.'

'What should I do, Inspector?'

'Leave him in peace . . . It's thanks to him, too, that you
don't live in a country run by Germans.'

'Yes, sir,' said Binazzi, and he ran away.

Bordelli grabbed his packet of cigarettes, then tasted a bitter,
disgusting patina on his tongue and put it back in his pocket.
Exchanging a glance with Piras, he thought he saw the young
man smile.

'What a pain in the arse,' he said.

Indeed. He could only guess the pain Inzipone would cause
him after that umpteenth round-up with no arrests.

'So, monkey, is your big bad headache going away?'

Rosa was standing behind him and massaging his face up
to the temples. She had spread cream all over his skin, and her
fingers seemed magical.

'Yes, it's going away, but don't stop,' said Bordelli. The former
prostitute was as pure as a child. After years of hard work in
brothels all across the region, she decided to quit when the
Merlin law was passed. She didn't like one bit the idea of
spending the whole night pounding the pavement. Luckily she
had always been a sort of squirrel and over the years had
managed to put away enough to buy herself this little flat with
a view of the roofs and Arnolfo's Tower,[3] and to live on her
savings until she grew old. She really had earned it all. 'I'm
the only one of the girls who managed to save up my money,'
she often said with a certain pride.

It was almost three o'clock in the morning. Bordelli lay on
the sofa with his shoes off, stroking the head of Gideon, Rosa's

white cat. The beast had curled up on the inspector's belly and was purring. After a day like the one he'd just been through, this was exactly what Bordelli needed. The cat had been used a year before as a Trojan horse to kill its owner, and the inspector had given the orphaned animal to Rosa.

'Are you hungry? Shall I make you a tartine?' she asked.

'No thanks. I don't feel like eating.'

'You look sad.'

Bordelli couldn't get the image of the dead little girl out of his head.

'This isn't a good time, Rosa . . . And tonight I had to conduct a round-up,' he said.

'Poor dear, I know how much you hate that.' Rosa stopped massaging him and went into the bathroom to wash the greasy cream off her hands. Gideon gave a full-mouthed yawn and, stretching, planted his claws in Bordelli's belly. Before curling up to go back to sleep, he turned round on himself once, his tail brushing the inspector's face.

Rosa returned and collapsed in the armchair.

'Would you like something to drink, monkey?' she asked.

'If you've got some of that cognac . . .'

'Of course I have.' Rosa got up again, lithe as a young girl, and went and filled two glasses. Handing one to Bordelli, she went to turn on the gramophone. She put *Vecchio frac* on the turntable and started to dance wistfully, swaying on the carpet. At a certain point she smiled sadly.

'That poor little girl must have gone straight to heaven,' she said, still dancing.

'Maybe she didn't feel like going there so soon,' said Bordelli.

Gideon stretched again and slid off him lazily, heading towards the kitchen, tail straight up. The inspector put his feet on the floor and slipped his shoes on.

'I think I'll go home to bed,' he said, yawning.

'Go and get some rest, dear. I'm sure you'll catch that madman.'

'Say a prayer for me,' he said, feeling discouraged. He downed the rest of his cognac and stood up. Overcoming a slight dizziness, he tucked his shirt into his trousers, then lit a cigarette. It tasted disgusting, but he kept smoking it anyway.

'I'm off,' he said.

Rosa accompanied him to the door and stroked his face, which was already rough with a growth of beard. The inspector took Rosa's hand in his.

'Sweet dreams, beautiful,' he said, kissing her fingers, and he started to go down the stairs, followed by Rosa's kisses, which echoed in the stairwell.

It was cold outside, and a fine, dense rain was falling. The light of the street lamps shone bright on the wet asphalt. A few illuminated windows could be seen here and there. An old man smoked on his balcony, watching the drops fall from the sky. It really did feel like November. No sign of spring in sight. Feeling a chill down his spine, Bordelli turned up the collar of his jacket. As he was unlocking his car, a raindrop fell square on the burning end of his cigarette and extinguished it. So much the better, he thought. He flicked the butt away and got into the car. He felt a great weariness in his legs, as if he had been walking all day. He couldn't wait to get into bed.

The Beetle whistled more than usual as he started it up, and coughed out a lot of smoke. The streets were deserted. He crossed the Ponte dell Grazie and turned on to the Lungarno, yawning all the while. A few minutes later he parked the car right outside his front door and dragged himself up the stairs.

As he entered his bedroom he heard some yelling in the street and went over and looked out the window. Two drunkards were quarrelling and cursing each other. Nothing serious. A rather normal occurrence in that part of town. He closed the window, turned out the lights, and threw himself down on the bed. He lit what was supposed to be his last cigarette, smoking it with eyes open, staring into the darkness. He thought of Valentina's mother. How old could she be? Twenty-five, thirty at most. No, not even thirty. Maybe twenty-eight. Whatever the case, she was very beautiful. He snuffed out the cigarette and turned on to his side. Just a minute before, he had felt sleepy, but no longer. Groping through the confused memories spinning round in his head, he remembered the time he had got trapped in German crossfire with ten of his men. They didn't know what to do and could only look at one another, wondering how they might ever get out of that bloody fix. They were lying belly down on the ground, faces in the tall grass, as the bullets flew a few centimetres over their heads. All at once Commander Bordelli started rolling down the slope like a log, arms folded over his face. The others all followed behind him as the German bullets ripped the grass from the ground. They all got away, but Bordelli never told anyone how afraid he had been at that moment, thinking they weren't going to make it that time.

That night he had a dream. Nonna Argìa had tied his hands to the sink so she could wash his face, and as she rubbed the soap over his mouth and nose she nearly suffocated him. He opened his eyes and sighed with relief. He couldn't remember his grandmother ever tying him to the bathroom sink, but as a little boy he had always been a bit afraid of that gaunt, bony woman, her skull sharply outlined under her brownish skin. She walked with a cane and wore black shoes laced up to the calf. She died when he was eight years old. His parents brought him to her deathbed for a last goodbye to Nonna. She was dressed all in black, hands folded on her chest, a crucifix between her fingers. In the penumbra a shaft of sunlight made the hair on her face gleam. He bowed his head to please his mother and recited a random prayer, but he was worried all the while that Nonna would sit up in bed, and he couldn't wait to get out of there . . .

He woke up with a start. It was already nine o'clock. He got up, aching all over. Feeling impatient, he phoned Diotivede.

'Have you done the girl?' he asked.

'I finished a short while ago.'

'Find anything?'

The pathologist told him he had no news and confirmed

what he'd already said before. The girl had been strangled and then violently bitten on the abdomen just after death, the teeth having penetrated rather deep. Nothing else.

'Shall we have lunch together?' Bordelli asked.

'I'm too busy. I'll have something delivered to the lab.'

'Ah, lovely.'

'Why do you say that?' said the doctor, sounding offended.

'Oh, nothing, nothing.'

'My work is no different from any other, Bordelli. Why can't you all get that through your heads?'

'You're too touchy . . .'

Diotivede hung up without saying goodbye, but Bordelli knew he would get over it soon enough. That was just the way the doctor was. He could joke about everything, but he wouldn't tolerate even the slightest irony about his job.

Bordelli put on whatever clothes he found within reach, shaved, and then got into his car to go to the office. The sky was clear, but a cold wind was blowing from the north. The kiosks were all plastered with giant headlines: SEVEN-YEAR-OLD GIRL MURDERED.

When he got to headquarters the inspector sent Mugnai down to the bar across the street to fetch him a coffee. He felt very tired, and his thoughts were muddled, as if he hadn't slept a wink all night. *night*

Late that morning Rinaldi came in to report the initial findings of the investigation into the murder of Valentina Panerai. They had questioned dozens of people who lived in the immediate area of the Parco del Ventaglio.

'We went door to door, Inspector. Nobody saw anything,' Rinaldi said in an almost guilty tone.

'Carry on.'

'Of course, Inspector.'

The policeman left in a hurry. Bordelli lit a cigarette and smoked it in front of the open window. He felt as if his feet were stuck in a bog. At a certain point his eye fell on the bottle of de Maricourt cognac he'd found in the olive grove, and he immediately thought of Casimiro. They'd talked a few days before, and the little man had said he would call again soon to tell him something important about that villa in Fiesole. He had seemed quite convinced and very agitated. The inspector had told him to forget about it, that it wasn't very important at the moment, but to all appearances Casimiro had taken a liking to playing cop.

'I'm getting close now, Inspector,' he'd said.

'Don't do anything stupid.'

'I never do anything stupid.'

Casimiro had hung up before Bordelli had a chance to reply, and the inspector hadn't heard from him since then. It might not be a bad idea to pay him a call and tell him to stop playing spy.

After their infamous evening together, Bordelli had even phoned the Fiesole police to find out whether anyone had reported the disappearance or killing of a Doberman, but there was nothing. It seemed quite strange.

Although at that moment Bordelli's thoughts were taken up with the murder of the little girl, this whole business had him worried. Especially as he hadn't heard from Casimiro. Every so often the man with the black mark on his neck, who had looked out from the garden balustrade, came into his head. He was almost certain he had seen him before, but he couldn't recall where or when.

He felt nervous and needed to move. After an afternoon spent fruitlessly ruminating, he decided to go back to the olive grove.

It was already dark when he got there. He left the car in the usual spot on the Via del Bargellino and climbed up the low wall. The same cold wind was still blowing, and he buttoned up his jacket. He crossed the stretch of woods and entered the olive grove with his Beretta drawn. It was darker than last time, and colder. The only sound was the dull hum of the city below, too far away to mar the silence. He kept his ears pricked as he walked along, never losing sight of the baron's great villa, which as usual loomed dark above him. Arriving at the foot of the massive buttresses, he looked around a little, raising his eyes repeatedly towards the top of the wall. All at once he felt like a silly fifty-four-year-old in search of adventure, and wondered what the hell he was doing in such a place. He put away his pistol and returned to his car. Descending back towards the city, he decided to drop in on Casimiro.

The Case Minime was one of the poorest working-class quarters of Florence, home to smugglers and brawling rival gangs. Bordelli left his Beetle in a courtyard criss-crossed with hanging laundry, and made his way into the labyrinth of hovels. He entered the tenement house in which Casimiro lived and walked to the end of a long corridor. He knocked on Casimiro's door, but nobody replied. So he knocked hard on the door opposite, and a moment later a huge man in singlet and socks opened up.

'Inspector! What are you doing here?'

'Hello, Beast.'

The Beast was an ageing smuggler who knew everyone. In his youth he had repeatedly landed in jail for the cartons of cigarettes the authorities never failed to find under his bed, but now that he was old, the police left him alone.

'Want to come in for a minute, Inspector?'

'Thanks, but I'm in a hurry. I was just wondering if you had any news of Casimiro.'

The Beast scratched an old scar that cut across his face, and said he hadn't seen the little guy for three or four days.

'He owes me five hundred lire,' he added.

'Does he often stay away for days like this?' Bordelli asked.

'Not usually.'

'Thanks, Beast. Take care of yourself.'

'Long live anarchy, Inspector.'

That was how he said goodbye, the way someone else might say 'God bless you'. Bordelli was about to leave, then changed his mind. Casimiro's strange absence had him worried.

'Beast, give me a hand breaking open Casimiro's door.'

'Lemme put something on my feet. I'll be right back.'

The giant went back into his flat and returned immediately,

shuffling in slippers. At the count of three, they put their shoulders to the door. The frame came detached from the jamb with the first thrust, and they were inside. Bordelli flicked the light switch, and a small ceiling lamp came on. The air smelled musty. Casimiro's den consisted of one big room with rotting plaster and almost nothing in it aside from two pieces of old furniture, a table, and a straw mattress on a platform of upside-down fruit crates, to protect against the humid floor. Beside the bed were a few carefully folded rags laid on top of a sheet of newspaper. A small door led to the loo, which was tiny and dirty. On the wall was a calendar of naked women, and hanging from the same nail was a crucifix.

'He's not here,' said the Beast, looking at a dusty glass full of cobwebs on the table. Then he went up to the girlie calendar and started thumbing through it.

Bordelli advanced a few steps into the room, looking around. He opened the only wardrobe, which was old and dirty. Inside were a few child-sized rags and a pair of shoes in bad shape. He closed the doors and looked up. On top of the wardrobe was a rather large brown suitcase. He reached up to grab it, but his arm wasn't long enough.

'Beast, you're tall . . .'

'I'll be right there.' The Beast dropped the naked women, grabbed the suitcase without much difficulty and set it down on the table with a thud. It seemed quite heavy. The inspector tried to open it, but it seemed locked.

'Shall I open it for you, Inspector?'

'Please.'

The Beast pulled out a penknife and in a few seconds had snapped the locks open. Opening the suitcase, Bordelli found a grim sight before him. Casimiro's dead body was wrapped up tightly in a sheet of transparent plastic, and his contorted face looked as if it was immersed in water. His wide-open eyes were upsetting. They looked alive.

'Fuck!' said the Beast.

'I don't think you'll be getting your five hundred lire back.'

'Fuck . . .' the Beast repeated.

The inspector leaned forward to have a better look at the dwarf. The body had been very carefully enclosed, and one smelled almost nothing. There was some dried blood smeared on the victim's head, matting the hair. The upper teeth stuck out unnaturally, as if the jawbone had been dislocated, and his forehead, blackened at the temples, looked as if it had been squeezed in a vice.

'Don't touch anything,' said Bordelli.

'I know, Inspector.'

'Do you remember exactly when you last saw Casimiro?' asked Bordelli, lighting a cigarette.

'Let me think . . .' The Beast concentrated for a moment, scratching his scar with his fingernails. 'I think it was three or four days ago . . . I ran into him in the hallway. He was going out as I was coming in.'

'What time of day was it?'

'It must have been about two o'clock in the morning.'

'Did he tell you where he was going?'

'He didn't say anything to me, and I didn't ask him anything. We just said hello,' the Beast said, shrugging, and he went back for another look at the calendar.

Bordelli looked around again, to see whether there was anything that might be of help. He started searching every corner very carefully, but found nothing.

'Where's the nearest telephone, Beast?'

'In the bar down the street, Inspector.'

The north wind bore holes in one's ears. As Bordelli was about to insert the key into the front door of his building, he was accosted by a lady of about seventy, very thin, almost transparent, with hair tinted a silvery violet and eyeglasses attached to a delicate chain. She was wearing a small black cap with a veil and hatpins.

'You're a police officer, aren't you?' she said, her voice whistling.

'More or less,' said Bordelli.

'*Carabiniere?*'

'What can I do for you, signora?'

The old woman cast a furtive glance around her, then looked at him and whispered something.

'Signora, if you talk like that I can't hear a thing,' said the inspector.

The woman came closer and partially raised her veil, uncovering only her chin.

'I am Signora Capecchi, and I have a very urgent matter to discuss with you. You should come up to my place for a moment,' she whispered a bit more audibly.

'All right,' said Bordelli, detecting an unpleasant scent of chestnut flour and stale sweets.

'Please follow me,' said Signora Capecchi, and she started walking briskly towards the Arno. Bordelli followed behind, thinking he would have done better to skip the whole matter.

'Don't walk so close to me, Marshal[4],' said the old woman, crossing over to the opposite pavement. The inspector let her go on a few steps ahead of him, still following her, and feeling more and more like a fool. When the woman got to Borgo San Frediano, she turned right, crossed the street, then immediately turned left, passing under the Volta di Cestello. Moments later she nodded complicitly at Bordelli and went through a door. The inspector waited a few seconds, then approached. When he arrived at the door, he hesitated, thinking it might be a trap, then shook his head and pushed the door open.

'You don't seem very alert, Marshal,' said the old woman, turning towards the staircase. She climbed it one stair at a time. She was wearing a dress too large for her and full of wrinkles. Bordelli followed her without saying a word. At the first-floor landing, Signora Capecchi stuck the key in her door, but before entering, she turned to Bordelli.

'Are your shoes clean? I certainly hope so, I spent the whole morning cleaning the place,' she said.

'I think so.'

The woman shot a glance at Bordelli's shoes, then opened the door. Once inside, she slipped on a pair of mules and began to walk about without raising her feet, sliding them across the floor. Bordelli followed behind her until they reached a small drawing room with a shiny waxed floor. There were a number of small glass-fronted cupboards with little lace curtains, and the walls were covered with trinkets, travel souvenirs and small paintings. Signora Capecchi sat him down in an armchair, sat herself down in front of him, and raised the little veil over the top of her cap. She had a big mole on one cheek, bristling with hair. Her kerosene stove was at maximum setting, and the room was unbearably hot. The air was dry and insalubrious; it smelled of rosolio[5] and old sofas. Bordelli started sweating and unbuttoned his shirt.

'Sorry,' he said.

'Not at all, Marshal.'

'What did you have to tell me?' Bordelli couldn't wait to get out of there. The old woman opened her eyes wide and raised a ring-studded hand in the air.

'The fact is that strange things have been happening in this building,' she said with an air of mystery.

'What do you mean?'

'People coming and going, up and down the stairs, above and below, laughing, shouting – the traffic never ends . . .'

'Oh really?' said Bordelli, feeling a drop of sweat roll down his neck.

'You have no idea the racket they make!' whispered Signora Capecchi, waving her hands in the air and making all her bracelets tinkle.

'A nasty business . . .' said Bordelli.

'You're telling me! And it's all the fault of that man on the top floor . . . the new arrival, Nocentini, he's called . . . a shady character, that one, with an ugly face. It's all his fault . . . Before him, Signora Meletti lived up there on the fourth floor, but then she died, poor thing . . .'

'I'm so sorry.'

'Would you like something to drink, Marshal?'

'No, thank you.'

'No need to be coy, now. An Alkermes,[6] perhaps?'

'Thank you, no, I don't want anything.'

'Good Signora Meletti . . . nobody ever so much as paid a call on her, poor dear. She was a tiny little woman, a delightful person, always polite, never missed a day of mass . . . Not like that little tart up there now, I can tell you . . .' And Signora Capecchi cast a glance upwards, in a specific direction, and shrivelled up inside her dress. Bordelli asked whether he could smoke and lit a cigarette.

'Can't you tell me any more about these noises?' he asked, hoping to get this over with quickly. The old woman nervously shuffled her slippers back and forth on the floor.

'Noises . . . There is . . . how shall I say? . . . a lot of commotion, slamming doors, raucous laughter . . . yelling that doesn't even sound human . . . and then a deafening sort of music that makes the whole building shake . . . But you could hardly call it music! It's just a lot of meaningless racket . . . What ever happened to the beautiful songs of Otello Boccaccini, or Rabagliati, or Spadaro, or—'

'What else can you tell me about this Nocentini?'

'Ah, he's a perfect boor, I tell you! Never says hello, always humming something through his teeth . . . and he puts out his cigarettes in the stairwell . . . and he spits, I've seen it with my own eyes . . . And he's always chewing that American filth . . . and he whistles at women . . .'

'Well, I think I'll go and have a chat with him,' said Bordelli, feigning disapproval. He was at the end of his tether.

'And when will you do that, sir?'

'I'll do it straight away, if he's in.'

Signora Capecchi blanched, shuffling her slippers again on the floor.

'Please, don't ever say it was I who sent him to jail,' she whispered, her eyes open wide.

'Don't worry, nobody will ever know.'

'Ah, thank God!' said Signora Capecchi, crossing herself.

And then she thanked Bordelli endlessly, saying how really very nice he was, for a *carabiniere*, extremely nice, in fact she'd never met a *carabiniere* so nice. Bordelli crushed his fag-end in a little dish from Lourdes and got up to leave.

'Will you keep me informed, Marshal?' she asked, sliding along the floor as she saw him out.

'The moment I've got any news, I'll give you a ring.'

'Soon, I hope.'

'That depends,' said Bordelli, glad to be leaving.

'Don't let that oaf intimidate you, Marshal. Put him in his place,' the old woman said as she opened the door.

'Don't you worry.'

'Don't pull any punches, Marshal. The hooligan may be big and fat, but you're a *carabiniere*, aren't you?'

'More or less.'

'Let me know when the trial date is set, I shouldn't want to miss it.'

'Goodbye, signora. Don't worry, I'll take care of everything.'

'Thank heavens. You have no idea how happy that makes me.'

At last Signora Capecchi closed the door, and Bordelli heard the sound of a hundred bolts turning. Shaking his head, he started up towards the top floor. He felt like an idiot. With all the things he had to do, here he was, doing the bidding of a crazy old woman. At the top of the stairs, he lit a cigarette. On the door on the right-hand side of the landing there was still a little plaque with the name *Meletti*. Bordelli knocked without conviction, but nobody came to the door. He knocked again. Nothing. The nasty fellow wasn't there. He descended the stairs at a leisurely pace, but before heading down the last flight he heard the front door open and close. Accompanied by a gust of cold wind, someone came in whistling a famous tune. Bordelli tried to remember the title, but it wouldn't come to him. The man took the stairs like a horse, and when he was face to face with Bordelli, he stopped whistling. He was tall and fat, and must certainly be him, the terrible Nocentini. He looked to be just over twenty years old, with clear eyes and a likeable face.

'Evenin',' he said, thrusting his hands in his pockets and continuing on his way.

'I beg your pardon, but what were you whistling?' Bordelli asked him.

The young man turned round and gave him a funny look, then smiled faintly, amused.

'I don't know, something French, I think,' he said, shrugging.

'Was it perhaps a song by Yves Montand?'

'Perhaps.'

'Are you Nocentini?'

'Yes. Why do you ask?' the man said, no longer smiling.

'Could I talk to you for a minute?'

'And who are you?'

'Inspector Bordelli. Let's go upstairs for a minute. I just need to ask you a couple of questions.'

'All right,' said the lad, frowning.

They climbed up to the top floor and went into his flat. It consisted of a narrow hallway with a room at each end, dirty walls, crates yet to be unpacked, rags strewn about, and a musty, closed smell that made one want to cough.

'I'm still getting settled,' said the young man, standing in front of Bordelli.

'Are you the one making all the racket at night?' the inspector asked.

'It was the old hag on the first floor who told you that, wasn't it? What the hell is her name . . .?'

'Couldn't you try to be a little quieter?'

'I am extremely quiet, but the minute the lady hears a fly buzz—'

'What about that record player?'

'I keep it turned down low.'

Bordelli went over to see what records Nocentini was listening to. Celentano, Carosone, Rita Pavone . . .

'Have you got a job?' he asked.

'I work at the central market. At five a.m. I'm already there unloading.'

The inspector looked up from the stack of records and headed towards the door.

'Well, I have to go now. Try not to make too much noise at night, or Signora Capecchi will keep bugging me.'

'Okay.'

'And see that you don't put out your cigarette butts in the stairwell.'

'I'll be careful not to.'

'It'll be better for everyone,' said Bordelli, knowing how annoying old ladies of that sort could be. He shook the lad's hand and went away trying to remember the title of that song by Yves Montand.

Ever since he had seen little Casimiro folded up inside the suitcase, Bordelli had felt guilty. But now all he could do was find who had killed him, and this he swore he would do.

Forensics had examined Casimiro's flat but found no fingerprints other than those of Bordelli and the Beast. The killer had taken great care not to leave any traces. Which was rather strange for the murder of a poor dwarf from the Case Minime.

Late the following morning, around midday, Bordelli got into his car with Piras and headed off towards Fiesole. On the way he gave his assistant a thorough account of everything he knew about the case, from the not-quite-dead man Casimiro had seen in the field to his last phone call to the inspector.

They left the car in the usual spot and walked as far as the olive grove. Bordelli had no clear sense of what they were doing, but Casimiro's last words led them to that villa, and that was where they should start. When they got to the buttresses, they noticed a great many torn ivy leaves on the ground. It looked as if someone had tried to climb up one of the buttresses by grabbing on to the vines' strongest branches.

'I like this story less and less, Piras.'

Bordelli was thinking of Casimiro, his wretched life and horrific death. It would have been better if he had never been born. At that hour maybe Diotivede had already opened up his belly.

Piras was looking carefully at the ground. At a certain point he spotted something in the grass and got down on his kness.

'Come and look, Inspector.'

Bordelli came closer and bent down to look.

'Shit,' he said. It was Casimiro's little plastic skeleton. He picked it up and turned it around sadly in his hand.

'Why did you say *shit*, Inspector?'

'Because this belonged to Casimiro.'

'Are you sure?' asked Piras.

'Quite sure. It was a sort of talisman. He was always fiddling with it.'

'Couldn't he have dropped it the night you came here together?'

'No, I remember specifically that he had it in his hand when I drove him home.'

'Shit,' said the Sardinian.

Bordelli put the little skeleton in his pocket and resumed looking around. He took a few steps back to get a full view of the villa. As usual, the shutters were closed and there was no sign of life within. Piras kept searching along the ground, looking for footprints, but it was no use. The dense carpet of grass didn't hold an impression for very long.

'Let's go up to the villa, Piras,' Bordelli said out of the blue. They returned to the car and, a few minutes later, pulled up at the big rusty gate. They went up to it and looked through the bars. In the daylight the garden looked even more neglected. The small stone fountain was dry and covered with moss, the weeds growing freely beyond the limits of the old flower beds.

'It looks like one of those haunted houses,' said Piras. If Bordelli hadn't seen the German woman come out with his own two eyes, he might have thought the same thing. He tugged the chain to the bell. They heard it ring inside the house, but nobody came out.

'Miss Olga!' Bordelli shouted. Again he had the feeling that someone was spying on them through the slats of the shutters.

'Are they watching us?'

'You can read my mind, Piras.'

The wind gusted and stirred up the dry leaves on the villa's patios. The effect was rather like a Sunday at the cemetery. Piras and Bordelli carefully checked all the windows one by one, trying to determine whether someone really was watching them, but they didn't see anything out of the ordinary. They only heard the rustle of the windswept leaves.

They got back in the car and returned to the city by way of the old road, so steep it was almost perpendicular. Bordelli kept thinking of the man with the black mark on his neck. Where had he seen that sort of mark before? Perhaps he was mistaken . . .

'Piras, a man with a dark spot on the neck from here to here,' said Bordelli, running his finger across his throat, 'does that ring a bell for you?'

'I don't think so,' said the young man.

'So, what do you make of all this?'

'Well, we know for certain that Casimiro was in that field and had perhaps tried to climb up the buttress, but that doesn't necessarily mean the villa had anything to do with the murder . . .'

'Quite so . . .'

'But I do wonder: where, exactly, was Casimiro murdered? At home or somewhere else? And if he was killed away from his home, why did they carry him all the way back there inside a suitcase? It would have been easier to dump him in the Arno or bury him out in the country somewhere.'

'Good question, Piras. Have you got an answer?'

'I'd really rather you didn't smoke, Inspector,' said Piras, seeing Bordelli reach into his jacket pocket. The inspector merely made a face that meant such things couldn't be helped, and lit a cigarette. Piras opened the window at once.

Diotivede heard him come in, but he kept his eye pressed up against the eyepiece of the microscope.

'What are you doing up at this ungodly hour?'

It was barely half past seven.

'Well, I know you start work early,' said Bordelli.

'But you don't.'

'I haven't been sleeping well lately.'

'I've already done your dwarf, but haven't written the report yet,' said Diotivede, turning a knob on the microscope.

'Tell me in person.'

'I know you knew him.'

'I first arrested him just after the war.'

The pathologist ceased combing through the cilia of bacteria and sat up straight. Every time Bordelli looked at him he was amazed. Diotivede was over seventy, but his face still had something childish about it.

'He died two days ago, between one and two o'clock in the morning.'

'From a crushed skull?'

'Wrong.'

'How, then?'

'He was poisoned,' said the doctor.

Bordelli's eyes widened.

'What about that blow to the head?'

'They did that later, almost certainly with a hammer.'

'What could it mean?' asked Bordelli, shaking his head.

'I was wondering myself. Perhaps your little friend had some muscle spasms as he was dying; that can happen with poisoning. And the killer, perhaps fearing he wasn't going to die, finished him off with a hammer.'

'Anything else?' asked Bordelli, feeling a keen desire to light up.

'His fingernails were broken, except for the thumbs. He seems to have scraped them against a very rough surface. The fingertips are also a bit chafed.'

'Could he have done it against a stone wall?'

'Certainly.'

'Go on.'

'His stomach was full to bursting. Want to know what he had eaten?' the doctor asked.

'Poor guy, I can guess . . . Black cabbage, beans . . .'

'You're on the wrong track.'

'What do you mean?'

Diotivede picked up a wrinkled sheet of paper from the table and read:

'Crayfish, gilthead bream, shrimp . . . there was even a fair amount of langoustine, and a lot of mayonnaise. The wine was a Gewürztraminer or something similar. I won't list the desserts, or you might gain weight.'

'You're joking, of course.'

'No,' said the doctor, a little smile on his face.

'Shit!' said Bordelli.

'There was no lack of cognac, either, though it was cut with cyanide.'

'Was it a painful death?'

'I'd say so,' said Diotivede, adjusting his glasses on his nose.

'Poor bloke . . .' Bordelli muttered.

'But there's another curious fact: it was rather unusual cyanide.'

'In what sense?'

'Old stuff, fashioned into very small tablets.'

'How old?'

'Very old,' said the doctor.

'From the last war?'

'Even before.'

'Can it keep for so long?'

'Depends on how you store it.'

Bordelli nervously fingered his chin.

'Anything else?'

'I don't think so. And now I'm sorry, but I have to finish the girl,' said Diotivede, pointing towards a gurney at the back of the laboratory. A cascade of blonde hair poured out from under a sheet, and at the opposite end, two very white, slender feet pointed upwards.

45

'Is she the one who was found in the dump?' the inspector asked.

'She is. That fathead Rabozzi's handling the case.'

'A prostitute?'

'Apparently not.'

'Raped?'

'I was just going to check.'

'Could I see her?'

'Go ahead.'

The inspector approached the gurney and raised the sheet a little, then lifted it completely. He looked sadly at the girl. She was barely twenty years old.

'Beautiful girl,' he said.

'She looks Parisian,' said the doctor.

'Do you know Paris well?'

'Almost as well as I know human intestines. I lived there for five years.'

'I didn't know that.'

'You don't have to know everything,' said the doctor.

Bordelli lowered the sheet. He too had been in Paris, in December 1939. He had met a beautiful woman and fallen in love with her like a teenager. Her name was Christine. Their three weeks together had been like a dream, and returning home hadn't been easy. They had started writing to each other. She, too, seemed in every way in love with him, and almost ready to come to Italy. Then Hitler's divisions entered Paris, and he never heard from her again . . .

Bordelli shook his head free of those memories and put a cigarette in his mouth, which he wouldn't light until outside the laboratory.

'I'm going. Once you've typed up your report, send it to me,' he said.

'Goodbye,' said Diotivede, getting back down to work.

When he reached the door, the inspector stopped.

'Sorry . . .' he said, turning round.

'Don't ask me if there's anything else, because there isn't,' the doctor interrupted him without looking up from the microscope.

'I just wanted to know if you know a cognac called de Maricourt.'

'Of course I do,' said the doctor.

'Oh, really? I didn't know it.'

Diotivede looked up from his microorganisms with a sigh and put his hands in his pockets.

'Nobody in Italy knows it. It's never been exported and hasn't even been produced for at least twenty years. The distillery was destroyed during the war and never rebuilt. The last reserves were carried away by the Nazis during the American advance.'

'Is it good cognac?'

'The best.'

'Diotivede, you amaze me. How do you know these things?'

'Culture.'

'Tell me something, how can you distinguish cognac from whisky or Calvados? In a dead man's stomach, I mean.'

'Don't think I taste it,' said the doctor, expecting another of those idiotic quips he'd been putting up with all his life.

'No, I mean it seriously,' said Bordelli. 'How do you tell them apart?'

'There are chemical tables of all the different kinds of alcohol, and each has its own characteristics.'

'I guess it doesn't get any easier than that . . .'

''Bye, Bordelli,' said the doctor, turning his eye back to the microscope.

But Bordelli wasn't leaving. He had started pacing back and forth, the unlit cigarette still in his mouth.

'Do you think you could also determine the brand of cognac that Casimiro drank?' he suddenly asked.

'That's asking too much,' said Diotivede.

'Forget I asked,' said Bordelli, who muttered goodbye and

walked out of the laboratory, leaving the pathologist in peace at last.

He returned to headquarters with his mind in a state of confusion. Climbing the stairs, he ran into Rabozzi. The big lug was wearing his usual mastiff-like grimace, which screwed his face up.

'Hello, Bordelli.'

'Hello. I've just seen the girl they found in the refuse dump.'

'Beautiful, no? . . . What's wrong? You look glum.'

'I can't get over what happened to Casimiro.'

'Your little dwarf friend?'

'Yeah.'

'What are you going to do if you find the person who killed him? Shoot him in the head?' Rabozzi asked, chuckling.

'Let me catch him first,' said Bordelli.

'If you send him to jail, between one buggering and another, he'll already be out in five years.'

'I'm going upstairs.'

''Bye, Bordelli.'

Rabozzi strode off with his avenger's swagger, and Bordelli went up to his office. He lit another cigarette. He had started smoking a lot again, blaming it on the hard times. The murdered child and Casimiro's death kept him in a state of constant tension. Despite the time of day, he opened a bottle of beer, flipping the cap off, as usual, with his house keys.

On the desk was a brand-new report: during the night a prominent businessman had caught a burglar in the act of robbing his villa at Bellosguardo and shot him with his hunting rifle, gravely wounding him. Self-defence, the businessman had called it. Bordelli knew the burglar well: Bernardo, an unlucky wretch who had never harmed a fly. He had simply gone to pick up a crumb of prosperity in an Italy with a few very rich people and a great deal of poverty, and for this he was shot with a hunting rifle. There was something about this that didn't make sense. Bordelli finished reading the report, shaking his head. He rang Mugnai on the internal line.

'Send me Piras, please.'

At that moment there was a knock at the door, and Piras poked his head inside.

'Mugnai, don't bother. He's already here,' said Bordelli.

He set down the phone and stood up, looking the young Sardinian in the eye.

'You know what Casimiro had in his stomach, Piras?' And he told him everything Diotivede had told him about the little man's last supper. Piras scratched his head.

'What a stinking mess,' he said.

Bordelli huffed, then picked up the bottle of de Maricourt cognac and started staring at it as if trying to read the truth in it.

That same night Bordelli returned alone to the olive grove in Fiesole. The sky was clear and full of stars. As it was almost the new moon, he'd brought along a torch. But he knew the place well by now, and managed not to turn it on.

He didn't really know what he'd come looking for. He wanted only to poke about a bit, in the hope of discovering something. He could have asked Judge Ginzillo for a warrant to search the villa, but for the moment he preferred to proceed with caution. He still had no idea who he was dealing with, and was afraid to make a wrong move. Anyway, Ginzillo was too timid, always clinging to legal quibbles like a vine, terrified of wrecking his judicial career with a single mistake. For the moment it was best to forget about Ginzillo, who would only waste a great deal of his time, as usual.

At last he came to a stop, at a spot from where he had a good view of the villa. As usual, the shutters were all closed and no light was visible. The air was still. There was deep silence. He leaned back against the trunk of a great, leafy olive tree and lit a cigarette, taking care to hide the flame of the match. On so dark a night, he risked being seen. He smoked with his hand cupped round the burning cigarette-end, the way he used to do in the war.

All at once he saw a window light up in the villa, but a few seconds later it was dark again. He tossed the butt to the ground and snuffed it out with his shoe. He suddenly felt like imposing on Miss Olga. He was about to return to the car when he noticed something. Turning round, he glimpsed a human silhouette in the distance, walking through the olive trees. He crouched instinctively and held still. He was almost certain he hadn't been seen. The man was strolling casually through the trees, as if he could see quite well in the darkness. The inspector waited for him to draw near, then popped out and came towards the man, shining the torch and pointing his pistol at him.

'Good evening,' he said. The man quickly sidestepped and stopped. Bordelli lit up his face, and for a moment he thought he was looking at a mask. The face was full of wrinkles, with two powerful eyes that seemed to belong to a wounded animal.

'Good evening,' said the man, body relaxing. Bordelli lowered the beam of light to the stranger's clothes. He clearly was not a vagrant, and actually seemed rather well dressed. Bordelli raised the torch again to the man's face.

'Were you looking for something?'

'Who are you, if I may ask?' the man said innocuously. He had the accent of a foreigner who had lived for a long time in Italy.

'Police,' said Bordelli. The man didn't seem the least bit surprised.

'Can I help you with anything?' he asked.

The inspector took a step forward.

'What are you doing here?'

'I was out for a stroll.'

'At one o'clock in the morning?'

'At one o'clock in the morning,' said the man, unflinching.

'Why don't you tell me your name, for starters?' said Bordelli, making the mistake of lowering his gun. The man muttered something in a strange language, then bounded forward and, before the inspector realised what was happening, punched him in the stomach. Bordelli fell to his knees, the wind knocked out of him, and the torch slipped from his hand. With some effort he raised his head, then saw the man's black silhouette running like a rhinoceros towards the wood. He took aim with his pistol and was about to fire but decided against it. What sort of bloody language was the big ape speaking, anyway? It sounded like something Slavic, or Arabic.

When he had regained his breath, he stood up, reeling, and with one hand on his liver, he staggered back to the Beetle. He felt like an ass. He sat inside the car for a few minutes, smoking a cigarette under the moon, which that night was as slender as the stroke of a pen. Tossing the butt out the window, he started the engine. He climbed up the Via del Bargellino and a moment later stopped in front of the villa's entrance. He got out of the car and went up to the gate. All was dark. He pulled on the bell insistently, not giving a damn that it was the middle of the night. Lights came on on the first floor, and then on the ground floor. A moment later the door opened, and Miss Olga appeared in silhouette in the lighted doorway.

'Miss Olga, please forgive me for coming at this time of the night,' he shouted. 'It's me again, Inspector Bordelli.'

The woman wrapped her shawl about her neck and came forward through the garden. She stopped a step away from the gate and did not open it. This time she was in a dressing gown, and her eyes looked very angry.

'I vas asleep,' she said, annoyed.

'I wanted to talk to you for a minute.'

'Then talk.'

'Has the baron returned?'

'No.'

'Do you know where he is?'

'Africa, I think.'

'And you don't know when he'll be back?'

'*Nein.*' Uttered drily by the puckered mouth of Fräulein Olga, that word brought Bordelli back to the war days. He stared at the woman, imagining her in an SS uniform.

'Does the villa belong to the baron?'

'*Ja* . . . Yes.'

'When did he buy it?'

'You can research zese things by yourself.'

'If you tell me now you'll save me a lot of time.'

'After the war,' the woman said with a sigh, increasingly irritated.

'Forgive me for asking, signorina, but does the baron by any chance have a large black spot on his neck?'

'I really sink you mistake him for anozzer persson.'

'And one last thing. Have you noticed anything strange around here lately?'

'If dare was somesing strange I call the police,' said Olga, staring at him. Bordelli tried to smile.

'When the baron returns, would you be so good as to tell him to come and see me?'

'Baron stays away long time, maybe months.'

'Well, if you're in touch with him by telephone, please tell him to give me a ring at police headquarters.'

'All right.'

'Thank you, and sorry to disturb you.'

'Good night,' said Miss Olga. She did an about-face, marched to the house and closed the great door behind her with a thud. You certainly couldn't call her hospitable.

One evening in January 1944, in a little town in the south, Bordelli and Gavino Piras, the father of Bordelli's young assistant, had gone out for a walk along the roads. They had put civilian coats over their uniforms. The 8th of September was still a recent memory,[7] and the area was still full of Nazis. It was foolhardy to be out like that, and they knew it. Round a bend they were stopped by a German military lorry and forced at gunpoint to climb aboard the flatbed, where there were other men, old and young, with fear in their eyes. They were all brought to a farmstead just outside the town and forced to dig a large pit in the muddy ground, perhaps to bury their dead. Bordelli and Piras were in a cold sweat. If the Germans ever discovered that they were with the San Marco Battalion, they would have them shot as traitors. And so they shovelled earth and mud with the others for almost three hours, with nobody opening his mouth, and then they were all released. Once they were round the corner, Piras and Bordelli burst out laughing. Not from amusement, but from the tension accumulated in their guts, which demanded release. It seemed almost impossible that they'd come out alive. They returned to camp and didn't tell anyone what had happened. They spent the night awake, smoking like chimneys.

Bordelli got up out of bed at six, without having slept. He still had that chilling adventure with Gavino on his mind. The ashtray emitted a nasty, sickly-sweet smell. He went and emptied it in the dustbin in the kitchen, then returned to the bedroom. He opened the window and looked out, shivering from the cold. It was still dark outside. A very light rain was falling, tiny little drops that glittered like diamonds in the light of the street lamps. He lit a cigarette and rested his elbows on the sill, thinking of the monster who had killed Valentina. Maybe the killer, too, was awake and looking at the same low sky, the same blanket of dark clouds. He tried to imagine the man. Perhaps he was lonely, rejected by all, half mad, and had killed on impulse, for reasons only God knew. And now he carried that horrible secret inside, crushed by guilt, unable to understand the monstrous force that welled up in him at certain moments. Or perhaps not. Maybe he was pleased with what he had done and was already planning another murder. Or maybe he was neither devastated by guilt nor pleased with himself, and simply carried on with his life, indifferent to everything. It was anybody's guess.

The inspector blew his smoke against the sky and ran a hand over his face. His brain was weary. He wished he could detach his head in order to stop thinking. He flicked the butt into the street below and lit another. It was disgusting and tasted like metal. Leaving the window open, he went and lay down in bed. To distract himself, he started studying the details of the room. He knew intimately every crack and stain in the plaster, the areas where the paint was flaking off the shutters, the cobwebs in the corners of the ceiling, the cardboard wedges under the bookcase, the worn-out spines of his books, which never changed place over the years. Sometimes he liked seeing everything stay the same; at other times he couldn't stand it. He blew the smoke forcefully out of his mouth . . .

The desire to kill . . . Perhaps it had deep roots in the heart of every man. An irrational force, an ancestral legacy that smacked of the survival instinct. Or perhaps it was the wish to learn something about death, to see it with one's own two eyes . . .

He remembered the time he had killed a lizard as a little boy. He may have killed many more, but that was the one he remembered. It was summertime. The lizard was a few yards away from him, immobile at the foot of a pine tree, peacefully sunning itself. It was nice and big, and very green. He had taken aim with his slingshot, driven by a will he didn't understand. He had let the elastic band go, and the stone had struck the lizard on the head, making it jump in the air. He had approached to look at it. The lizard lay on its back, a line of blood round its neck. Its belly was white and scaly, and its tail was still moving, as if it refused to die. He stood and watched it for several minutes, horrified and fascinated by that pointless death. The decision to kill had been entirely his own, and now he felt all the weight of that irremediable act on his shoulders, unable to understand why he had done it . . .

In the two years of war following the Armistice, he had killed many Nazis, but at least he knew why. He had wanted to fight them face to face. That was why he had asked to join the San Marco Battalion after spending three years on boats and submarines. When April 1945 arrived, he had twenty-four notches carved in the butt of his machine gun, and they were only for SS men that he was certain he had personally killed. Looking at those dead bodies, he had felt something entirely different. Mostly nausea. Nausea for all those dead, for himself, for war.

He snuffed out the fag-end and put his hands behind his head. He half-closed his eyes, to rest them. No, maybe the monster wasn't awake after all. Maybe he was sleeping as he did every other night, normally, like one who has come home tired from work, disappointed and resigned, or melancholy, depending on the day. And he was curled up in bed, clutching the pillow, as he himself often did. If he lived in Florence, he breathed the same air as Bordelli, walked the same streets, saw the same buildings, the same churches, was one of the many on whom he happened to rest his gaze for a second. Perhaps they had even looked each other in the eye once or twice in the street, or brushed shoulders, as so often happened with so many people.

He sat up to look at the alarm clock. Quarter to seven. He switched off the light and turned on to his side. It was almost dawn. His head felt heavy, enveloped in the vapours of a sleepiness that clouded his vision without ever delivering the *coup de grâce*. A cold breeze blew in through the open window. He didn't feel like getting up, and wrapped the covers round himself, clutching the pillow tightly to his chest. His bronchial tubes were inflamed from the cigarettes. He felt more numb than ever, but couldn't stop thinking. It was as though someone were ceaselessly turning a crank connected to his brain. He thought about the war, childhood, the fact of being fifty-four years old, Rosa's massages, Casimiro balled up inside the suitcase . . . He thought about the absurd, wrongful death of Valentina, and her mother sleeping in a hospital, pumped full of sedatives . . . He thought about the time that—

The telephone rang, and in the darkness his hand found the receiver.

'Yeah?'

'Is that you, Marshal?'

'What is it, Signora Capecchi?'

The old lady seemed quite agitated.

'Things are going from bad to worse here. Zillo has disappeared!' she said.

'Who is Zillo?'

'My canary . . . He's gone! The cage is empty! He's been kidnapped! And I think I know who did it . . .'

'Nocentini?'

'That hooligan wants to frighten me! He wants to make me die . . . Ohhh!'

'What's happening, signora?'

'Buricchio . . . he's got feathers in his mouth . . .'

'Who is Buricchio?'

'My cat . . .'

'Ah, I see.'

'Buricchio, come here! . . . you naughty, wicked cat . . . What have you done with Zillo?'

He got to the office at about ten o'clock, pumped full of coffee, after leaving the Beetle at the police department's garage for a check-up. He had slept barely two hours. His ears were ringing. He put out the cigarette he had just lit and went to see Porcinai in Archives.

The archivist raised his powerful head and rubbed his eyes, two big, round, gentle eyes like a sheep's.

'Hello, Bordelli.'

'What are you eating?'

'*Sommommoli*.[8] Want one?'

'No, thanks.'

Porcinai lived in the darkness of the archive from morning to evening, always sitting. He didn't even get up to eat. It was too much of an effort. He would bring mysterious packages from home, stick them in a drawer and then nibble a bit of everything all day long, getting his fingers greasy and wiping them on his trousers. A bright white lamp lit up the desktop, which was littered with papers and folders. The rest of the large room remained almost always in darkness.

'What do you need, Bordelli?'

'I can manage by myself, thanks. Just turn on the light for me.'

Porcinai flipped a switch he'd had installed under the desk, and the fluorescent tubes came on, one after another. The inspector made his way through the stacks, which stretched to the ceiling, looking for the records of criminal offenders. He

pulled out a folder from the shelf marked ABA–CES. It was full to
bursting. He brought it over to a table and started thumbing
through it listlessly. It was just a way for him to feel as if he was
doing something. He was thinking about the man at the villa with
the bloody black spot on his neck. He read the names and looked
at the faces: Abitanti, Vito; Abbate, Angelo; Abelamenti, Nicola;
Abissino, Giuseppe; Accursio, Tommaso . . . but he felt that he
wasn't going to find anything of interest in these files, only the
normal faces of normal criminals. In the end he gave up. He put
the folder back in its place and stopped for a few minutes to
chat with Porcinai, sitting down on a corner of the desk. Then
he patted him on the back and went back to his office.

He collapsed into his chair, sighing. He hadn't made an inch
of progress on either of the two murders and felt an over-
whelming sense of powerlessness.

It was almost noon. A steely sky weighed down upon the
city, the cold air pressing against the windowpanes, steaming
them up. And yet it was mid-April.

He reread the reports on the little girl for the thousandth
time. He looked at the photos, thinking that the killer, too, had
witnessed that scene. This gave him an unpleasant feeling, as
if a very fine thread linked him directly with the killer. If only
he could follow that thread, inch by inch, without ever pulling
on it, all the way to the culprit . . .

He jotted something down on a notepad, hoping this might
grant him some sort of foothold for moving forward. But after
a few minutes, he crumpled the paper into a ball and tossed
it into the waste basket.

He picked up the telephone receiver and asked Mugnai to
go and get him another coffee at the bar in Via San Gallo.

'Drink whatever you like and have them put it on my tab,'
he said.

'Thanks, Inspector.'

While waiting for his coffee, he was summoned by the
commissioner. And so he went upstairs one floor, with no desire
whatsoever to do so. Knocking faintly, he pushed the door

open without waiting. Commissioner Inzipone greeted him properly and offered him a cigarette.

'Thanks, I've got my own,' the inspector said, sitting down. The commissioner looked at him with concern.

'Did you want to talk about the round-up?' Bordelli asked provocatively.

'Never mind the round-up, I don't feel like quarrelling,' said Inzipone, pressing his eyes with his fingers. It took the murder of a little girl to make him get over those stupid round-ups, thought Bordelli.

'Tell me what it is you want, sir, I haven't got much time,' he said impatiently.

'I want to know how far we've got with the case of the little girl.'

'We're still at square one, unfortunately . . . As soon as I return to my office I'll ring the hospital to find out if I can talk to Valentina's mother.'

Inzipone rested his chin in his hand, looking grave.

'People expect a lot from us, Bordelli,' he said, his head bobbing.

'I do too, I assure you.'

'Try to speed things up . . . And what can you tell me about the Robetti murder?'

'I'm sorry . . . Who is Robetti?'

'The dwarf you found in the suitcase.'

'Oh, you mean Casimiro.'

'Any leads?'

'I'm working on it,' said Bordelli, standing up.

'Keep me informed.'

'Of course.'

'All right, then, you can go.'

Conversations like this made no sense, the inspector thought as he closed the door behind him. When he got back to his office, the coffee was already cold, but he drank it anyway. Then he picked up the phone and called Forensic Medicine. After ten rings, somebody picked up.

'Yes?'

'Hello, Diotivede, it's me.'

'I'm a little busy,' the pathologist said. Bordelli imagined him with someone's spleen in his hand.

'Just one question . . . do you have any recollection of a man with a long black spot on his neck?' he asked. Diotivede thought about it for a moment.

'It does seem to ring a bell, but I can't recall anything specific,' he said.

'Well, I tried . . . How are things down there among the dead?'

'It's the only place where I don't have to hear that sort of nonsense.'

'What about the girl from the rubbish dump?'

'Raped by three men.'

'The animals . . .'

'I'm going back to work.'

'Ciao.'

Bordelli hung up and shook his head, hoping those three soon ended up in Rabozzi's hands. He started staring at the wall in front of him, but still saw only the same things: the little girl lying on the ground with her arms spread, Casimiro's stiff, misshapen body crammed inside the suitcase . . . Poverty, death, injustice . . . He couldn't stand it any more. He noticed in the waste basket the bottle of beer the dwarf had drunk that famous night, and he angrily lit a cigarette. He didn't know which way to turn, and this pissed him off no end. He unwrapped a chocolate that had been sitting on his desk for months. It must have melted in the summer and resolidified in the winter, as it was white and smelled like soap flakes. He ate it just the same, rolling the tinfoil wrapper tightly in his fingers.

He was getting increasingly worked up. He tried to grasp on to some shred of an idea, any idea, even the most insignificant, just to feel as if he was making a little progress in the two murder cases. But nothing came to him. He thought again of Ginzillo and getting a search warrant for the villa in Fiesole, but this still seemed like a bad idea. Even if Casimiro's killer really did live in that house, the person had already managed in time to regroup and remove all traces before the murder was even discovered.

In the end Bordelli gave up and tried to busy himself with the little he had. He picked up the phone and called Santa Maria Nova hospital to see whether he could talk to Valentina's mother. He asked for Dr Saggini.

'She's still very weak, Inspector,' the doctor said.

'I only want to ask her a few questions.'

'Try calling me tomorrow morning. Maybe she'll feel a little better then.'

'Thanks, Doctor.'

The inspector hung up and sent Mugnai down to the bar again, this time to pick up a few beers. He felt at a loss. All he was doing was ruminating, without result, never advancing a single step. It was even worse than walking in the rain during the war, in boots weighed down with mud.

Casimiro's murder disoriented him. A great many things had happened around that villa in Fiesole, things which, at first glance, might appear disconnected. Perhaps they really were only coincidences that had nothing to do with the murder; or perhaps they were part of a bigger, still invisible design. For the moment it was hard to understand any of it. He flipped the cap off a beer bottle and distractedly opened the bottom drawer, the most private, of the filing cabinet. It was full of odds and ends, strange, useless objects – he couldn't even remember where he had got them: empty little boxes, colourful ribbons, a magnet with bits of iron stuck to it, old postcards signed by strangers, crumpled scraps of paper with meaningless telephone numbers written on them. At once he found a small, yellowed sheet of paper, folded in four. Unfolding it, he recognised his own handwriting. It was a letter he had written to his mother during the war. It was dated 9 September 1943, the day after the Armistice. A letter full of lies: '*Dear ones, we are leaving. We are on the move, to a destination unknown. We are perfectly calm. Do not worry about me, or about anything, even if you do not hear from me for a long time. I will write if I can. Love and kisses to all, F.*' He reread that brief, lying letter several times, shudders running up his arms. He well remembered when and where he had written it, and the mood he was in. After that date, the real inferno began. Farther down on the same sheet of paper his mother had written: "*'43 to '45 = War. N.B. Franco, aged 33, was taken away. For 12 months until September '44 we had no news of him, neither the Vatican nor the Red Cross could answer our questions. For 12 long months this note was our sphinx! Then two soldiers of the San Marco brought word to us, though he didn't write anything else until the end of the war.*' It was true. He had written nothing else. A few months after the liberation he had returned to Florence without telling anyone. It was a night in June. When he got to the house he went into the garden without ringing and looked in through a ground-floor window. His mother was sitting at a small table full of votive candles, and in the middle of all the little flames was a photo of her only son, whom everyone by now believed lost. He saw her praying in the shadows, her face perfectly still. He waited a few minutes, blood pounding in his temples as he looked on. Then he knocked on the windowpane. His mother stiffened and stopped praying, and even before she had turned round, she cried, 'Franco!' Then she stood up, planting her hands on the table, and went and opened the window, remaining silent for a moment, just looking at her son who had come back from the dead, face darkened by sun, cheeks hollow, eyes glistening like those of certain animals. 'You must be hungry,' she said. He climbed over the window-sill, tossed his backpack to one side, and lifted his mother in the air as if she were a little girl. 'I'd love some spaghetti,' he said.

He folded the letter up again and put it back in the drawer. He ran a hand over his eyes to try to suppress the emotions at the heart of that memory, then lit another stupid cigarette and stared at the wall, spellbound. The image of his mother in front of that shrine to her son stayed with him for a long time.

Midway through the afternoon he remembered Aldo Bandiera, an old friend and fellow-thief of Casimiro's. Perhaps the little guy had confided in him, he thought. It might not be a bad idea to pay him a visit. He decided to go there at once. On his way out he gestured to Mugnai.

'If anyone asks for me, I'll be back in an hour,' he said. Mugnai came out of his booth and followed him into the street.

'My sister is very worried, Inspector,' he said. 'She has two little girls and lately she's taken to keeping them always at home.'

'There's nothing else we can do at the moment, Mugnai. But we'll catch him soon,' the inspector said with conviction. He didn't want anyone to notice that he was worried. He slapped Mugnai on the shoulder by way of goodbye and went to the department's garage to pick up his Beetle. Sallustio was just lowering the bonnet as he walked in.

'Ciao, Sallustio.'

'Inspector, are you sure this tractor ran before you brought it in?'

'It ran the way it always does. Why?'

'The spark plugs were in pretty sorry shape. I had to use a hammer just to unscrew them.'

'Everything all right now?'

'Everything's just fine, Inspector. You'll feel the difference . . . But I'm keeping the old plugs as souvenirs. I want to show them to my sons.'

'German cars.'

'If it had been down to these road-rollers, the potato-heads would have won the war.'

'Let's not think about that, Sallustio, it's too frightening.'

He said goodbye to the mechanic and revved the engine as he left, to see whether he could feel this supposed difference, but he didn't notice anything different. The Beetle ran as well as it had always done, noisy as ever, German as ever.

When he got to Le Cure,[9] he parked the car in front of Bandiera's shop, which consisted of a glass-paned door giving on to a small room chock full of geegaws of every sort. The light was on inside, and a sign hung from the doorknob saying: I'LL BE RIGHT BACK. Bordelli got out of the car and looked in through the glass. There really was everything there, from wooden mannequins to used washbasins. He knew that Aldo lived round the corner, so he went there on foot.

He passed through the main door of a building with a dirty façade. Unable to find a light switch, he ascended the stairs in darkness. He let his hands brush against the wall to orient himself. He counted three storeys, then knocked on a door with his fist. He could hear a television going at full volume inside. Nobody came to answer the door. The inspector knocked harder, and finally heard the sound of a chair scraping against the floor. At that same moment a woman on the floor below screamed at her child, triggering the hysterical puling of a number of little children. Bandiera's door suddenly opened, and Bordelli found himself looking at Aldo's old mug, which bore the signs of a harsh, bitter life. The man had two enormous ears full of hair. By now he must be nearly eighty years old. As he hadn't turned down the television set, Bordelli had to raise his voice.

'Hello, Aldo, could I come in for a minute?'

The old man didn't look overjoyed to see him.

'That's what somebody else said, Inspector, when they came to arrest me.'

'I just want to ask you a couple of questions.'

Leaving the door open, the old man turned round and walked towards the room with the blaring television, dragging his feet, with Bordelli following behind. He collapsed in a chair and glued his eyes to the cartoons on the screen. A large drop hung from the tip of his nose, but it refused to fall, not even with the trembling of his head. One wanted to wipe it away for him, even without his permission. Bordelli sat down in front of him.

'Could you turn down the telly, please?' he asked.

Aldo pricked his ear with a finger.

'What?' he said, wrinkling his nose.

'The telly . . . Could we turn it down?' Bordelli yelled. The old man stood up reluctantly, went over to the television and lowered the volume.

'I wanted to watch *Felix*,' he said, sitting back down.

'I'll only take five minutes of your time.'

'At my age, five minutes is a lot of time.'

'Have you heard about Casimiro?'

'I read it in the papers. If you find who killed him, send him here to me, Inspector. I'd like to have a few words with him, in my own way.'

'When did you last see Casimiro?'

'He came by a few days before he died.'

'Did he say anything to you?'

'He talked about a villa up Fiesole way, which he'd been spying on for several days.'

'Do you know if he'd discovered anything?'

'He didn't tell me anything else. The little guy always liked to be mysterious about things.'

'I'll find his killer, you can be sure of that.'

'He was a good dwarf,' said Aldo, staring at him. Bordelli got up to go. He'd reached another dead end.

'Thanks, Aldo. I'll let you watch your *Felix*.'

Aldo stood up to see him out.

'No need, Aldo, I know the way,' said Bordelli. The old man slumped back in his chair.

'Goodbye, Inspector,' he said, turning his eyes to the television screen just as Felix was scratching his belly and laughing wildly . . . *The End*.

'Hell,' said Aldo. Fortunately another cartoon started at once, also *Felix the Cat*, and the old man gave a sort of smile. Bordelli went out, leaving him in peace. He descended the stairs in the dark, afraid he might stumble. The little children were finally starting to pipe down, and on the top floor a woman was singing, as an old person somewhere else coughed and coughed.

The following morning, round eleven o'clock, Bordelli phoned Santa Maria Nova hospital again, to see how Carla Panerai, Valentina's mother, was doing.

'You can come now, Inspector, but please don't tire her out,' said Dr Saggini.

'Five minutes is all I need.'

'Ask for me when you get here.'

'Thanks. See you in a bit.'

The hospital wasn't far from Via Zara. Since the sky was clear, Bordelli decided to go on foot. He walked at a brisk pace, trying to empty his mind for a few minutes at least. As soon as he came out into Piazza San Marco he heard someone call him and turned round. Before him he found an unpleasant but familiar face.

'Bordelli! Don't you recognise me? I'm Melchiorri.'

'Hello, how are you?' said Bordelli.

So that's who he was. That prick Melchiorri. He still had the same big head covered with yellow hair, the same stupid blue eyes. Bordelli had never liked Melchiorri.

'I'm well, and yourself?' said Melchiorri.

'No complaints.'

'It must be thirty years, no?'

'Even longer,' said Bordelli, already bored. He looked at Melchiorri's motley tie, wishing he'd never seen it.

'I live in Milan nowadays . . . A splendid city. The only truly Italian city. But my parents stayed behind, so a couple of times a year I come down to see them.'

'Ah, good.'

'Do you remember the row we used to kick up in class sometimes? The class from hell!' Melchiorri said, cackling with laughter.

'Right.'

Bordelli didn't feel like talking. He didn't know what to say.

He never knew what to say to people like Melchiorri, but the blockhead gave every indication of wanting to stand there and chat for a while.

'Remember the Latin teacher? Mrs Vizzardelli . . . walked like this, all stiff, like she had a pole up her arse? Poor thing, she's dead, you know. Guerrini told me . . . Remember Guerrini? I saw him again, he married a black girl. He'd always been a bit strange, that one. I even thought he was a poof! And remember Francesca Caselli? Ah, la Caselli! The most beautiful bottom in the class . . . I saw her again a couple of years ago at a restaurant with her husband and three children and, you won't believe it, but she's still beautiful . . . Her husband's some sort of writer, I didn't quite get what he writes, he's got the face of an undertaker . . . Speaking of which, did you know about Fantecchi? Hanged himself about ten years ago, they found him dead in his kitchen . . . I was sorry to hear it. He was a nice guy, in his way, always let me copy his homework . . . But best of all was Coppini! Do you remember how he dressed? He went through all of grammar school with the same pair of shoes . . . And when I saw him again last year, guess what he had? A Giulietta Sprint! Got married to a very rich woman, pretty too, I'm told. Can you imagine it? A twerp like that! And what about yourself? You seen anyone from back then? I even ran into Gonnelli . . . the moron! Inherited his dad's butcher shop, the drip couldn't have managed any other way. Remember what he used to do to Latin? Oh, and I also saw Degl'Innocenti again, the little guy, remember him? The one with the funny teeth who used to fart all the time . . .'

The inspector had stopped listening, and it slowly came back to him that Melchiorri had once reported him to the headmaster for playing truant with a girl. No, he'd never liked the creep, who hadn't changed at all. He still had the same useless face as before, the same air of a respectable mediocrity who only breaks the rules on the sly. He probably voted for the Christian Democrats and felt like a revolutionary for it.

'. . . and what about Mazzanti? D'you know he married Luisa Tombelli? The curly-haired girl who used to chew her pens? I don't know, I could never do anything like that, marry someone who's been in your bleeding way all through grammar school! Except for the fact that la Tombelli . . . remember her? One year she's a little girl, and then the next, pow! What a dish! But the sexiest girl in the whole school was Marisa Conti . . . Remember her? Dark and dusky with green eyes . . . Damn, she was hot! . . . Yeah, those were the days . . . Oh, right, did I forget to mention whatshisname, come on . . .? Panichi! You know what he's up to these days? He works for the railways, the brute . . . And Chiara Magini! Jesus, was she ever ugly! . . . Poor thing . . . She was sweet on Fantechi for a good five years, but he wouldn't touch her with a ten-foot pole! . . . Boy, have the years ever gone by! So, what do you do for a living? Me, I deal in sanitation. If you ever need a toilet, just give me a ring. It's not a bad job . . . a bit like a mortician's, people will always need coffins and toilets, now, won't they? So, what do you do yourself? How are you getting along?'

'Me? I'm a pimp,' said Bordelli, all serious.

'What's that?'

'I've got a couple of girls working for me. The pay's pretty good, you don't lift a bloody finger all day long . . . Why are you making that face?'

'What face?'

'I've even got a little drug business going on the side, just to round things off.'

'Oh, really?' Melchiorri felt uncomfortable, even scared. Bordelli lowered his voice.

'You wouldn't need a bit o' coke now, wouldja? I just got some yesterday from Bolivia. I'll give you a good price.'

'No, thanks . . . Look, I'm sorry, but I have to go and buy some bread.'

'Listen, why don't we organise a big dinner for the whole class? I could bring my girls.'

'Of course, why not? Let's think about it . . . I'm so glad to have run into you, really. We'll try to meet again, okay? But now I've really got to go.'

Melchiorri quickly said goodbye and ran away without turning round. Bordelli began to feel better at once. He lit a cigarette and continued on his way. He had never liked Melchiorri.

When he got to Santa Maria Nova, he asked the first nurse he saw for Dr Saggini. She made him wait in a long corridor lined with closed doors. The doctor arrived a few minutes later with a bouncy, athletic step and white hair combed back. He took Bordelli immediately to see Valentina's mother, but before they entered the room, he reminded him not to tire her out.

'She's still in pretty bad shape,' he said, shaking his head.

'Is she alone in the room?' the inspector asked.

'There are two other patients.'

'If she can get up, I'd rather talk to her alone.'

They entered the room. The woman was dozing in her bed. She had dark circles round her eyes, and her dirty hair clung to her cheeks. She looked as if she'd lost a lot of weight. She was like a small, abandoned child.

'How are we feeling today?' the doctor asked her. The woman looked at him absently, then nodded as if to say she felt fine. It was clear she was under the influence of sedatives.

'Do you think you could get up? The inspector would like to ask you a few questions.'

'Yes,' she said. She was very weak, and unsteady on her feet. The doctor helped her stand up from the bed. They walked with her into an empty room and eased her into a chair.

'I'll leave you two alone now,' said Dr Saggini, darting a glance at Bordelli, and then he left, closing the door behind him. The inspector sat down in front of the woman.

'Signora Panerai, I'm sorry, but I have to talk to you about what happened,' he said.

Valentina's mother looked at him with a stupid smile on her face, not batting an eyelid. Bordelli hated questioning people in these conditions, but he knew it couldn't be helped. The slightest clue might prove important. He believed that the killer might strike again, and felt he was in a race against time.

'May I begin?' he asked.

'Yes.'

'Do you have any enemies?'

'Enemies?' she said, squinting a little. She was quite feeble minded from the drugs.

'Someone who hates you so much they might wish to harm you in this fashion?'

'No.'

'What sort of work do you do?'

'Sales.'

'Where?'

'With the big wholesalers.'

The woman replied slowly, and always with that hint of a smile on her lips. Bordelli left long pauses between questions, so as not to tire her.

'Are you married?'

'No.'

'Do you have a boyfriend?'

'I don't have anyone.'

Although she was thin, she sat as if her body felt very heavy to her.

'And Valentina's father?'

'He lives in Turin . . . He was already married with children, but I discovered that a little late.'

'Is that why Valentina doesn't have her father's name?'

'When she was born, he didn't want . . . how do you say it?'

'To acknowledge paternity?'

'Yes . . .' she said, shrugging slightly.

'Why not?'

'He didn't want any trouble for his *real* family,' the young woman said, a furrow between her eyebrows.

'Forgive me for asking, Signora Panerai . . . But didn't he help you at all?'

'He sent me a little money every month. Though that certainly wasn't what I had in mind when I met him.'

'So, you couldn't say you've maintained good relations with him,' the inspector said.

The woman shook her head.

'I tried every way I could to make him say that Valentina was his daughter. A few years ago I even filed a complaint against him . . . We ended up in court, but he kept on denying everything. He could afford a good lawyer, and so it all came to nothing . . . In the end I gave up,' she said, looking at him through empty eyes. Saying more than a few sentences seemed to have tired her out.

'Did he ever come and see Valentina?'

'Three or four times a year.'

'Was he fond of her?'

'What?'

'Valentina's father . . . was he fond of her?'

The woman nodded faintly.

'Her, yes . . . He wrote her many letters and was always giving her presents,' she said.

'Has he been told what happened?'

'Yes.'

'How did he take it?'

'He cried . . .' the woman said, her eyes vacant. Bordelli left her alone for a bit, to let her rest. Then he resumed.

'I'm sorry, signora . . . but I have to ask you a few questions about that afternoon.'

'Ask whatever you like,' she said, seeming tired.

'Did you notice immediately that your daughter was missing?'

'No.'

'How did you lose sight of her?'

'She did it all the time.'

'Ran away, you mean?'

'Yes.'

'Why did she do that?'

'She liked to hide,' the woman said, staring at the wall with an unhappy smile. Her eyes looked huge in her gaunt face.

'What time was it when you last saw Valentina?'

'I don't know . . . about half past five, I guess.'

The girl was found around six. And in that half-hour she had been killed.

'Did you go often to the Parco del Ventaglio with your daughter?' Bordelli continued after another pause.

'When it wasn't raining . . .'

'Do most of the people who go to the park know each other?'

'Yes.'

'Lately, had you noticed anyone you hadn't ever seen there before?'

'No,' she said, shaking her head repeatedly. Bordelli waited for her to calm down, then continued.

'Do people sometimes come to the park alone . . .? I mean, people without children?'

'A few old men with dogs.'

'And had anyone ever bothered your daughter in the past?'

'No.'

'Had anyone ever bothered any other little girls?'

'I've never heard any mention of it.'

The woman was beginning to seem impatient. She looked exhausted.

'There wasn't anybody in the park who you think could have . . .'

'No,' she said, shaking her head. She squeezed her eyes shut, then reopened them and looked out the window. The sun was still shining, but some dark clouds were approaching from the north.

'One last thing, signora . . . What school did your daughter go to?'

'Via Fibonacci.'

'Thank you. Well, for now I don't have anything else to ask you. I'm sorry to have disturbed you.'

'It doesn't matter,' she said.

The inspector went over to help her stand up. She had left a wet imprint on the seat of the chair, and there was a strong smell of urine.

'Let me walk you to your room,' said Bordelli. Carla grabbed hold of his arm. After they had taken a few steps towards the door, she froze.

'I just don't understand why,' she said, a gleam of madness in her eyes.

'We'll catch him,' said Bordelli, squeezing her hand. He accompanied her back to her room, helped her lie down, and pulled the covers over her.

'Goodbye, Signora Panerai,' he said, looking at her fleshless face submerged in the pillow.

'We'll catch him . . .' she muttered, as if saying goodbye. At that moment a nurse came in and gave her an injection in the arm.

At one o'clock he decided to go and have a bite to eat at Da Cesare. It was already a few days since he'd last put in an appearance. So long an absence was unusual, but lately he hadn't felt like stuffing himself and was happy to eat a panino at the bar. That morning, however, his appetite had reawakened, perhaps as an antidote to the frustration he'd had to stomach over the past few days. He needed a break, to clear his head.

He slipped into Totò's kitchen, feeling relieved, and flopped on to his stool.

'Ciao, Totò.'

'Inspector! Where've you been hiding?' the cook yelled, coming up to him. Bordelli squeezed his arm to avoid his greasy hands.

'I was a little busy,' he said.

'I'm not surprised . . . with that maniac at large!' said Totò, making a disgusted face. The inspector tried to change the subject.

'Cook anything good today . . .? No, wait. Let me guess,' he said, sniffing the air. Totò looked at him defiantly. '*Baccalà alla livornese*?' Bordelli asked.

'Bravo, Inspector! Except that it's my own variation.'

'And you've ruined it, I'm sure . . . And what've you got for the first course?'

'Spaghetti *à la however I want it.*'

'And how do you want it?'

'Do you trust Totò?'

'Absolutely.'

'And you're right . . . just one minute, I'll be right back.'

Totò ran and stirred the contents of a big pot, filled five or six bowls with pasta, and set these down on the sill of the serving hatch. Then he dumped some spaghetti for the inspector into the boiling water and stirred for a good minute, humming *Stai lontana da me*[10] to himself. He then put the *baccalà* on a low flame and turned about suddenly, like a cowboy ready to draw his gun. After Casimiro, he was the shortest man Bordelli had ever seen.

While they waited for the pasta, they ate some toast and shrimp together. At a certain point Totò folded his arms on his chest and looked Bordelli straight in the eye.

'What do you say, Inspector? Are you going to catch that maniac or not?'

'I'm going to catch him, Totò, and soon.'

'Let's hope so . . . These disgusting things happen where I come from, too . . . Right after the war some half-mad bloke killed the chemist's ten-year-old daughter, a beautiful little girl. They found her in a straw rick with her throat slit and all bloodied. The madman had even bro—'

'You're not overcooking my spaghetti, are you, Totò?' said Bordelli, to make him stop talking. The last thing he wanted to hear about was murdered little girls.

'Don't worry, Inspector, I've got a clock up here,' said the cook, pointing to his temple.

'You never know.'

'As ~~was~~ I was saying, Inspector . . . the madman had even broken her legs, just snapped them in two, like toothpicks. Poor little thing. I even saw her . . . she looked like a chicken *alla diavola*. Her parents seemed dead . . . they couldn't get a single word out. Thank God they caught the maniac straight away . . . The whole town gathered in front of the *carabinieri*'s

73

headquarters . . . "Out with him!" they cried. "We want the monster!" The women were raving even worse than the men . . . The sergeant got scared, and he fired a shot in the air and shouted to us all to go home . . . But nobody budged . . . Without too much trouble they broke down the door and pulled the madman out of his cell, dragging him by the hair all the way to the church square, where they tore him to pieces . . . A disgusting scene, Inspector, but not so unusual in my parts . . .'

'Totò, the spaghetti . . .'

'We're almost there, Inspector . . . Just one minute to go . . . Another time there was a massacre in the town next to mine, and they caught that maniac straight away, too. He'd cut up two little sisters into pieces, an' they were found in a—'

'Excuse me, Totò, you wouldn't happen to have a drop of wine, would you?'

'You might want for water sometimes around here, Inspector, but . . .' said the cook, chuckling. He went off to get a flask, and Bordelli got ready to change the subject. He wanted to enjoy the spaghetti without getting an earful of Totò's tales of the macabre. They made him feel too sad, especially at a moment like this. It grieved him also to hear that those murderers had been caught, while *his* was still free . . . free to kill again. He couldn't stop thinking about it. He was becoming obsessed. The cook returned with the wine and filled his glass to the brim.

'Have a taste of this, Inspector, it's from my town.'

Bordelli took a sip.

'Nice. Is it made by some relative of yours?'

'My uncle. He's the artist.'

'Oh, really? So, how does he make it?' asked Bordelli. Totò scratched his brow.

'Inspector . . . don't tell me you don't know how wine is made. It'd be like saying you don't know what an arsehole is.'

Bordelli threw his hands up and played dumb. He had hit upon a subject that could distract Totò from killers of little girls, and he wanted to exploit it to the utmost.

'I have a vague sense of it, Totò, but I'm sure there isn't only one way to make wine . . . How does your uncle do it?'

The cook ran to the back of the kitchen to drain Bordelli's pasta, then yelled so the inspector could hear him.

'Making good wine begins with the pruning,' he said. 'Some people prune only once a year; my uncle does it twice.'

'And does it really make a difference?'

'You bet it does!' Totò put the spaghetti in a bowl, poured an orange-coloured sauce full of clams over it, and brought it to the inspector.

'Smells good,' said Bordelli, a scent of the sea regaling his nostrils.

'Totò's own invention . . . When you're done you can tell me if you like it.'

The inspector tasted the pasta. It was excellent, of course.

'You're a great chef, Totò. And you can tell your mother I said that,' he said, raising another forkful in the air.

'You're too kind, Inspector, too kind.'

'No, I mean it . . .'

'And you haven't even tasted the *baccalà* yet,' said Totò.

'One thing at a time . . . And, anyway, you still haven't told me how your uncle makes his wine,' said Bordelli, fearing that Totò would start in again with his stories about the monsters of Apulia.

The cook looked up and resumed explaining to Bordelli how his father's brother made wine. He went into great detail, completely forgetting the story of the two slaughtered sisters, to the inspector's immense satisfaction. And, going from theory to practice, they drank several more glasses of the wine.

Bordelli left Totò's kitchen after a bowlful of *however I want it*, two platefuls of *baccalà*, one black coffee, a great deal of wine, and several grappas. Feeling he had eaten and drunk too much, he decided to go for a stroll along the Mugnone.[11] He walked slowly, cigarette dangling from his lips so he wouldn't have to take his hands out of his pockets. He started watching people passing by along the road. There wasn't much movement. A freezing woman, a few bored old men, some stray dogs. He liked walking along these empty roads with the cold stinging his face. It helped him to think . . .

He remembered a moonless night in March 1944. The cannon-fire echoed without cease from the Allied rear lines, and the Germans answered in kind. Gennaro had started singing the Neapolitan songs of his homeland, making everyone cry. Poor Gennaro, with his big, oval face and childish eyes. He was out of his element among the scoundrels of the San Marco squadron. Only a few days later he was thrown high into the air by an anti-tank mine. His body flew like a rag doll some thirty feet away, falling back down with a thud into the bushes. The rest of them went and recovered it. His legs were all mangled. He looked like a chicken carcass, and was bleeding like a fountain. Raising his head, he looked at Bordelli with eyes already dead.

'Isa . . . bel . . . la,' was all he said. He coughed twice, spraying blood from his mouth. Then he died at once, without so much as a shudder. His eyes remained open, and Bordelli closed them. They wrapped him in a blanket and carried him back to camp. Poor Gennaro. Poor Isabella . . .

The inspector stopped a moment to light another cigarette. A very fine drizzle started to fall, so light it swirled like snow. It landed on his hair without seeming to wet it. He kept on walking aimlessly, leaving each block behind without noticing. Then he suddenly thought of Valentina's mother, seeing her again in the chair, circles of grief under her eyes and that strange smile on her face. He took his time returning to the station, then spent the afternoon smoking, locked in his office.

The following morning, at about ten o'clock, a woman phoned police headquarters. She was very agitated and stammering, and impossible to understand. Only after a few minutes did she manage to say something comprehensible about a dead little girl, and so she was put through to the inspector's office.

Bordelli charged out of his room, cursing, then yelled Piras's name. Doors opened, heads peered out all down the hallway, but nobody said a word. A moment later Piras arrived on the run, and as soon as he saw Bordelli's face, he knew what it was about.

They got into the Beetle and raced off to the Parco delle Cascine, engine roaring. They drove over a grassy meadow that already had a number of squad cars on it with lights flashing. A strong wind was blowing, but it was a sirocco, and it felt almost hot. At the far end of the grassy expanse, before a grove of oak trees, was the usual crowd of rubberneckers being held back with difficulty by the police, as well as a few journalists.

Rinaldi spotted the inspector and immediately came up to him, face glum.

'Where's the child?' Bordelli asked.

'Over there, Inspector,' said Rinaldi, pointing towards the oak wood. As he walked alongside Bordelli, he whispered to him that a lady had said she had seen the killer. It was the same woman who had called the police.

'She's a bit upset,' he added.

'Try to calm her down, and I'll be there straight away,' said Bordelli, shuddering and exchanging a glance with Piras. The idea that he could now start a proper investigation electrified him.

'And the photos?' he asked, still walking towards the wood.

'They've already been taken, Inspector,' said Rinaldi.

'What's the girl's name?'

'Sara Bini. Five years old.'

'Is her mother here?'

'The little girl was with her grandmother, Inspector. She's the one crying down there.'

'Has the mother been told?'

'Scarpelli's taking care of it.'

'Did the grandmother see anything?'

'No, Inspector. She had started talking to a friend on that bench over there, and kept on turning round to keep an eye on the little girl, who was playing near that tree down there. At a certain point she noticed that the child was gone, and so she called her name, but the girl didn't answer. And so she went looking for her but was unable to find her. Then she heard a woman scream and went in that direction . . .'

'Send all these people away, including the journalists.'

'Straight away, sir.'

Rinaldi headed quickly towards the crowd thronging the grass. Bordelli and Piras went down the small lane that cut the oak wood in two, passing through dense, untended vegetation, and fifty yards later were at the scene. Two policemen stood guard over the girl's dead body. Bordelli answered their salute with a nod and bent down to look at the child. She was laid out behind a bush at the edge of the lane, amidst the dead leaves. Blonde, with green eyes gaping wide to the heavens. Her neck bore the same red marks found on Valentina's. The buttons had been torn off her little red overcoat, and there were marks of a human bite on her belly.

'The same bite, Piras.'

'It's like some kind of signature.'

'Maybe he wants us to know he's the killer.'

'Here comes Diotivede, Inspector.'

The old doctor approached them with the light step of a child, his overcoat flapping in the wind. He looked grim. He made a single hand gesture and got right down to work. Bordelli left him in peace and, followed by Piras, returned to the policemen at the edge of the oak wood, where only a few journalists remained, scribbling furiously in their notebooks.

'Where's the witness, Rinaldi?'

'It's that lady down there, Inspector, the one in the brown coat.'

She looked to be about fifty and was well dressed. She was pacing back and forth in front of a bench. Bordelli made a gesture to Piras, and they walked towards the woman. After they had introduced themselves, she grabbed hold of Bordelli's jacket.

'I got a good look at him – it was him all right! I knew he wasn't normal, I knew it . . . I'd always said he was a degenerate, but nobody would ever believe me!' Then she crossed herself two or three times. Piras looked at her with some suspicion.

'Please calm down, signora,' said Bordelli. The woman was made up and well coiffed. Not unattractive, though there was something unpleasant about her, and she had a grating voice.

'He bent down over that poor little girl and started kissing her head, the swine! And when he saw me he took to his heels in a hurry! But I recognised him just the same, I did!'

'You must calm down now, signora,' Bordelli repeated, glancing over at Piras. The Sardinian sighed, resigned to putting up with the woman.

The sky was hopelessly overcast, despite the strong wind. Bordelli lit a cigarette, protecting the flame for a long time with his hands. He was stalling. He was in a terrible rush, but he was stalling. He wanted to prolong as much as possible this moment of feverish hope and the electrifying feeling of already having the killer in his hands.

'Meanwhile, please tell me your name,' he said, to slow the pace.

'Cinzia Beniamini,' the woman said, raising her chin as she said it, as if everyone was supposed to recognise so famous a surname. The inspector turned again towards Piras, to see whether he was ready to start writing. The Sardinian already had his notebook in his hand, and with a look of disgust on his face he wrote down the woman's name. Bordelli took a deep drag on his cigarette, then blew the smoke far away.

'Now, Signora Beniamini, tell me calmly what you saw. And please start at the beginning.'

'The beginning?'

'The beginning,' Bordelli repeated. The woman rolled her eyes, as if at a loss. She tried to collect the impressions in her memory and set them in order. She shot a glance at Piras, then again at the inspector, clearly the more important of the two. She looked at his face, but not directly in the eye. She seemed to focus on his lower lip.

'I was talking to a friend,' she began, 'over there, where those benches are. Then at one point we got up to walk a little . . .'

'What time was it?'

'I don't know. It must have been half past nine or so, perhaps a bit later . . . Does it matter?'

'Go on.'

'As I was saying, I was chatting with my friend, Marcella. We were sitting on that bench down there. We sometimes meet here early in the morning, to have a little walk before we go into town to do our shopping. At one point we stood up and went in that direction, just to stroll a bit. We wanted to go as far as the Arno and then back to the car, as we often do. And so we turned down that little lane over there, the one through the trees, and from a distance we saw the silhouette of a young man in sporting clothes walking ahead of us.'

'Was he coming towards you?'

'No, he too was going towards the Arno. He was moving his arms about the way they do in gymnasiums.'

'How far was he from you?'

'I don't know . . . More or less as far as those trees over there.'

'Write "about thirty yards",' Bordelli said to Piras, then he turned back to face the woman.

'Were there other people around?'

'I don't think so.'

'Go on.'

'At a certain point the young man stepped off the path and bent down to the ground. We couldn't tell exactly what he was doing, because it's always very shady under those trees, even during the day. So we continued on our way, and when we got closer, we saw that he was on all fours, hunched over something colourful that we hadn't noticed until then. Marcella got scared and stopped, but I was curious, and so I went on ahead. When I got fairly close to the man – perhaps fifteen paces or so – he was still on all fours, but he seemed to be vomiting. I thought he was unwell – what else could I think? And so I called to him. "Are you unwell, sir?" I said. Until that moment he hadn't noticed us, because he shot to his feet like a spring . . . And I recognised him at once. He's a misfit, a maniac who lives not far from me . . .'

'And where do you live, Signora Beniamini?'

'In Via Trieste.'

'What happened next?'

'The young man ran off like a rabbit. And so I went up to look at that red thing on the ground, and saw that it was a little girl. I let out a scream to signal for help, but nobody came . . . And the lad disappeared at the end of the path.'

'How old is this person?' asked Bordelli, who had noticed a furrow of disappointment on the woman's brow.

'About twenty-five, I'd say,' she said.

'What's his name?'

'Simone Fantini. He also lives in Via Trieste, at number thirty-two.'

The inspector sighed and tossed his cigarette butt aside.

'Does he live with his parents?' he asked.

'No, he lives alone.'

'Tell me, signora, are you absolutely certain that the young man you saw was Simone Fantini?'

'What do you mean? I see him almost every day, I'd recognise his sick face anywhere!'

'Why do you say he's sick?'

'You should see the way he looks at women.'

'How does he look at them?'

'It's as if he wants to eat them alive. And he does it to my daughter Ottavia. You should see how pretty she is . . .'

'If she's pretty, then everyone must look at her,' the inspector commented.

'Not the way *he* looks at her, I tell you,' said Signora Beniamini, eyes narrowing in contempt.

'Has this Fantini ever bothered your daughter?' Piras asked provocatively.

'He wouldn't dare . . .' the woman said without even looking at him.

'Have you anything else to add?' the inspector asked her, feeling rather discouraged.

'Why, haven't I told you quite a lot already?' said the woman, looking offended.

'Thank you, Signora Beniamini, I'll send for you if I need anything else,' said Bordelli, cutting things short.

'He killed her,' the woman said, staring hard at the inspector.

Piras closed his notebook and looked at the woman as if he wanted to make her disappear.

'Goodbye, signora,' said Bordelli.

'He's a monster,' she continued, goggling her eyes, then she turned and walked away, ladylike, towards the lane. Piras shook his head and exchanged a glance of disappointment with the inspector.

Diotivede had finished jotting down his initial observations on the corpse of Sara Bini and was waiting for the inspector with medical bag in hand, standing motionless in the middle of the path. The wind was gusting straight into his frowning face, which was as pink as a child's, despite his seventy-one years. Seeing him from afar, Bordelli and Piras quickened their pace and got to him in a hurry, anxious to know what he'd found.

'At first glance, everything's exactly the same as with the first murder,' the pathologist said.

'Will that bite be of any use to us?' asked Bordelli.

'I don't think so. Tooth marks on such a soft part of the body are very imprecise.'

'Anything else?'

'No, not for now.'

Bordelli shook his head, feeling more and more discouraged.

'Want a lift?' he asked the doctor.

'I've got a car waiting for me.'

'Call me the minute you've got any news.'

'I'm already sure there won't be any,' said Diotivede, frowning darkly. Nodding goodbye, he headed towards the grassy meadow. Piras stared into space. The deaths of these little girls were having a bad effect on everyone.

'Wake up, Piras, we're going to go look for that young man.'

'He didn't do it,' said Piras, following behind him.

'I'm well aware of that,' said Bordelli, shrugging. Signora Beniamini had seen Simone Fantini walking ahead of her, and the corpse of the little girl lay farther ahead. Only afterwards did Beniamini see Fantini step off the footpath and bend over the girl, who was already dead. What sense would there be in the murderer coming back and kneeling down over his victim right after killing her?

They got into the car, and as they were leaving the meadow, they saw two technicians from Forensics arrive. Bordelli waved at them and noticed that they, too, looked very tense.

'What should I do with Signora Benianimi's testimony, Inspector? Shall I put it in the report?' asked Piras, already knowing what Bordelli would say.

'Forget it, Piras . . . If it ended up in the hands of you-know-who, it would trigger a useless manhunt.'

Piras tore Beniamini's deposition from the notepad, crumpled it up and put it in his pocket. Ginzillo would never get to read it.

They parked in Via Trieste and rang the buzzer to Fantini's flat, but nobody answered. It was a fine stone building, with big windows and a monumental entrance.

'What should we do, Inspector?'

'Let's hear what the neighbours have to say,' said Bordelli, pressing another button at random. A few seconds later they heard the front door unlock with a click and then open. The atrium was spacious and luminous, and a number of large potted plants created a nice effect.

They began to climb the fine granite staircase. A girl was waiting for them on the second-floor landing with a wooden spoon in her hand. She was wearing a blue apron and a white bonnet.

'Was it you who rang?' she asked, looking at them with big green eyes. She was quite pretty, and Piras ran a hand through his hair to smooth it down.

'Police,' said Bordelli.

'The masters of the house aren't here,' said the girl, a bit frightened. She shot a quick glance at young Piras and felt embarrassed, as he was staring at her insistently and puffing his chest like a rooster.

'Do you know Simone Fantini?' the inspector asked.

'He lives upstairs, on the fourth floor . . . Why, what did he do?'

'What kind of a person is he?'

'He's very nice,' said the girl, blushing slightly.

'As far as you know, does Fantini have any friends in this building?' the inspector asked.

'I see him often with the Sicilian girl who lives across the landing from him. She's called Sonia.'

'Is she his girlfriend?'

'I don't think so.'

'Does Fantini have a girlfriend?'

'I don't know. For a while he was with a girl who lives across the street, but she left him a few months ago.'

'Ottavia Beniamini?' asked Piras.

'Yes,' said the girl, rather surprised. Bordelli and Piras both gave a hint of a smile and exchanged a glance of understanding.

'Do you know by any chance at what time we might find Simone at home?' the inspector asked.

'He's usually at home studying at this hour,' the girl said in a ringing voice. Then, realising she had spoken with too much enthusiasm, she blushed again.

'Thank you, and sorry for the disturbance,' said Bordelli.

'Not at all,' said the girl.

Bordelli and Piras headed upstairs. The girl remained standing in the doorway, watching them, and when Piras turned round to look at her, she quickly ducked back inside.

There were two doors on the fourth-floor landing. They rang

the doorbell to Fantini's flat, but again there was no answer. On the door opposite was a plaque with the name *Zarcone*. Bordelli rang the doorbell and heard a sweet *ding-dong* sound within. The door opened, and there stood a tall blonde girl with green eyes, totally different from how one might expect a Sicilian to look. She was wearing a form-fitting black sweater that looked very good on her, and a red skirt that ended well above the knee.

'Hello,' she said, somewhat perplexed. Bordelli flashed his badge before those smiling eyes.

'Police,' he said. 'Are you Sonia Zarcone?'

'Yes,' she said, her smile fading.

'Can we come in?'

'Has something happened?'

'Nothing serious,' said the inspector. The girl looked first at one, then the other, with a confused expression. Piras's face brightened in a broad smile, to the great surprise of the inspector, who had never seen him smile like that.

'We'll only take a minute of your time,' said Piras, casting another furtive glance at Sonia's legs, which were as beautiful as a movie star's.

'All right,' she said, pulling the door open and standing aside to let them pass. They followed her into a fairly large room, rather unusually furnished. It was a lovely apartment to begin with, but the girl's imagination had made it even more pleasurable, with its combination of antique and modern furnishings.

'Please sit down,' said Sonia, gesturing towards a black-leather sofa, then sitting down opposite them in an old armchair that had probably belonged to her grandmother. Piras studied the girl's figure, eyes wandering everywhere. She, too, was an interesting mix of antique and modern, he thought.

The primordial female and the woman of today, combined in the best manner possible. The Sardinian liked her. A lot, in fact. It was the first time since he had arrived 'on the continent' that he had met a girl he really, truly liked. He even liked her Sicilian accent, which got all the O and E sounds wrong. Bordelli noticed Piras's admiration for the girl but said nothing.

Sonia, meanwhile, had recovered her smile, and her eyes spark-led with a hint of vanity. She, too, seemed to notice how Piras was looking at her. She asked the policemen whether they wanted something to drink, then blushed as if she had said something silly. They were hardly a couple of guests paying a social call.

'Please don't bother, thank you,' Bordelli replied for both of them. 'We only wanted to ask you a few questions.'

'Go right ahead,' said Sonia, her curiosity aroused. She rearranged her hair and crossed her legs, much to the embarrass-ment of Piras, who couldn't stop looking at all those wonders of nature. The inspector grabbed his packet of cigarettes.

'May I?' he asked.

'Of course,' said Sonia.

Bordelli lit up, took a deep drag, and exhaled the smoke towards the ceiling. Piras was too busy with other concerns to grimace with irritation. It was the first time he had failed to do so.

'Are you really Sicilian?' the inspector asked. Sonia smiled.

'You Northerners seem to think Sicilians are all four foot tall and black as coal,' she said. 'But there are a lot of people like me.'

'Because of the Normans,' said Piras.

'Very good,' she said. Piras smiled with satisfaction. Staring at the girl, he felt glad that the Normans had passed through Sicily.[12] The inspector glanced at his watch: almost noon.

'The young man who lives across the landing, Simone Fantini . . . is he a friend of yours?'

'Yes. Why? Has something happened?' asked the girl, alarmed.

'No need to get upset. Do you know where we can find Simone?'

'Normally he's at home at this time of day.'

'We tried, but nobody answers,' said Bordelli.

'He must have gone out for a walk, or to study at a friend's house.' Sonia seemed rather concerned, which brought a slight furrow to her brow that Piras liked very much.

'What does Simone do?' the inspector asked.

'He's in his last year of Engineering, but his real passion is writing.'

Sonia had a lovely voice, warm and deep, and a vague smile in her eyes which never faded. It was a pleasure just to look at her. Every so often she shot a quick glance over at Piras, who was getting as excited as a little kid. Bordelli witnessed everything and smiled to himself.

'Forgive my asking, miss,' said the inspector, 'but are you and Simone just friends or are you . . .?'

Piras pricked up his ears, staring at a tiny mole on Sonia's lower lip while awaiting the reply.

'We're just friends . . . why do you ask?' she said.

Piras relaxed. Bordelli brought his cigarette over to a little pot that looked like an ashtray, but before tapping it with his finger, he looked at Sonia for approval. She nodded and Bordelli knocked off some ash. At that moment he felt a bitter surge of bile rise up through his oesophagus and burst at the back of his throat like a rotten flower. He'd been having digestive problems the past few days.

'You wouldn't happen to have the keys to Simone's place, would you?' he asked, repressing a grimace.

'Yes, I would. Why?'

'We'd like to go and have a look.'

'Maybe he's at home and doesn't feel like answering the door,' said the girl, embarrassed.

'Let's go and see,' said Bordelli. There were a few seconds of silence, a few quick exchanges of glances.

'You really don't want to tell me what's happened?' Sonia asked with a worried smile.

'Nothing serious, but we need to talk to Simone as soon as possible,' said Bordelli.

'Has he done something wrong?'

'Please, I beg you . . .'

'I'll go and get the keys,' she said, standing up. She crossed the room, devoured by Piras's gaze, and disappeared behind the door, which she closed behind her.

Piras sought the inspector's eyes. A gleam of suffering shone in his black pupils. Bordelli smiled.

'Pretty, eh?'

'Not bad,' Piras said indifferently.

Sonia returned with the keys, and they followed her out to the landing. She had a beautiful body, and Piras didn't miss a single movement. Those two fine legs stretching out from under her skirt were good for his health.

Before going into Simone's flat, the girl rang the doorbell and knocked several times, but there was no answer. In the end she made up her mind to unlock the door. Sticking her head inside, she called out loudly to her friend. The apartment was dark and all was still.

'He's not here,' she said needlessly, then automatically turned on the light and let the two policemen inside. From her movements it was clear she knew the space well. The flat was messy but pleasant.

'This is the conversation room,' said Sonia, going through the first door they encountered in the hallway. It was a big room covered with carpets and large cushions strewn across the floor. One wall was entirely taken up by a bookcase painted blue and overflowing with books all the way to the ceiling. Bordelli went up to it and started reading the spines: Dostoyevsky, Mann, Kafka, Leopardi, Svevo, Lermontov, Flaubert, Primo Levi, Poe, Foscolo, Tolstoy, Simenon, Chekov, Bulgakov . . . All good stuff, he thought. On one shelf was a framed photo of a young man with black hair, intense eyes, and a large, imperfect nose that nevertheless looked good on him.

'Is this Simone?' the inspector asked. Sonia nodded.

'Handsome, isn't he?' she said, picking up the photo. Piras craned his neck to have a look, and a furrow appeared between his eyebrows. Simone really was handsome, he had to admit. This discovery troubled him, and in reacting to it he smiled like an idiot. Bordelli had never seen him look so asinine. Sonia put the photo back in its place and folded her arms over her breasts, awaiting instructions.

'I'd like to have a look around the place,' Bordelli said.

'I'll come with you,' said the girl.

The inspector raised a hand.

'Thanks, there's no need. Meanwhile Piras will ask you a few questions.'

'Don't you want to tell me what's happened?' Sonia persisted.

'Well, not now, anyway,' said the inspector.

'Then when?' she asked.

'Piras, be sure to write everything down.'

'Of course, Inspector,' said the Sardinian, blushing. Bordelli suppressed a smile and left the room, leaving Piras in Sonia's hands. There was no need to ask Sonia anything. He had merely wanted to play a little trick on Piras. Or do him a favour.

At the end of the hallway he pushed open a door and entered a large room that looked on to Via Trieste. More shelves full of books. It must be Simone's room. The bed was unmade. On the wall was a poster of a film starring Virna Lisi, the most beautiful of Italian actresses. A few books lay scattered across the desk, along with a full ashtray, a typewriter and a number of typescripts stapled together or bound with paper clips. They must be Simone's stories. The inspector picked one up at random and started reading the first page. It wasn't bad, though there was a certain immaturity in the fanciness of the words. He put it back in the pile, picked up another, and began to leaf through it, reading a passage here and there. All the same, there was something powerful in his way of writing, a sincerity that one read with pleasure. But this wasn't the time for it. He put it back down and continued thumbing through the typescripts, reading only the titles: *The Paralytic*; *The Contract*; *Love's Darkness*; *Half the House*; *Betrayal* . . . The last in the stack was *The Tower*, a rather short story. He read the first page. It wasn't bad, so he continued . . .

All at once the sound of Sonia's laughter floated lightly down the hall. Apparently Piras was keeping himself busy. Never mind those who say Sardinians are closed and taciturn. Bordelli smiled and continued reading Simone's story, which was slowly drawing him in. He'd remained standing beside the desk and kept on turning the pages, one after the other, increasingly engrossed in the horrific tale. Holding his breath as he read, every so often he felt a tingling at the back of his neck. And, almost without realising it, he read it through to the end. Then he looked up and shook his head. The lad might very well become a writer, he thought, but for the moment he had better not let that story end up in Judge Ginzillo's hands, since it told of a little girl who was raped and then killed.

He heard Sonia laugh again. Could Piras possibly be so amusing? Normally he spoke little and laughed even less. The inspector folded *The Tower* in two and put it in his jacket pocket. He opened the desk drawers and rummaged about without much interest, then resumed looking around. It was a beautiful room, with a coffered ceiling and big windows. He opened the wardrobe. There were few clothes inside, but a number of shelves were covered with stacks of typescripts of every imaginable length. There was something for everyone. Simone obviously spent a lot of time at the typewriter. The inspector closed the wardrobe and, after one last look around, went back into the hallway. He stuck his head into the bathroom: light blue tiles, a dark, wood-framed mirror, a plant by the window and, next to the toilet, a shelf with some ten books. He closed the door and, accompanied by Sonia's laughter, found his way to the kitchen. A stack of dirty dishes rose up from the sink. On a marble table were some half-empty packets of pasta, a wilted head of lettuce, a few apples, and many dirty glasses. There must have been a party. On one shelf of the glass-fronted cupboard was a collection of coffee pots from different eras, some of them quite strange.

Bordelli continued his tour and, after having seen everything, he returned to the 'conversation room' and the two youngsters. Before entering, he eavesdropped at the half-closed door and heard them talking quite animatedly. They weren't making much sense, but they were laughing a great deal. As soon as they saw the inspector, they stopped.

'Signorina Zarcone, where can we find Fantini?' Bordelli asked.

'You mean now?'

The inspector nodded. The girl shrugged and gestured as if throwing up her hands.

'I don't know . . . He's often at his cousin's,' she said.

'What's this cousin's name?'

'Francesco Manfredini,' said Sonia, as Piras kept on looking at her.

'Where does he live?'

'Nearby, in Via Stibbert.'

'What number?'

'Seventy-seven . . . You really don't mean to tell me why you're looking for Simone?' Sonia asked yet again, though she no longer seemed too worried.

'We just want to have a little chat with him,' Bordelli said curtly.

'Someone like Simone would never do anything bad,' she said sweetly. When he heard her affectionate tone, Piras's expression changed. Bordelli noticed and looked at him with amusement.

'I'm very sorry, Sonia, but we have to take Simone's photo away with us,' he said, gesturing towards the small frame on the shelf.

'Please, Inspector, tell me what this is about,' Sonia insisted, looking to Piras for help. Bordelli threw his hands up and shook his head in a definitive way. Piras went and picked up Simone's portrait, stared at it for a few seconds, then took the print out of the frame and handed it to the inspector.

'Let's go, Piras,' said Bordelli, putting the photo in his jacket pocket. The girl accompanied them out to the landing and then locked Simone's door. The Sardinian continued to feast his eyes on her, clenching his jaw.

Suddenly Sonia put her hand over her mouth.

'Oh no!' she said. The door to her flat had closed by itself, and she had left the keys inside. Piras started to shake in his clothes and seemed to grow three inches taller.

'You go on ahead to Via Stibbert, Inspector,' he said. 'I can take care of this.'

'What do you mean, Piras?' said Bordelli.

'I was just thinking that . . . I could go look for a locksmith and then meet back up with you at the station,' said the Sardinian, eyes sparkling.

Bordelli looked at him with affection and bent down to have a look at Sonia's lock. A few years back he had taken a few lockpicking lessons from his friend Botta, a professional thief and swindler, and ever since, he had been able to pick about seventy per cent of the locks on the market.

'If you'll allow me, I can give it a try,' he said.

The girl looked at him with hope in her eyes. Bordelli took out his wallet and extracted his lockpicking tool, a simple piece of firm iron wire bent into a hook at one end. He got down to work and, a few seconds later, the lock clicked open. Sonia clapped.

'Oh, thank you!' she said, smiling brightly. Her teeth glistened like wet pebbles.

'The pleasure's all mine,' said the inspector.

'I'd already filled the bathtub,' she added with a sigh of relief. The statement had a powerful effect on Piras, who immediately imagined the girl in the water with her hair all wet.

'It's probably cold by now,' he said in an almost grieving tone.

'Well, I can just add a bit more hot water,' Sonia said, smiling, flattered by all the attention. Bordelli nodded faintly.

'Goodbye, Sonia . . . We can go now, Piras.'

He took the lad by the arm and pulled him away. Piras barely had time to make an awkward gesture of goodbye to the girl, to which she replied with a smile full of shiny little white teeth. As they were descending the stairs, the inspector put another cigarette in his mouth.

'What's wrong with you, Piras? Did you see a fairy with turquoise hair or something?'

'I was just trying to make myself useful,' said Piras, having turned very serious again.

The Beetle's engine rumbled in German down the street, sounding like something that could never break. The windscreen was covered by a very fine yellow sand that came from Africa, and a drizzle began to fall. The windscreen wipers were old and didn't work very well.

'I can't see a bloody thing, Piras . . .'

'Watch out for the pavement, Inspector!'

They turned on to Via Stibbert and started going uphill. Piras had opened his window and was studying the numbers on the front doors with a rather imbecilic expression on his face. You could tell he was still thinking about the Sicilian girl. They pulled up in front of number 77 and got out. It, too, was another fine old building, with a stone façade and sculpted mouldings. They rang Manfredini's bell several times, but nobody answered. Bordelli threw down his half-smoked cigarette, which was wet with rain.

'Got any intelligent ideas, Piras?'

The Sardinian made an idiotic face.

'Let's go back to Sonia's . . . Maybe we could ask her—'

'I said "intelligent", Piras, not "pleasant".'

'I was just thinking that we—'

'Let's go, we can try again later,' Bordelli cut him off. They got back into the Beetle and drove down Via Stibbert. Then they turned on to the Viali[13] and slowly headed back towards the Parco delle Cascine. A fine drizzle continued to fall as they got out of the car, but the wind had died down. There was still some activity in the meadow. The inspector gestured to Rinaldi, and the officer came running, water dripping from the brim of his cap.

'Has the mother arrived?' Bordelli asked.

'She left just a few minutes ago, Inspector.'

'How did she take it?'

'She just stood there staring at the child without saying anything. She didn't want to talk to anybody.'

'Any other news?'

'No, sir, nothing to report.'

Bordelli stood there in silence, staring at the little path that led into the oak wood. He looked hypnotised. Then he snapped out of it and ran a hand over his eyes, as if trying to wipe something away.

'Come on, Piras, let's go back to Via Stibbert.'

'It hasn't even been half an hour, Inspector.'

'Maybe he'll come back for lunch,' said Bordelli, walking down towards the car. Piras shrugged and followed him. The rain was rapidly gaining in strength and, to judge from the sky, it wasn't going to let up any time soon. Before shifting into third, Bordelli lit a cigarette. Piras opened the window and started waving his hand around.

'Couldn't you smoke a little less, Inspector?'

'Not now, Piras.'

Bordelli was driving at a snail's pace, to kill a little time. When he finished his cigarette, he lit another, to Piras's great joy. It started raining harder. There were very few people about.

By the time they began driving down Via Vittorio Emanuele it was pouring. They turned on to Via Stibbert and parked in front of Manfredini's building.

'Don't you have an umbrella, Inspector?'

'I've got several, but not here.'

'Well, it's just water,' said Piras.

They dashed out of the car and took shelter in the great doorway of Manfredini's building. They rang his buzzer, but no one answered. Piras repeatedly wiped the rain off his face.

'What are we going to do, Inspector? It's almost one.'

'Are you hungry?'

'Not terribly, but I would gladly eat a . . .' Piras stopped talking, distracted by a guy with an umbrella who had stopped in front of the entrance to number 77 and was searching his pockets for the keys. He looked to be about thirty and was short, with round glasses and a rebellious shock of hair on his head. As he slipped the key into the lock, he cast an inquisitive glance at the two strangers standing motionless out of the rain.

'I beg your pardon . . .' said the inspector. The man looked at them with a serious expression, his gaze moving quickly from one to the other.

'Yes?' he said. He had skin as delicate as that of a young child, and two dark, intelligent eyes behind the lenses of his glasses.

'Do you know Francesco Manfredini?' the inspector asked.

'And who are you?' the man said, rather provocatively. Bordelli took out his badge.

'Inspector Bordelli. He's Piras.'

'I'm Manfredini.'

'Could we have a little talk with you?'

'What about?'

'It'll only take a minute. Could we go up to your flat?' Bordelli asked, indicating the rain with a gesture. Manfredini didn't say anything, but just pushed the great door open and turned on the light. The staircase lit up with a yellowish glow, as if the light itself was from the past. They climbed the stairs in silence, water dripping from their clothes. Manfredini's heels made noise against the stone, and he was continually running his hand through his wet hair. On the third floor he opened the door to his flat and showed them in. The entrance was bare, but the ancient flooring sufficed to give the space a certain warmth. A long hallway leading into darkness gave the impression of a rather large apartment. Manfredini slid his umbrella into a tall earthenware vase, took off his coat and, without saying a word, led them into the drawing room, a great big space with ceilings nearly fifteen feet high and frescoed by some naif seventeenth-century painter. There was a vague scent of old wood and wax in the air. The chandelier gave off a faint, wan light, and a dark, enormous armoire covered nearly the whole wall between two tall, curtained windows. Two sofas were set up facing one another, with a small, oval table between them.

Walking silently across the carpet, Manfredini went and turned on a twenties lamp on a corner table, immediately giving the place the feel of a brothel.

'What did you want to tell me, Inspector?' Manfredini asked with a nonchalant air, turning towards the two policemen and stopping a short distance from them. All three had remained standing.

'How long has it been since you last saw your cousin Simone?' Bordelli asked.

'I saw him yesterday. Why?'

'Do you know where we can find him?'

'Did you try his place?' Manfredini asked, a little disingenuously.

Bordelli glanced at Piras, who was staring at Manfredini with an air of suspicion. Then he calmly lit a cigarette and inhaled deeply.

'Signor Manfredini, if you know where Simone is, you'd better tell us straight away.'

'I don't know where he is, I've already told you . . . Could you please tell me what this is about?' Manfredini asked, getting more upset than was warranted. He no longer seemed so nonchalant. Bordelli had the distinct impression that he was lying, and decided to get straight to the point.

'Your cousin is in a lot of trouble, and I'm sure he won't come home for a good while. If you know where he is, I advise you to tell me.'

'What kind of trouble?' asked Manfredini.

'He's suspected of killing a little girl.'

'What rubbish . . .' said Manfredini, feigning the utmost nonchalance. But he was a terrible actor. The inspector went up to him, looking him straight in the eye.

'Listen to me . . . I am almost convinced he didn't do it, but if Simone keeps on hiding, it will worsen his chances.'

'There must be some kind of misunderstanding. It's absurd to think—'

'Your cousin is taking a very grave risk,' Bordelli interrupted him. 'If you know where he is, you'd better tell me.'

'I assure you I don't know where he is, Inspector,' said Manfredini, trying to smile but trembling slightly. Outside it started thundering. It was pouring, and one could hear the sound of the rain violently striking the asphalt of Via Stibbert. Piras shook his head and started pacing back and forth behind Manfredini.

'Perhaps you haven't fully understood the situation,' he said.

'No, indeed I haven't,' said Manfredini.

'Let me explain it to you . . . A witness saw your cousin kneeling over the corpse of a little girl and swears that he was the killer . . .'

'That's absurd!'

'Let me finish. The inspector and I are practically convinced your cousin Simone is innocent, but if he was at the scene where the murder took place, he may have seen something that could be of use to us.'

'We need speak to him as soon as possible,' Bordelli added.

'I'm sorry, but I don't know where he is,' Manfredini repeated, staring at the inspector with a nervous look in his eye.

'You're making a mistake,' Piras said in a wicked tone, stopping right beside him. Manfredini put a hand behind his neck and started sweating. He seemed very tense, and Bordelli tried to take advantage of this.

'If we don't speak immediately with Simone, that testimony will end up on Judge Ginzillo's desk, and that will mean big trouble,' he said to frighten him. Manfredini bit his lip, trying to control his nerves.

'But why would anyone listen to that . . . that woman?' he stammered.

'How did you know the witness is a woman?' asked Piras.

'You told me yourselves, didn't you?' said Manfredini, head sinking into his shoulders.

'No, we didn't,' said Piras, staring at him.

'Of course you did, I remember it clearly—' A very close thunderclap rattled the windowpanes and Manfredini gave a start.

'Tell us where he is,' said the inspector. Manfredini looked him long in the eye without speaking, as if he were torn.

'I swear I don't know where he is,' he finally said. Bordelli sighed impatiently, jingling the car keys in his pocket.

'Pay close attention to me, Francesco, I'll put it to you another way. It makes no difference whether Simone is guilty or innocent. If you know where he is and you don't tell us, you can be charged with aiding a suspect. Think it over very carefully.'

Manfredini was having trouble breathing, and his face was shiny with sweat.

'I don't know where he is, I haven't seen him since yesterday,' he said, nearly hysterical.

The inspector crushed his cigarette butt in a small silver platter.

'Let's go, Piras,' he said drily. He gestured to his assistant, and together they headed towards the door. Manfredini followed them, face hardened with tension. In the doorway, Bordelli turned and looked him straight in the eye again.

'What you're doing is very serious, Signor Manfredini,' he said severely.

'I'm not doing anything,' Francesco muttered.

The inspector thrust his fists into his pockets and started descending the stairs, with Piras following behind.

They came out on to the street. It was raining frightfully hard. Pulling their jackets up over their heads, they dashed inside the Beetle, already soaking wet.

'We've got to put him under twenty-four-hour surveillance and tap his telephone,' said Bordelli, drying his face with his handkerchief.

'For the telephone we're going to need Ginzillo's authorisation,' said Piras, already knowing what the inspector would say.

'Never mind Ginzillo, he'll only waste our time,' said Bordelli, shrugging.

'What about Simone's place?' asked Piras.

'Same thing.' Bordelli took Simone's picture out of his pocket and handed it to Piras. 'Have a hundred copies made and send them to every police station in town and in the surrounding villages,' he said, starting up the car.

Piras took the photograph as if it were scalding hot and stuffed it into his pocket without looking at it.

It was not quite midnight. Bordelli was still at the office, limp with fatigue in his chair. That afternoon he had dashed over to the cemetery to attend Casimiro's burial. Then he'd dropped in on Diotivede to find out whether there was any news about

Sara Bini, but the pathologist hadn't yet had the time to work on her and told him that it was best not to get one's hopes up. Bordelli had come back to the station as taut as a drum, and organised, with Piras's help, the shifts of surveillance of Simone Fantini and his cousin Francesco Manfredini. After a long dinner in Totò's kitchen, he'd returned to the office and set about comparing the reports on the two murdered girls. He had smoked a great deal and felt that he needed to relax a little. He thought of paying Rosa a quick visit. On his way out of the station, he stopped at Mugnai's guard booth.

'If there are any urgent developments, you'll find me at home, or at this number,' he said, and he dictated Rosa's telephone number to him.

'Very well, Inspector,' Mugnai said, adding a little chuckle of understanding. Bordelli ignored him and went out. He got into his Beetle and drove through the centre of town in the rain. Pulling up in Via Neri with two wheels on the pavement, he parked the car next to the front door of Rosa's building. Dashing out of the car to avoid getting too wet, he collided with a short, hairless man who was walking fast in the middle of the street. The little man mumbled an apology with his head bowed and continued on his way, but Bordelli grabbed him by the arm and stopped him.

'Romeo! Don't you say hello to me any more?'

'Inspector! I didn't see you.'

As it was still raining hard, Bordelli pulled Romeo towards him under the jutting cornice of a building.

'I'll bet you're running off to some shady business deal of yours.'

'I swear I'm not, Inspector,' Romeo said between coughs.

'Don't swear.'

'I've taken your advice, Inspector: no more fake money.'

'And how's the blonde?'

'What blonde?'

'The one you showed me a picture of the other day, a good-looking blonde you'd fallen head over heels for.'

'Ah, her . . .'

'You don't like her any more?'

'She's dumped me for some prick from up north, Inspector . . . The man's a chicken thief. A woman like that is worthless.'

'Too bad . . .'

'It doesn't matter, I'm a lot better off alone.'

'Try not to get into any trouble, Romeo, and stay away from the big circuits. They're not for you.'

'From now on, just safe deals, I swear. I don't want to go back to jail.'

Bordelli patted him on the shoulder.

'Best of luck,' he said.

'I'll need it.'

Romeo made a gesture of goodbye and walked away in the rain, coughing hard. Poor Romeo. There was good reason to hope he never ended up in jail again. With those lungs, he would never come out alive.

Bordelli turned up the collar of his jacket and ran to Rosa's front door. He rang the buzzer three times, then paused, then rang three more times. It was their code for when he arrived late at night.

Rosa welcomed him with her usual good cheer, even though she had already gone to bed and didn't like people to see her without make-up. She was wearing a rather transparent pink dressing gown and strange slippers with heels. Sitting him down on the sofa, she took off his shoes, poured him a glass of *vin santo* and ran into the kitchen to make him something to eat. Bordelli tried to relax, but it wasn't easy. His brain was moving all by itself, ploddingly, like an earthworm stuck in mud.

Rosa returned a short while later with a plate full of colourful tartines and a maternal smile that deformed her lipstick-covered lips. She had also been to the bathroom to put on some make-up.

'You're a dear,' said Bordelli, chewing.

'For so little, monkey?' she replied.

'Where's Gideon?'

'Out and about over the rooftops.'

'In this rain?'

'He's got a lot of girlfriends.'

'Lucky guy.'

The inspector took one last bite and downed the rest of the *vin santo* in his glass.

'You spoil me like a baby,' he said. Rosa looked very proud of herself. She blew a kiss at him and went and poured him a glass of cognac.

'You know, Rosa, I just can't get those two little girls out of my head.'

Rosa squeezed her eyes shut in horror.

'Poor little things. Who knows what terrible moments they went through in the hands of that madman,' she said.

'If this goes on much longer, I'll go mad myself . . . I can't even manage to move an inch forward on Casimiro.'

'Poor little man. What did he ever do to end up that way?'

Bordelli collapsed horizontally on the sofa, listening to the sound of the rain pelting the roof tiles. From the window giving on to the terrace he could see rooftops cluttered with chimneys and antennae and, farther on, Arnolfo's Tower.

As nobody had come forward to claim Casimiro's mortal remains, the dwarf was buried early that afternoon in Soffiano cemetery, at the city government's expense. Only Bordelli and the priest, motionless in the rain, each with his own umbrella, watched him being lowered into the grave. The matter was over in minutes, after a few words of farewell and a handshake with the priest.

Rosa had grown somewhat sad, which didn't happen very often. She lit a little ball of incense and a few candles, then turned off all the lights except for the standing lamp beside the couch, and collapsed into the armchair with a sigh. From a canvas bag she extracted some knitting work and started knitting without a word. Gideon came home soaking wet and shook himself on the carpet. Then he yawned and went and lay down at Rosa's feet.

Bordelli closed his eyes. It was nice just to lie there listening to the sound of the rain and the clicking of Rosa's needles, but his thoughts continued to oppress him. He was obsessed with the case of the little girls, and for the moment there was no hope of stopping the killer. He felt very discouraged, more than he had for a long time. Even finding Simone Fantini would probably serve no purpose. The sooner he realised this, the better.

Then there was the murder of Casimiro. Here too, total darkness. Too many questions he couldn't answer. Who was that man with the black spot on his neck? And who was the foreigner that had punched him in the liver? Did the two men know each other? Had they been involved in the killing, or were these only stupid coincidences? Most importantly, who could have any interest in killing a miserable little dwarf who never frightened anyone? Had he discovered something big?

'What are you thinking about, monkey?' Rosa suddenly asked, startling Bordelli.

'Can't you imagine?'

'Don't obsess, dear. You'll catch that monster soon . . . Another drop of cognac?'

'Thanks.'

Rosa filled the glass very nearly to the brim. Cognac was never lacking in her household. A girlfriend of hers sent it to her periodically from Paris.

The inspector took little sips, warming the glass in his hands. Though he tried not to think of those things, his mind always came back to them, like flies to shit. Feeling suddenly hot from the alcohol, he unbuttoned his collar. Rosa carried on knitting with her usual slowness.

'What are you making?' Bordelli asked.

'A winter sweater for you . . . Do you like the colour?'

It was a nondescript light green.

'It's lovely,' said the inspector.

As often happened, they started talking about days gone by. Rosa loved to tell stories, and Bordelli loved most of all to listen. In some respects she was proud of her life . . . She would often say that she felt as if she had lived three or four lives instead of just one. As a little girl she had known hunger and cold. Then she'd grown up, and since she was very pretty and very poor, she found herself surrounded by admirers of all ages, from spineless youths to old wankers who got right to the point without any fuss, opening their fat wallets straight away. 'Whores are made,' she used to say with a bitter smile. Then, during the war, she'd had the pleasure of meeting Fascists and Germans, she said, and she told stories to make your hair stand on end.

'The world is full of cowards and sons of bitches,' she said, knitting away like a grandmother.

Slowly the candles reached their end. Rosa got up to light some more and then sat back down. It was almost two o'clock.

'You know, monkey . . . I just love sitting here with you and talking,' she said, crossing her once-beautiful legs.

'Me too.'

'I've never told you this, but ever since I met you, I've always thought that something would happen between us. I think it has yet to happen, even though I don't quite know what it is.'

Bordelli handed his empty glass to Rosa for her to refill. Her comment stuck in his head and wouldn't go away: 'something has yet to happen . . . has yet to happen . . .' Perhaps the murder of Casimiro should be interpreted in a completely different way. Perhaps the dwarf had stumbled upon something that had yet to happen and was kicked aside like a clod of dirt in the road . . . The inspector shook his head. Enough was enough. At night, at least, he had to stop thinking about these things. Anyway, it was pointless to fill his head with conjectures. He downed his glass and slid his feet into his shoes. Rosa put down her knitting needles and went and sat down beside him, preventing him tying his shoes, like a little girl wanting attention.

'C'mon, Rosa . . .'

She chuckled. 'Do I bother you?' Gideon, too, came up to him and started sharpening his claws on Bordelli's trousers. The inspector pushed him away, and the tomcat went off, snapping his tail.

'When are you going to come and see your Rosina again?' she asked, sticking a finger in his ear.

'You know I can't stay away from you for very long.'

'I can believe it! Where are you going to find somebody else like me? Eh? Where?'

'Now, I couldn't say . . . But a few years ago, at that little villa up on the Lungarno del Tempio,' said Bordelli, already shielding his face with his hands.

'Bastard!' she said, giggling as she tried to slap him. She had bony little hands that could inflict damage. In the end Bordelli managed to tie his shoes. He stood up and kissed Rosa's fingers.

'You are so beautiful,' he said.

Rosa blushed and couldn't suppress a giggle. She loved this sort of thing, perhaps because for most of her life she had been treated quite differently. She saw her monkey to the door, her arm looped through his, and after their last kisses she slipped into his pocket a small, blue silk sack full of something and tied with a blue ribbon.

'Put this in your underwear drawer, it'll make everything smell nice.'

'What is it?'

'Lavender and rosemary.'

The inspector thanked her by kissing her hand again. Then he descended the stairs, fingers squeezing the scented little sack that made his pocket bulge. He couldn't remember whether he actually had a drawer just for underwear.

He was dreaming . . . Before him stood Mereu, the most illiterate member of the San Marco Battalion, looking at him and smiling, and the next second flying through the air after stepping on a mine. The scene kept on repeating itself, and each time Bordelli failed to warn him in time . . . He would run over to him and then find his head in a bush, still smiling . . . Then he'd see him stepping on the mine again, he would run over to him and find his head in the bush again . . . And it would start all over again . . . Mereu would smile, step on the bloody mine and . . . All at once Bordelli heard an infernal ringing, boring through his brain. It took him a moment to realise it was the telephone. Groping wildly in the dark, he seized the receiver.

'Yeah . . . Who is it?'

'Marshal, did I wake you?' asked a woman's voice in an excited whisper. Bordelli was thick tongued, still seeing Mereu's face in the dark . . . but he realised at once that he needed to do something decisive.

'The marshal is in Spain on an investigation and won't be back for three or four months,' he said, faking a Neapolitan accent.

'And who, may I ask, are you?'

'A relative.'

'Another *carabiniere*?'

'Plumber.'

'Oh, what a shame! Strange things are happening in my building, very strange things . . . Had the marshal mentioned them to you?'

'I don't think so.'

'Please do me a favour. If you hear from the marshal, tell him to phone me at once. I am Signora Capecchi, he'll understand.'

'I'll pass it on,' said Bordelli, hanging up before the old woman could say anything else. He turned on to his side, hoping to fall back asleep at once, but in the haze of his forced awakening, the image of the loutish young Nocentini, who chewed gum like an American and spat in the stairwell, kept coming into his mind. He was unable to fall asleep again. In the end he turned on the light and started staring at the ceiling. He felt dead tired, but his brain was as busy as ever. There was no point in trying to sleep any more. He got up out of bed and started rummaging through the pockets of his jacket. He'd remembered Simone Fantini's short story, which he'd snatched from the young man's desk. *The Tower*. Good title. He went back to bed and started reading. He already knew what would happen, but kept on reading with the same curiosity

as the first time. The story had something at once horrifying
and sweet about it, something he had difficulty fully understanding. When he had finished reading it, he let it slide off
the bed. It really was quite a coincidence that Fantini had
written a story in which the protagonist was suspected of raping
and killing a little girl. But it was a good story and, still thinking
of Fantini, he fell back asleep with the light on.

He woke up past eight, heavy headed. He shaved in a hurry
and went out. The sky was still full of clouds, but it wasn't
raining. He went on foot to buy matches, as usual passing
through the streets where he had played as a child. He remembered that period well. The games they played were never
peaceful; they were harsh tests of courage, wild, dangerous
challenges, slingshot battles, and often one of them ended up
at the Misericordia to get stitched up. Nothing had changed
in those streets since then; the atmosphere was the same as
when he used to set out on his bicycle from the distant Cure
to come to these narrow streets full of mystery and misery.
Walking through Piazza Piattellina, he turned to look at the
wall where four little pricks from Ponte di Mezzo had once
smashed Natalino's face. It was as if he could still see the stain
on the stones. They left him on the ground half dead, blood
pouring out of his nose. Natalino had ended up spending
several weeks in hospital. The doctors had put his face back
together as best they could, but his features were never quite
the same after that. After he recovered, he went to take revenge,
and somebody nearly got killed. All this over a girl . . .

The inspector passed in front of a closed metal shutter
covered with rust and slowed his pace, head full of memories.
This used to be the shop of the Captain's Wife, the tobacco
lady who in the early days of Fascism had lived in Africa. He
remembered her well. She had rotten teeth, and when she
laughed it was a horrific sight. Her shop was always filled with
the fog of a thousand cigarettes. She sold everything imaginable, and very rarely sent a customer away unsatisfied. She was

the only person who ever went into the back room, and she always returned with the right thing. She died before the war. The shop was shut down and had never reopened. The Captain's Wife had no relatives. Her only companion was Gertrude, a furious little monkey that used to run about the shop with its teeth bared, terrifying customers. When the old woman died, it was given to a circus passing through.

He bought matches in Piazza Tasso and went back to get his Beetle. He was in a bad mood. He drove along looking at people's faces, trying to imagine who they were and what sort of lives they led, to keep his head uncluttered for a bit. But the same ugly stories kept coming back to him.

He crossed the Arno and in Piazza Santa Trinita saw a man who made him start. He slowed down to have a better look. It was indeed him, the stranger who had punched him in the liver in the olive grove at Fiesole. He had come out of a side street and turned down Via Tornabuoni. He looked to be in a big hurry and was taller than Bordelli remembered. Well dressed, but not wearing a tie. If he had seen him only from behind he might not have recognised him, but the face was unmistakable. A face with heavy features, covered with wrinkles and as though marked by an ineradicable horror that emanated mostly from the eyes.

Bordelli accelerated, turned on to Via della Vigna Nova and parked the car with two wheels on the pavement. He got out in a hurry and walked back to the corner of Via Tornabuoni. He waited for the guy to pass and then fell in behind him. The man was walking serenely, without turning round. He seemed not to have noticed anything. He turned onto Via de' Giacomini, walked its entire length, then turned right on to Via delle Belle Donne and, after another thirty yards, slipped into a doorway, having opened the great door with a key. As soon as he saw him disappear inside, Bordelli sprinted for the door, but got there too late, finding it locked again. There were five buzzers outside the door. He rang one at random, pressing several times, but nobody answered. He then tried another, at the bottom, and a few seconds later heard the door click open. Climbing the stairs in a rush, on the first-floor landing he found a very old woman waiting for him in her doorway.

'I'm sorry, signora . . . Did a man enter your home just a few moments ago?' asked Bordelli, approaching her.

'And who are you, may I ask?'

'Police.'

'Oh my God, what's happening?' she cried, taking a step back.

'Please remain calm, nothing is happening.'

'Is there a criminal in the building?'

'Lock yourself inside and don't worry,' said Bordelli, leaving her to chew on her fear and heading upstairs. There was only one apartment per landing. The second-floor flat had no name on the door. He rang the bell and heard footsteps approach. The peephole darkened for a couple of seconds, and then the door opened and Bordelli found the person he would least have expected to see standing before him.

'Hello, Inspector . . . You're still an inspector, aren't you?' said the man, smiling tensely.

'Dr Levi! What are you doing in Italy?' On top of his surprise, Bordelli felt delighted to see this intelligent man after fifteen years. He hadn't changed in the least . . . He had the same skin tightly pulled over the bones, the same hard eyes, even when laughing. He was rather short, but his gaze added another six inches to his stature.

'Please come in, Inspector, I'll get you something to drink,' the doctor said, standing aside. Bordelli entered, and Levi led him down a corridor of closed doors.

'To what do I owe your lack of surprise, Dr Levi?' Bordelli asked.

'After my holiday in Poland, I don't think there's much left that can surprise me, Inspector.'

Levi had spent over a year in a concentration camp, and a painful smile remained forever etched on his face as a sort of suspension of judgement of humanity.

They entered a rather large room. There were two sofas with

a small, low table between them, a desk covered with closed portfolios, a filing cabinet with many identical drawers, and a glass-fronted cupboard full of bottles. Bordelli rifled through all his pockets in search of cigarettes, but couldn't find any.

'Are you sure you weren't expecting me, Dr Levi?' he said.

'You are always welcome here.'

'You didn't answer my previous question . . . how is it you're in Italy?'

'I live here, didn't you know?'

'I have to confess I didn't.'

'You didn't answer me, either. Are you still an inspector?'

'More or less.' Bordelli at last found the cigarettes, but the packet was empty. He crumpled it up and put it back in his pocket.

'Would you like one of these?' said Levi, holding out a cigarette box for him.

'Thank you.'

Levi also took one, and they lit up. Bordelli looked around. He couldn't tell whether the room was an office or a drawing room.

'Are you still involved with that stuff, Levi?'

'Water under the bridge. I'm retired now.'

Levi had worn the white-and-blue striped pyjamas from January 1944 until the fall of the Third Reich. When the Russians found him, he weighed less than five stone. It had taken him more than six months to get back on his feet, but he had recovered rather nicely. In '47 he became a member of the White Dove, an organisation founded after the war, secretly financed by Zionists and headed by the tenacious Simon Wiesenthal. The task of the Dove was to hunt down to the far corners of the world those Nazis who had escaped trial at Nuremberg. They had headquarters on every continent, the fugitives having spread across the globe with the help of ODESSA, an organisation financed by German industrialists to help Nazi chiefs hide while they waited for the utopian recapture of power by survivors of the NSDAP.

Every detachment of the White Dove had the authorisation to involve, in their area of operation, anyone they deemed necessary to their ends, obviously taking maximum care to vet the persons in question as thoroughly as possible. In '48 Bordelli had caught the eye of the organisation's Italian chapter, owing primarily to his anti-Nazi past, and it had been Levi's job to contact him. He had explained to Bordelli what they were about, and the inspector had agreed to work with the Dove without a second thought, happy to keep on fighting Hitler's followers. At the time the organisation was working on the case of Dr Christopher Möng and his wife Elfi, who had disappeared from Berlin one month before the Führer committed suicide. Möng, like his counterpart Mengele, had worked on human guinea pigs in a variety of Polish camps, and Elfi, like a good wife, had stayed by his side, preparing cotton wads, passing him surgical instruments, compiling dossiers, numbering corpses, washing the blood away from the laboratory. They conducted every conceivable kind of experiment, all as useless as they were cruel, and their notes were a catalogue of monstrosities. Reliable intelligence had located them in Italy as of late 1946. All that remained was to discover their new identities and perhaps their new faces. Bordelli had studied secret archives and documents, looked at never-released photographs and films. The research was slow and arduous, but the eventual satisfaction was great. Bordelli was fifteen years younger back then and felt that he was working for the good of humanity. A few months later, Möng and his wife were tracked down in a farmhouse in the Po Valley and executed by the White Dove. Bordelli received a word of thanks, and Levi left for Uruguay, where it seemed there was a veritable colony of Nazis.

'Have you found any other bigwigs since Eichmann?' Bordelli asked.

'What would you like to drink, Inspector?'

'Do you have any news of Mengele?'

'What can I get for you?'

'A cognac.'

'At this hour?'

'There are people who do even stranger things,' said Bordelli.

'I don't doubt it . . . Have any preferences?'

'Yes, I'd like some de Maricourt.'

Levi's face tensed for a fraction of a second, as if from a jolt of electricity. Then he smiled.

'I don't know it. Would you be content with a Hennessy?'

'We all have to suffer.'

Levi went and got a bottle and two beautiful glasses from the cupboard, sat down in the armchair, and poured the cognac.

'So, Inspector, what do you have to tell me?' Levi asked with a friendly smile. Bordelli took a sip of Hennessy and felt a wave of warmth over his whole body. Levi wasn't drinking. He had left his full glass on the table, looking over at it from time to time.

'The man I saw enter this building was coming to your place, wasn't he?' Bordelli asked.

'Why were you following him?'

'Tell me first who he is.'

'Aaron Goldberg, a dear friend of mine.'

'Well, a few nights ago your dear friend put my liver to the test,' said Bordelli, miming a punch.

'So it was you,' said Levi, looking rather amused. Bordelli took another sip of cognac. It was excellent, even first thing in the morning.

'You're not drinking, Dr Levi?'

'At this hour I'm content with the aroma. I'm rather attached to my liver.'

'Well, then, I advise you not to stroll through the countryside at night,' said Bordelli.

'I'll keep that in mind.'

There was a hint of tension in the air, but neither of the two would ever have admitted it.

'Tell me, Dr Levi, what was your friend Aaron doing in such a place at one o'clock in the morning?'

'You were there, too, Inspector.'

'Be nice, Levi, tell me everything . . . Is it some job for the Dove?'

'Do you really want to know?'

'Yes.'

Levi looked him straight in the eye for a few seconds, smiling coldly, then heaved a sigh of resignation.

'All right, but you must swear not to tell anyone.'

'Of course.'

'Goldberg had gone to dig up some documents.'

'Oh really?'

'Personal letters of Himmler and Goebbels.'

'Who buried them?'

'One of ours, when things got difficult. And now the time has come to bring them back into the light of day. They are of great historical importance,' said Levi, smiling faintly.

'Ah, I see.'

'Everything clear now?'

'So, in short, you're still working for the Dove . . .'

'As I said, I'm retired now. I just do odd jobs now and then, when they ask.'

Bordelli took a long draught of cognac and shook his head.

'I must say I would have expected better of you, Dr Levi.'

'Is the cognac not very good?' said Levi, with an air of concern.

'I was one of yours, Levi. I worked with your people on Möng, I personally met Wiesenthal . . .'

'Let's not dig up the past, Bordelli, there's no point, for any of us.'

'Then let's talk about now . . . Why are you feeding me all this bullshit?'

'Because it's the pure and simple truth.'

They exchanged an intense glance, as if wanting to tell each other something. Then Bordelli smiled.

'All right, then, let's drop it. Is your friend Goldberg at home?'

'He's here.'

'I'd like to shake his hand. Would that be possible?'

'If it really means that much to you . . .'

'It does.'

'Goldberg!' Levi called in a low voice. A few seconds later a door opened, and Aaron's face peered in. Levi gestured to him to come, and the man entered the room. Seen indoors, he looked even taller. He didn't seem terribly surprised to find before him the man he had floored in the olive grove.

'Let me introduce to you Inspector Bordelli,' said Levi. The inspector stood up and went up to the beast, smiling.

'My dear Goldberg, so pleased to meet you,' he said.

'Sorry about the other night,' Goldberg said in a strong foreign accent, without changing expression. From up close his eyes looked like two holes burrowing all the way through his brain.

'I've already forgotten about it,' said Bordelli, but instead of shaking the man's hand, he sucker-punched him in the liver. Goldberg brought his hand to his side without so much as a groan. He seemed to be having a little trouble breathing, and his face had turned a sickly white. Bordelli rubbed his closed fist with his other hand, marvelling at the silence of the other's suffering.

'I just wanted to communicate my admiration for you, Goldberg. I worked for your people in '48 and it was a real pleasure, believe me.'

Goldberg slowly recovered his wits and glanced over at Levi to know what he should do.

'Go now, Goldberg, we'll talk about it later.'

Goldberg left the room with a hand over his liver, without saying a word. The inspector sat back down on the sofa and picked up his glass of cognac.

'Your friend wasn't offended, I hope?' he said.

'Are you satisfied now, Inspector?' Levi's tone of voice was exactly the same as before, without the slightest modulation.

'He's a dear friend of yours, and yet you both use the formal address,' Bordelli observed.

'It's an old habit.'

'Dr Levi, I'm the first to admit I'm a bit dim witted, but don't expect me to believe your story about buried documents. It makes me feel upset.'

'If you don't want to believe it, there's nothing I can do about it.'

'You could tell me what is actually going on, for example.'

'You still haven't told me what *you* were doing in that place at one o'clock in the morning . . .'

'Worried?'

'Just curious,' Levi said serenely.

'I was stargazing.'

'And I believe you, Inspector,' Levi said, smiling.

Bordelli's thoughts kept returning to the man with the black mark on his neck, but he decided not to mention this to Levi. He wanted Levi to think he knew nothing at all about anything.

'All right, then we've said all we're going to say to each other,' he said.

'It was a pleasure to see you again, Inspector,' said Levi, standing up.

'But you didn't drink with me,' said Bordelli, remaining seated. Levi's cognac had remained on the table the whole time, abandoned.

'Come and see me some time in the evening, Inspector, and I'll gladly drink with you.'

When he'd reached the door, Bordelli turned round.

'I'm going to ask you one more time, Levi . . . Tell me the truth. It could help me to get to the bottom of something of great importance to me.' He was thinking of Casimiro.

'I've told you the truth, the whole truth, and nothing but the truth,' Levi said, smiling.

'I'll return the favour some time,' said Bordelli. He already had his hand on the doorknob when, behind Levi, there appeared a dark, beautiful girl with a mass of hair tied behind her head.

'Hello,' said Bordelli, holding out his hand. She had two dark eyes as intense as a panther's. She looked to be about twenty-five, and he liked her at once, in a way that he hadn't felt for a long time. A bit like Piras with the Sicilian girl.

'Pleased to meet you. I'm Milena,' said the girl.

'Inspector Bordelli.'

They shook hands, and Bordelli imagined to himself that Milena had squeezed his fingers in a very special way. Levi forced a smile.

'I won't keep you, Inspector, I know you're very busy,' he said.

'See you again some time,' Milena said with a smile, and she walked away, followed by Bordelli's gaze. Levi went up to the inspector, so close he could almost touch him.

'Please don't tell anyone what you've learned,' he whispered with an ironic gleam in his eye.

'You can sleep easy; I don't feel like being laughed at.'

'I knew I could trust you, Inspector,' the Nazi hunter said with a cold smile.

'See you soon, Dr Levi. I always come back to see people I like.'

'Come whenever you wish, it's always a pleasure.'

Bordelli waved goodbye one last time and headed slowly down the stairs. He descended the first flight, then the second, and only then did he hear Levi's door close. When he reached the first-floor landing, he stopped, waited for the light in the stairwell to go out, and then went quietly back up to the second floor. Approaching Levi's door, he put his ear up against it. He heard a door slam inside, then Levi's angry voice. A few clipped sentences, like tiny explosions. He was speaking Hebrew. There was the sound of another door slamming, then nothing. Bordelli waited a little longer, ear pressed against the door. A good minute went by. In the silence he heard Levi's voice call Goldberg again. The tone was less aggressive, but more worried. Bordelli heard them walking fast and speaking intensely to one another. When they came towards the door, they suddenly lowered their voices to a whisper. The inspector ran and hid himself round a corner wall to avoid being seen through the peephole, and one second later the light in the stairwell came on. As Bordelli had expected, the two had looked out the window to see when he exited the building, perhaps with no real reason to do so, as one sometimes does after a visit from an unwanted guest. When they didn't see him leave, they had grown alarmed. Bordelli had played this little game merely to find out whether Levi was indeed concerned about the unexpected visit, and now he no longer had any doubt. He didn't believe that story about the buried documents for a minute. Obviously something much bigger was at stake.

As soon as the light in the stairwell went out, he dashed down the stairs, stopping only when he heard Levi's door open. Flattening himself against the wall, he felt as if he was playing cops and robbers. The light remained off, and a few minutes later he heard Levi's door delicately closing. Bordelli continued on down the stairs, and when he reached the ground floor, he looked for a secondary exit. Spotting a door behind the stairwell, he tried this and found it open. It led into a sort of empty warehouse. He crossed this, lighting his way with matches, then opened another door and found himself in the entrance hall of another block of flats on the Via del Sole. And so he went out into the street without Levi seeing him and, pleased with himself, headed towards his car. He had succeeded in playing a little joke on the White Dove, and he had even seen a woman he liked very much.

The sky was still blanketed with grey clouds, and thunder rumbled in the distance, but it still wasn't raining. Bordelli gripped the Beetle's steering wheel tight, an unlit cigarette in his mouth. Even were the world to end, he wouldn't light it until after he got to the station. He felt sort of excited. If the White Dove was mixed up in this business, he knew exactly where to find the man with the black spot on his neck.

Big headlines leapt out from the newspaper kiosks: THE MONSTER KILLS AGAIN. The words tormented him, as though shouted in his face.

By the time he parked in the courtyard of Via Zara, it was

already past ten o'clock. The moment he entered his office he lit the bloody cigarette and collapsed in his chair. Although running into Levi had opened a little crack in the investigation of Casimiro's murder, Bordelli still felt the same sense of power-lessness weighing down on him in the case of the little girls.

On his desk he found Forensics' report on Sara Bini. Inhaling the smoke deeply, he read it from beginning to end, but in vain: nothing of any importance had been found on the child's clothes or around her lifeless body.

He picked up the telephone and dialled the inside line.

'Mugnai, find Piras for me at once.' He always asked Mugnai because the man always knew how to find everyone.

'He was just now on his way out, Inspector. I'll send him up.'

'Tell him to be quick about it.'

While waiting, Bordelli rang Diotivede in the lab to ask about Sara Bini.

'All I can tell you is that it's the same killer, but you already knew that,' said the pathologist.

'So you didn't find anything that might be of use to me?'

'It's possible the murderer wears gloves when he kills, since there wasn't the slightest trace of scratching on either of the little girls' necks. But he could also have very short fingernails.'

'Nothing else?'

'No, unfortunately.'

'Could it be a woman?'

'I doubt it. Normally it's men who commit this kind of murder.'

'Are you sure we can't determine from the bite who it was? We could start researching the local dentists' records, for example.'

'It would be pointless, as I said. The flesh is very soft in that part of the body, and the tooth marks are not very clear.'

'Bloody hell. I'm at wits' end, Doctor. I don't know which way to turn.'

'You've got to get busy, Inspector. I don't want to see any more of these little girls on my table,' said the doctor, hanging up.

The inspector remained immobile, watching a fly collide with the windowpane. He identified with it. When Piras walked in, Bordelli gave him a surly look.

'Any news on Fantini and Manfredini?' he asked.

'Manfredini went out early this morning in his car. Gennari followed him, but he didn't do anything unusual.'

'Who's watching their residences?'

'Rinaldi has just now gone to Manfredini's, and Moretti will be at Fantini's till eleven.'

'And after eleven?'

'I'll be taking over, Inspector.'

'You?'

'What difference does it make whether it's me or someone else?'

'I get it, Piras, it's because of the girl.'

'What girl?'

'Go on, Piras, it's getting late.'

The youth glanced at his watch, assumed a serious expression, and left in a rush.

Bordelli remained seated, thinking, leaning back in his chair. He gazed out the window as he smoked. He thought again of Levi. The fact that the White Dove was interested in Baron von Hauser's villa gave him food for thought. He was convinced that Levi was hiding the truth from him, and he was determined to discover it. Casimiro's death might well be connected to this affair. Or it might not. What a mess.

He picked up the telephone and rang Archives on the internal line.

'Hello, Porcinai, do you know where I might find some photos of Nazis?'

'Let me think . . . Try talking to Professor Vannetti; he's in the literature department at the university. He's the top Italian expert on the Third Reich.'

'Thanks.'

He hung up and rested his chin in his hands. Vannetti, literature department. He had to find the time to go there.

An annoying drizzle started to fall. It tinkled against the windowpanes and then dripped like drool. It was rather cold outside. The spring really couldn't make up its mind to arrive.

The telephone rang and Bordelli answered distractedly.

'Yes?'

'Inspector, this is Ennio.'

'Ciao, Botta, I'm told your trip to Greece went rather well.'

'Not too badly, Inspector, I'll tell you more about it when I see you. And I hear you've got a pretty tough nut to crack.'

'I don't want to hear about it.'

'They also told me about Casimiro . . . Poor bloke.'

'This is a shitty period, Ennio.'

'I realise it's not the best time for this, Inspector, but I wanted to tell you that we can do another dinner at your place whenever you like.'

'I can't wait.'

'But this time I'll pay, just as I promised.'

'Let me catch this bastard, Botta, and then we can arrange a nice dinner.'

'See you soon, Inspector. If you need me, you know where to find me. Break a leg!'

'Thanks . . . 'Bye, Botta, I hope I'll be coming by soon to bother you.'

Late that morning, Bordelli went to the home of Emanuela Bini, Sara's mother, to ask her a few questions. He had phoned her the night before and agreed to come by her place the following day around midday. She lived in Via Masaccio, in a lovely apartment on the third floor.

The woman saw him into her living room and sat down in front of him. She was about forty years old and quite beautiful. She had reacted differently from Valentina's mother. She'd hardened; her eyes were like glass marbles.

'Signora Bini, please forgive me if I ask you some unpleasant questions . . . It's just that I'm trying to pick up a trail, and I can't afford to—'

'Ask me anything you like,' she interrupted him. Bordelli thanked her with a nod.

'Are you married?' he asked.

'Yes . . . but not to Sara's father.'

'Have you maintained good relations with the girl's father?'

'I have no idea where he is,' the woman said, shrugging her shoulders.

'Does he know he has a daughter?'

'Yes, we broke up when Sara was two months old.'

'And was that the last you ever saw of him?'

'I haven't heard from him since, and I've never sought him out.'

'Why not?' the inspector asked, with the unpleasant feeling that he should mind his own business. The woman made an expression of disgust.

'I wished I had never even met him . . . What happened between us was just one big mistake.'

'Does your husband know what happened?' asked Bordelli. The woman shot him a resentful glance.

'Whatever are you thinking?' she said.

'It was only a question.'

'My husband knows everything; I have never hidden anything from him.'

'I didn't mean to offend you . . .'

'And he's been a perfect gentleman about it. He loved Sara as if she was his own daughter,' she continued, a little upset.

'I don't doubt it for a minute . . . Where is he now?'

'At the office, as usual. He's working even harder than before, to avoid thinking,' the woman said, eyes blinking nervously.

'You must forgive me, Signora Bini, but in my position I can't afford to neglect a single detail,' Bordelli said, trying to calm her down.

The woman heaved a long sigh and nodded.

'Is there anything else you'd like to know?' she said wearily, pressing her temples with her fingers. Bordelli felt uneasy in the presence of this devastated woman, but he had no choice but to carry on.

'Do you have any enemies that you know of?' he asked.

'Why do you ask?'

'I'm simply looking for clues that might put me on the right track.'

'I have no enemies, not that I know of,' said the woman.

Bordelli wondered whether the killer was merely a madman who murdered at random, or whether he chose his victims according to a specific criterion. Knowing this would already be a big step forward.

'Did the girl go often to the Parco delle Cascine with her grandmother?' he asked.

'Usually it was I who took her there.'

'Every day?'

'Fairly often, but I had a doctor's appointment that day.'

'Had you noticed anything unusual in recent days? Say, a person following you, or any strange behaviour in your daughter?'

'No.'

'Do you know the mother of Valentina Panerai, the little girl who was killed in the Parco del Ventaglio?'

'No.'

Bordelli stood up from his chair, smiling with resignation.

'Thank you, Signora Bini. That'll be all for the time being.'

'Please come back whenever you like,' she said with empty eyes. She saw the inspector to the door.

'We *will* catch him,' said Bordelli, squeezing her hand tight.

'For Sara it's too late,' the woman murmured.

Descending the stairs, Bordelli lit a cigarette. Emanuela Bini's empty gaze remained etched in his mind. He felt quite discouraged. Nothing had emerged in the murder of the little girls that might open the slightest crack in the case. He got into his car and rolled down the window so he could blow the smoke out. It was still raining, and every so often he felt a drop land on his face. He was desperately searching his brain for something that might help him take one small step forward in these murder cases. He couldn't bear the feeling of immobility any longer. He felt a painful restlessness in the calves of his legs, like someone condemned to remain seated for eternity. He couldn't make a single move, nothing that might give at least the feeling of moving in a specific direction. He couldn't stand it. He tossed the cigarette butt out of the window and opened the glove compartment, looking for a sweet he recalled having seen there some time before. He found a Rossana,[14] unwrapped it with the help of his lips, and crushed it between his teeth.

While he was stopped at an intersection, he thought of Dr Fabiani, the psychoanalyst he'd met a few years back during a nasty murder case. It had been a while since he'd heard from him. Perhaps the doctor would be willing to talk to him about the two little girls. Not that Bordelli expected much, but it was better than sitting on his bum, going round in circles and smoking.

He glanced at his watch. Half past twelve. He stopped at a bar, looked up Fabiani's number in the phone book, and rang him at once. The doctor must have been in the garden, as usual, tending his flowers, since he picked up only after many rings.

'Yes?'

'Dr Fabiani, this is Bordelli.'

'Inspector . . . How nice to hear from you.'

'How are you?'

'I'm fine, thanks, I was just fertilising the azaleas. Why don't you drop in on me one of these days?'

'If you don't mind, I'd like to come by right now.'

'All right, then, I'll be waiting for you.'

'See you soon.'

The inspector got back into his car and, at the intersection with Viale Don Minzoni, turned towards Le Cure. It had stopped raining and the sky was slowly clearing. The weather had been undecided for a good two weeks now. The pavements were full of little children just out of school, their mothers leading them by the hand. In Viale Volta the inspector passed the house he had lived in as a child, slowing down and turning round to look at the garden and the ground-floor windows. The shutters were open, and he saw some white curtains. Every time he passed it, he was tempted to stop and ask the current residents whether he could see those rooms again, but he always put it off.

Before Piazza Edison, he turned left on to Via di Barbacane, climbing up the steep old street for a distance and then pulling up in front of Fabiani's little villa. The hedgerow of bay along the metal fencing had grown, and a cherry tree struggled to open its first blossoms.

Bordelli stood on tiptoe and peered into the garden. The psychoanalyst had heard the sound of the Volkswagen and was coming towards the gate. He was wearing his work smock, and the tip of a pair of gardening shears stuck out from one of the oversized sleeves like a crab's claw. Seeing the inspector, he raised a hand and quickened his step. As he opened the gate, it seemed to Bordelli that old Fabiani's eyes looked less sad than usual.

'It's been a long time, Inspector. How are you?' the psycho-analyst said with a smile.

'Not too bad, thanks. And yourself?'

'I can't complain.'

Bordelli entered the garden, and as they walked towards the house, he looked around. He felt good in this place, amidst all the greenery and earthenware pots with every imaginable sort of plant and flower sprouting from them.

'Did you know I've reopened my practice, Inspector? But I'm treating only a couple of patients. I don't feel up to any more than that.'

'I'm glad to hear you're working again.'

'I was about to make tea, Inspector.'

They went into the house. Dr Fabiani put the kettle on the stove and got the teapot ready on the table. He opened a box of biscuits as well. Through the open window in the sitting room one could see the doctor's pagoda, covered with the naked, sinuous branches of a white wisteria beginning to blossom.

'I seem to have gathered that you wanted to ask me something, Inspector,' said the psychoanalyst.

'How could you tell?' said Bordelli, grinning. Fabiani ran a hand through his snow-white hair.

'Well, it wasn't too hard,' he said. The inspector picked up a biscuit and bit into it.

'I wanted to ask you what you think about the two little girls who were killed,' he said.

The old man nodded as if he'd been expecting this question, and he threw his hands up. His white hair stood out against the dark blue smock like a splash of water.

'What can I say? The killer's a psychopath. We psychoanalysts abhor that kind of patient . . . Sorry, I hear the water boiling.'

Fabiani went into the kitchen and returned with a steaming kettle. After pouring the water into the teapot, he sat back down with a sigh.

'If we don't catch him he'll probably kill again,' said Bordelli. Fabiani shook his head sadly. The inspector lit a cigarette and crumpled the empty packet.

'I'm completely in the dark, Dr Fabiani, and I thought perhaps you could help me.'

Fabiani filled the teacups and moved the sugar bowl closer to the inspector.

'Lemon or milk, Inspector?'

'Neither, thanks.'

They sat there for a while without speaking, sipping their scalding-hot tea. The sun had come out, making the wet grass in the garden sparkle. A bumblebee buzzed amidst the silence, in search of flowers . . . At that moment Bordelli felt a sort of tingling in his gut, and realised that spring had finally arrived.

'Tell me more about those murders,' Dr Fabiani suddenly said.

Bordelli set his cup down, still half full, on the table, and told him all the details of the killings, trying not to leave anything out. The psychoanalyst listened very attentively, and when the inspector had finished talking, he folded his hands around his legs.

'Psychopaths are almost always people who themselves have experienced some great trauma, some tragic event that their minds are unable to accept. But how exactly they work out this trauma, and what factors lead these individuals to act in one way or another, is hard to understand.'

'Could the killer be a woman?'

'I doubt it. These sorts of crimes are almost always committed by men.'

'How old do you think he might be?'

Fabiani raised his eyebrows, unsure.

'One can never tell, but usually such individuals aren't too young,' he said.

'Are they lucid when they kill, or in a state of frenzy?'

'Both things are possible, but I think in either case their will is dominated by an uncontrollable force, even when the murder has been planned well in advance.'

'Are they guilty, in your opinion?'

'You may not like to hear this, but I have to be honest and say no. In a moral sense, I mean.'

A bumblebee entered through the open window, passed once over their heads and went back out to the garden.

'Thank you, Dr Fabiani. I'll leave you to your azaleas,' Bordelli said, standing up. The psychoanalyst got up with him, and they went out into the garden.

'I also need to plant my basil,' said Fabiani, pointing to a large basin resting atop a little pillar of bricks and shining in the sunlight.

'Do you think I could grow basil on my little kitchen balcony?' the inspector asked.

'Of course. You need only water it daily.'

'I'll give it a try.'

'When will I see you again, Inspector?' Fabiani asked at the gate.

'As soon as I settle this case, I'd like to have another dinner party at my place, with Botta at the cooker.'

'I'll be happy to join you.'

'I'm counting on it.' They exchanged a firm handshake.

'Good luck, Inspector,' said Fabiani, hinting at a smile.

'I'll catch him soon,' Bordelli muttered. The doctor made a last gesture of goodbye, then shut the gate and walked slowly back towards his plants.

When Bordelli got to the police station it was almost nine o'clock, but he wasn't very hungry. The moment Mugnai saw him, he came up to him with a piece of paper in his hand.

'A certain Manfredini phoned for you, Inspector. He said to call him at once at this number.'

Bordelli snatched the scrap of paper from his hand.

'What time did he call?' he asked.

'About half an hour ago.'

Bordelli raced upstairs to his office and rang Manfredini. Someone picked up after the first ring.

'Yes, hello?'

'What is it, Manfredini?'

'Inspector, could you come to my place immediately?'

'What is it?'

'Do you still want to talk to Simone?'

'Where is he?'

'Could you come to my flat?'

'I'll be right over.'

The inspector hung up the telephone and dashed out of the station. He felt less hungry than ever. He drove up Via Bolognese, and when he turned on to Via Trieste he saw Piras parked at the corner of the street staring at the front door of Fantini's building. He pulled up alongside and honked the horn. The Sardinian rolled down the window.

'Nothing to report, Inspector.'

'Piras, don't tell me you've been here since eleven . . .'

'It's no great effort on my part, sir,' said the young man, ears turning red.

'Get in my car.'

'What's happening?'

'Hurry.'

Piras locked his car and got into the Beetle.

'Where are we going?' he asked, puzzled.

'To Manfredini's.'

'Some new development?'

'Apparently we're going to talk to Simone.'

'Shit!'

They drove down Via Trieste and then back up Via Stibbert. The sky was blue and cloudless. They rang Manfredini's buzzer and the door opened at once. The young man was waiting for them at the door to his flat. He shook the two policemen's hands and showed them into the drawing room. All three remained standing, looking at one another in silence. Then Manfredini sighed.

'Simone is ready to talk to you,' he said.

'Where is he?' Bordelli asked.

'First tell me something, Inspector . . . Will you arrest him?'

'Where is he?'

Manfredini stared long and hard at Piras, as if trying to understand from him what was about to happen. Then he looked back at the inspector.

'Simone's here,' he said.

'Was he here yesterday?'

'He was hiding downstairs in the cellar.'

'Bring him in.'

Manfredini nodded, went out of the drawing room and quickly returned with his cousin. Bordelli and Piras were still standing in the middle of the room. Simone was even more handsome than in the photos. His dark, slanted eyes glowed with an intense light.

'Hello, Inspector,' he said. He had a beautiful voice, and even Piras, despite himself, could only look at him in admiration. The fact that he was so friendly with Sonia was hard for him to swallow.

'Shall we sit down?' said Bordelli. All four sat down.

'Is it all right if I stay?' asked Manfredini.

'I've got nothing against it,' said Bordelli. Simone was very tense, and looked at the two policemen with suspicion.

'I didn't do it,' he said suddenly.

'I know,' said Bordelli.

'How can you be so sure?'

'You tell him, Piras.'

The Sardinian sat up and looked Simone straight in the eye. He really is beautiful, he thought, before beginning to speak.

'Signora Beniamini saw you from behind, walking down the path when the little girl – who was already dead – lay a good distance up ahead. Only afterwards did she see you go off the path towards the trees. Why on earth would the killer go back to look at the girl right after killing her?'

Simone shook his head.

'I saw something red on the ground and went up to it without realising what it was. And then I saw that it was a little girl, and so I bent down over her, thinking she was unwell. Only afterwards did I realise she was dead. Then, when I saw that witch, Beniamini, I thought I was done for . . . That woman hates me.'

'Because of her daughter Ottavia?' asked Piras.

'You already know?' asked Simone, stunned.

'*We* do – it's Ottavia's mum who doesn't know . . . She thinks you don't even know each other,' said Piras with a smile of satisfaction. Simone shrugged.

'What were you doing in that park, Signor Fantini?' Bordelli asked, taking out a cigarette.

'Why do you ask? So you don't believe me . . .' Simone said, upset.

'Calm down. I've already told you what I think. All I want to know is whether you saw anyone in the general area that morning.'

Simone ran a hand over his sweaty face and nodded.

'Shortly before finding the little girl under the trees, I saw a man. He was coming towards me, and we walked past each other. He seemed calm to me, not—'

'What time was it?'

'About half past nine, more or less.'

'Where, exactly, did you see him?'

'On a small path parallel to the one where I saw the girl.'

'Are there usually many people around there?'

'I hardly ever see anyone. They're usually all on the grass or by the river.'

'What sort of man was he?'

'Slender, about my height.' Simone looked to be about six feet tall.

'How old do you think he was?'

'About fifty, maybe a bit older.'

'Would you recognise him again?'

'I didn't get a good look at him. He was wearing a hat and a scarf that covered almost half his face. At first he looked as if he had a toothache . . . but I didn't pay much attention . . . I never imagined at the time that anyone would ask me what he looked like . . . Anyway, I'm not very good with faces.'

Bordelli shook his head and crushed his cigarette in an ashtray.

'I did notice, however, that he was missing a finger,' Simone added.

'Are you sure about that?'

'Absolutely. When he was just a few yards away from me, he started taking his gloves off. At that moment his hat was blown off by a gust of wind and fell practically at my feet. I picked it up to give it back to him, and as I was handing it to him I noticed that he was missing the little finger on one hand, the left hand. I always look at people's hands, I don't know why.'

'Do you remember anything else?'

'Ask me some things.'

'Hair?'

'Dark and very short.'

Francesco Manfredini had sat down to one side and was silently following their conversation.

'What sort of gloves was he wearing?' Bordelli continued.

'Black leather. I remember thinking: how strange, wearing gloves in this heat. But it was just a thought . . .'

'Shoes?'

'I didn't notice.'

'What sort of hat did he have?' asked Piras.

The young man thought about this for a moment.

'I think it was black, with a wide brim . . . Come to think of it, when I grabbed it, I noticed a name inside: Beltrami.'

'That's a shop in the centre of town, right, Piras?'

'I think it's in Via Roma,' replied the Sardinian.

'Can you think of anything else?' Bordelli asked Simone, who stared at the floor, searching his memory. He remained that way for a few seconds, then looked up.

'There was one thing that struck me. When I gave him his hat back, he didn't react – didn't even thank me with a nod or gesture . . . I can't remember anything else,' said Simone, staring into space.

'Tell me something. Did your friend Sonia know you were hiding?' Bordelli asked, which made Piras give a start.

Simone squirmed and then exchanged a glance with his cousin.

'No need to say anything, I already know the answer,' said the inspector, thinking that, unlike Francesco, the Sicilian girl was a very good actress. Then he gestured to Piras and they stood up together.

'If you remember anything else, ring me at once,' said Bordelli.

'Of course,' the young man said, rising to his feet. Francesco joined the group, and they all headed for the door. Shaking hands, they said goodbye, taking care not to cross arms.

'Ah, incidentally, Fantini, Sonia let us into your flat, and I stole a short story of yours,' Bordelli said, looking him in the eye.

'Which one?' Simone asked, slightly alarmed.

'*The Tower*,' said Bordelli, pretending not to notice the lad's unease.

'And what did you think of it?' Simone asked, exchanging a glance with his cousin. Piras didn't know what they were talking about and looked on with curiosity.

'It's a good story. I'd like to hang on to it,' said Bordelli.

'That's not what I meant . . . I was referring . . . to the subject,' Simone stammered.

'Coincidence,' said the inspector, shrugging his shoulders. Simone remained silent for a few seconds, then smiled faintly.

'You can keep it,' he said.

'Thanks . . . Let's go, Piras.' They gestured goodbye and headed down the stairs.

The sun was high in the sky, with small white tufts of cloud that looked like cotton wads. Piras was frowning, as though not understanding something. Once they were in the car, Bordelli stuck a cigarette in his mouth, but let his assistant understand that he wouldn't light it and that this cost him great effort.

'Thanks, Inspector . . . What was that story you mentioned to Fantini?'

'Something he wrote himself. Want to read it?'

'All right,' said Piras, mouth tense. He seemed afraid to discover that Simone was not only good looking but also a good writer. Bordelli opened the glove compartment, took out the story and put it on the Sardinian's lap.

'Don't lose it,' he said, then turned on the ignition and started driving down Via Stibbert. Piras opened the first page of *The Tower* and fixed his eyes on it, but immediately stopped because reading in a moving car made him feel like throwing up.

The sun had warmed the seats of the Beetle. Spring was finally starting to make itself felt.

'What do you think of Simone, Piras?'

'He's certainly good looking,' said the Sardinian, pretending to be perfectly calm and therefore objective. Bordelli smiled.

'I meant what do you think of what he said,' he specified.

The level crossing at Via Vittorio Emanuele was closed, and so the inspector turned on to Via Trieste.

'I think he's telling the truth,' said Piras.

'I agree. Anyway, don't worry, I'm almost positive Sonia and Simone are really just friends. Although . . .'

'Although?' asked Piras, holding his breath.

'Nothing,' said Bordelli, lighting the cigarette, since at that moment Piras wouldn't even notice.

'Well, those things are none of my business,' said the Sardinian, squeezing Simone's manuscript.

'What about the man with the missing little finger? What do you think of him?'

'He's worth tracking down,' said Piras.

'Exactly,' Bordelli murmured.

When they passed in front of Sonia's building, Piras looked up at her windows. Realising this, Bordelli started laughing.

'Are we already so far gone, Piras?'

'I was just looking at the sky, Inspector,' said the Sardinian, taking longer than necessary to put Simone Fantini's story in his jacket pocket. Bordelli downshifted to second and, seeing that nobody was coming, turned on to Via Bolognese.

'What time do shops reopen, Piras?'

'Four o'clock.'

'At any rate the beautiful Sicilian girl made monkeys out of us both, my dear *sardegnolo*.'

'*Sardegnolo* is only used for dunces,' said Piras, fairly miffed.

At ten minutes to four, the Beetle was parked in Via Roma in front of Beltrami's haberdashery, smoke floating out of its open windows. Piras was pacing back and forth on the pavement so he wouldn't have to breathe the foul air inside the car.

At four o'clock sharp a man of somewhat simian appearance and with a large head stopped in front of the Beltrami display window, pulled out some keys, unlocked and raised the rolling shutter with the ease of habit, entered the shop and turned on the lights. Bordelli got out of the car and waited for Piras to join him in front of a display window full of berets and bowlers. They went in together. The shop was very deep and smelled musty. On the walls hung hundreds of hats of every kind.

'Good day, gentlemen, may I help you?' the man asked in a strong Florentine accent. He didn't seem terribly intelligent and smiled the way certain clothes merchants in the centre of town smiled, like high-class servants.

'Inspector Bordelli. Pleasure. He's Piras.'

The man looked at them with some concern, but kept smiling.

'What can I do for you, Inspector?'

'Are you the owner of this business?' Bordelli asked.

'I am Signor Beltrami in person,' the shopkeeper said in a self-important tone that made Piras smile.

'I would like to ask you one question,' said Bordelli.

'By all means.'

'Do you recall ever noticing, among your many clients, a man missing the little finger on one of his hands?'

Beltrami thought about this for a few seconds, then shook his head.

'I don't think so. Is it very important?' he asked, face still smiling.

'Think it over carefully,' said the inspector. Beltrami thought about it again, carefully, as the inspector had asked, with an empty expression in his eyes, as if he were multiplying in his head.

'No, I really don't think I've ever seen a man like that,' he said after his effort.

'Are you certain that all your clients have five fingers on each hand, or could you simply not have noticed?' the inspector asked.

'There's no way I couldn't have noticed, I'm a keen observer . . . Might I ask what this is about . . .?'

'Does your business also sell to other retailers?' Bordelli cut him off.

'Our line is sold only by us,' Beltrami said proudly, raising his big hands in the air.

'And is this shop the only outlet?' asked Piras.

'Of course not, we have other retail shops as well.'

'Where?' asked Bordelli.

'In Milan, Rome, Ven—'

'Here in town?'

'We're the only shop in town, and we've been here in Via Roma since 1915.'

Bordelli shot a disheartened glance at Piras, who was staring at the shopkeeper with a detached air. The Sardinian rarely liked anybody, but this sort of person particularly got on his nerves. The inspector's thoughts had wandered off, and he stared at Beltrami's face without seeing him.

'Do you also sell leather gloves?' Piras asked.

'We don't deal in leather,' the shopkeeper said with a certain disdain.

'All right, then, that'll be all. Sorry to have bothered you,' said Bordelli, rousing himself.

'No bother at all, Inspector, I'm glad to be of help,' said Beltrami, face smiling again.

The inspector said goodbye again and headed for the door, followed by Piras. After they got into the Beetle, Bordelli immediately lit a cigarette.

'Where the hell are we going to look for this man, Piras?'

'Maybe Beltrami isn't quite the *keen observer* he says he is. We could ask him for a list of his regular clients and—'

'And spend the next several days spying on them to see how many fingers they've got.'

'Have you got a better idea, Inspector?' said Piras, waving his open hand slowly in the air to send the smoke back towards Bordelli.

'I want to catch him soon, Piras. Let's get busy,' said the inspector, not giving a damn where his cigarette ash fell. Piras said nothing, apparently distracted. Bordelli on the other hand was quite agitated. He started up the car and put it in gear, but at that moment Piras opened his door and put a foot outside.

'Wait, Inspector.'

'What's wrong, Piras?'

'I'm going back inside for a minute,' said the lad.

Without another word he got out of the car and rushed back into the hat shop. Bordelli sighed with fatigue and turned off the engine. Taking advantage of being alone, he blew his smoke wherever he felt like it, meanwhile trying to think of a way to track down the man with the missing finger. It wasn't going to be easy.

Piras reappeared almost at once, got back in the car and made his usual disgusted face because of the smoke.

'So?' said Bordelli, crushing the butt in the ashtray.

'Beltrami has a female employee, Inspector. Normally women are much more attentive to certain things than men.'

The inspector shook his head.

'I guess I was too tired to think of that,' he said, embarrassed by his own lack of attention.

'The woman is out on an errand, but she should be back in half an hour,' said Piras, checking his watch. The inspector looked at him with satisfaction.

'You drive, please,' he said, getting out of the car.

'Where are we going?'

'Feel like a panino with prosciutto?'

When they got to the San Niccolò quarter, they turned on to Via San Miniato, where until just a few years earlier there had been a public washhouse, where women used to slap their wet linens against the stone basins. Now the people went there only to get water from the fountains, probably the best in Florence.

They drove past Porta San Miniato and stopped at a tavern that everyone called *Fuori Porta*, 'Outside the Gate'. At that hour there were few clients. Bordelli knew the owner, the gigantic Leone, a former smuggler who had managed to get out in time and buy the tavern with the fruits of his labours. He hadn't seen him for a good while, among other reasons because he knew that if he went to his establishment to drink, Leone wouldn't allow him to pay.

After exchanging a few slaps on the back with the inspector,

Leone put three tumblers on the marble counter and filled them to the brim with red wine.

'Have a taste of this, Inspector. It arrived yesterday from Tavernelle.'

'You wouldn't happen to have a glass of water, would you?' said Piras, who didn't want to get all muddled at a moment like that.

'Wine strengthens the blood, water makes you weak in the knees,' said Leone, appalled by the request, putting the glass of red in Piras's hand.

'To all the sons of bitches who wish us ill,' he added in a low voice, barely raising the glass. All three took a swig together.

'Nice and strong,' said Bordelli.

'Thirteen and a half,' said Leone.

'Could you also make us a couple of panini with prosciutto?'

'Sit yourselves down and I'll bring them to you straight away.'

Bordelli pointed to a table and he and Piras went and sat down. Practically every inch of wall space in the tavern was covered with wine-flasks of every shape and form, and the whole place had a pleasant smell of pressed grapes.

'My dad used to come here when he was young,' said Bordelli, looking at the old photos hanging high on the wall over the door. Piras looked around absently, as if his mind was elsewhere. The inspector, too, withdrew into his thoughts, and they both remained silent until the panini with hand-cut prosciutto arrived and roused them from their reveries. Piras opened his up and started removing the fat. The inspector sunk his teeth confidently into his own, looking pained as he watched the Sardinian's operation.

'If I wasn't so tired, I would have thought of it myself,' he said, chewing.

'What was that, Inspector?'

'I said, it would have occurred to me, too . . . to question the saleswoman . . . but I'm too tired . . .'

'It could happen to anyone,' said Piras. He put his panino back together and started eating it. The inspector shrugged.

'Anyway, talking to her may not lead to anything,' he said, to ward off bad luck.

'It's worth trying,' said Piras, taking a big gulp of wine.

'How's your father?' said Bordelli, changing the subject.

'I talked to him on Sunday, he's fine. He's planted the tomatoes and hot peppers.'

'Give him my best.'

Bordelli imagined Gavino Piras walking through his big, sun-drenched garden, cursing for having given one of his arms to the Germans and having only one left for planting and watering . . . Once, in '44, Gavino overcooked the only spaghetti that Bordelli and his comrades had seen for at least six months. He claimed that was how they were prepared where he came from: overcooked and with little salt. Everyone else ate them with gusto. Bordelli was unable to; overcooked pasta was disgusting even on the front lines . . .

Still thinking of that inedible spaghetti, he looked down and noticed a cut on the surface of the table that looked as if it had been made by a knife, and this set his memory going again . . . He remembered how, during the long night-time lulls, when awaiting orders from the rear lines, he and his men used to amuse themselves by playing a game. They would take turns putting a hand on the table, with fingers splayed out fan-like, while another was supposed to jab the tip of a knife in the spaces between the fingers, from the thumb to the little finger and back, with ever increasing speed and force. They were young and foolish, and often the wooden tabletop would become stained with blood. One time the bottom person was Gavino, and Bordelli nearly cut off his right index finger, from the same arm he would leave on the battlefield one year later.

'Oh, shit. Sorry,' Bordelli had said. Gavino hadn't even so much as moaned and, looking at the wound, had only said: 'You're a lot better with a machine gun, commander.'

Some time before that, in a rare moment of calm, they'd

had a shooting contest with machine guns. Everyone had set his weapon to single fire, and the targets were the still-green walnuts hanging from a tree. The magazines had forty bullets in them, and every one of them had to be fired. Commander Bordelli won, hitting thirty-nine walnuts . . .

'Eh?' said the inspector.

'We can go back to Beltrami's now,' Piras said for the second time.

'Let's go.'

They emptied their glasses and stood up. Bordelli went up to the counter to pay.

'It's on Leone,' said the ex-smuggler, wiping his hands on his apron.

'If that's the way it is, then I won't come back.'

'That's why I do it, Inspector,' said the gorilla, laughing.

Bordelli put his wallet back in his pocket and waved goodbye to him. As they walked towards the car, Piras's legs felt heavy and his head light.

'You want to drive, Inspector?' he asked.

'But wine strengthens the blood,' Bordelli said, laughing.

They drove back to Via Roma, got out of the car and, as they approached Beltrami's shop, they saw a dark-haired, barefoot girl in the display window arranging some new hats. She had her back to the street, but even so, she looked quite pretty. Bordelli threw away his cigarette butt, and they entered the shop together for a second time. When Beltrami saw the pair, he smiled exactly the same way he had done an hour earlier, and came up to them looking as if he knew exactly what they wanted.

'Signorina Gisella is back. I haven't told her anything, just as you asked,' he said, looking at Piras with a reassuring expression.

'Thanks,' said Piras.

The shopkeeper went towards the display window, stuck his head inside and whispered something to the girl. Gisella put down her hats, gave the two policemen a long look, then stepped down from her footstool and put her shoes back on.

'Cute . . . but Sonia is prettier,' Bordelli whispered without moving his lips. Piras gave him a nasty look but said nothing.

Gisella came up to the two policemen looking a bit scared, with Beltrami at her side.

'You wanted to talk to me?' she said. She really was very pretty. She had a pouty, tenacious look about her, sparkling eyes and very natural movements, like an animal pup. The inspector shot a glance at Piras to tell him to ask the question himself. Piras was a little awkward – as he was whenever a pretty girl appeared before him – but he recovered quickly and coughed into his hand a couple of times before speaking.

'Signorina Gisella, can you recall whether any of your clients is a gentleman who is missing a finger?' he asked in the steadiest voice he could muster up. He even raised a hand in the air and touched his little finger. The salesgirl didn't have to think twice.

'Of course, he's one of our regular clients,' she said.

Bordelli felt a shiver down his spine, like a panther that has scented its prey. He really hadn't been counting on this. He'd been careful not to get his hopes up, so as not to be too disappointed.

'Who is he?' he asked, butting in on Piras.

'Dr Rivalta is his name . . . Davide Rivalta.'

Beltrami gave a look of surprise.

'Oh really? I hadn't ever noticed,' he said, a little embarrassed.

Keen observer my arse, thought Piras, without taking his eyes off the girl.

'Do you know where he lives?' the inspector asked her.

'In the Porta Romana area, I think.'

'Are you absolutely certain he's missing a finger?'

'The little finger on his left hand,' Gisella said with great self-assurance.

'Thank you,' said Bordelli. Giving a quick goodbye, he grabbed Piras by the arm and dragged him outside. As soon as they were in the Beetle, he slapped him on the thigh.

'You see, Piras? I'm right to bring you along with me!'

The Sardinian looked at him as if he felt offended.

'What did Sonia have to do with any of this?' he said very seriously.

'That's just the way we are around here. When somebody falls in love we like to rib him a little . . . Don't you do that in Sardinia?'

Piras made a stern face and merely stared at the road.

'I'm not in love,' he said.

An hour later, after finding Davide Rivalta's address in the phone book, Bordelli and Piras turned on to Via delle Campora, a narrow street that began at Via Senese and ran all the way to the Charterhouse of Galluzzo. They went about fifty yards and pulled up in front of number 24 bis. Rivalta lived in a two-storey nineteenth-century villa surrounded by a garden. On the somewhat neglected lawn were some large earthenware pots full of flowerless geraniums. The house stood about twenty yards from the road. Next to the wrought-iron gate was a porcelain plaque that said VILLA SERENA. The shutters were all closed. They nevertheless tried ringing the doorbell, but nobody answered. They rang a few more times, then gave up.

'Damn!' said Bordelli.

'I agree,' said Piras.

They got back into the Beetle and returned to the police station. Bordelli was very tired, and the fluorescent lights in the corridors hurt his eyes.

'When are we going back to Rivalta's house, Inspector?' Piras asked, biting his lips.

'Stick around. I'll come and get you when it's time.'

Bordelli went into his office and took advantage of the opportunity to phone the literature department. He asked for Professor Vannetti, who wasn't in, and he was given the professor's home phone number. He called him at once.

'Professor Vannetti?'

'Who's this?'

'Inspector Bordelli. Sorry to bother you, but I need your help on a matter concerning Nazism.'

'What can I do for you?'

'I'd rather not say it over the phone. When could we meet?'

'Could you come here, to my place, tomorrow morning around ten?'

'Perfect. Where do you live?'

'Via San Zenobi, number 230.'

'Thank you so much, Professor.'

'See you tomorrow.'

Impatient to find out whether Rivalta had returned, Bordelli tried phoning him at home. There was no reply, and he hung up. He stuck his hand in his jacket pocket to look for cigarettes and found Casimiro's little skeleton instead. It was rather dirty and was missing a hand. He propped it against his pen-holder, thinking that this time the dwarf's good-luck charm hadn't worked. He saw the little corpse again in the suitcase and continued to feel guilty. Even if it meant upsetting the plans of the White Dove, he wanted to find out who had killed him. But he had to proceed carefully. If there really were ex-Nazis mixed up in this, then he had to handle the matter with kid gloves.

He opened the window to get rid of the smoke. The sky was clear. He picked up the telephone and sent Mugnai to get a few Peronis from the bar across the street. He opened the first with his house keys and drank straight from the bottle, rocking the spring mechanism in the back of his chair. A sluggish fly walked slowly on the ceiling. A typewriter clattered in the room next door. Time stood still. The inspector snuffed out his cigarette butt and picked up Casimiro's little skeleton again. It was funny. Its mouth was open, and the tiny red glass of its eyes sparkled in the light.

Round about seven o'clock he tried phoning Rivalta again, and after the third ring, somebody picked up.

'Yes, hello?' It was a man, with a nasal, cultured voice.

'Giacomo?' said Bordelli, masking his voice.

'Wrong number,' said the man, hanging up.

Bordelli put on his jacket and went to look for Piras. He found him in the radio room, reading Fantini's short story.

'I rang Rivalta again. There's somebody there now,' he said, sticking a cigarette between his lips. Piras grabbed his jacket on the run and they left. They got into the car and went up the Viali all the way to Porta Romana without saying a word. Then they took the Via Senese for a short distance and finally parked in Via delle Campora, in front of Rivalta's villa. Piras was glad to get out of the smoke-filled car, muttering between his teeth about that stupid vice.

'The windows were down, Piras.'

'You can smell it just the same,' said the Sardinian.

The lights on the first floor of the villa were on. A black Lancia Flavia, sparkling clean, was parked in the garden. They rang the bell. A few moments later a window opened and a man appeared. Seeing the two men outside the gate, he closed the window. Seconds later the lights in the garden came on. The villa's front door opened and a man came out. He was tall and thin, with very short black hair. The appearance fitted the description given them by Simone. The man walked towards the gate and stopped about a metre away. He had a long face and a big, hooked nose.

'Yes?' he said.

'Are you Dr Rivalta?' asked Bordelli.

'Yes. Who are you?'

The inspector recognised the nasal voice that had answered the telephone.

'I'm Inspector Bordelli, he's Piras. Could we come in for a moment?' he asked, flashing his badge. Rivalta didn't budge. He had his hands in his pockets, and it was impossible to see whether he was missing a finger.

'Do you mind telling me what this is about?' he said.

'We just want to ask you a few questions. Would you please open the gate?'

Rivalta didn't answer. He had two very dark, deep eyes that shone with intelligence. At last he took a step forward and opened the gate.

'I hope this won't take up too much of my time,' he said.

'Just a few minutes,' said the inspector.

Rivalta turned and headed towards the villa, with the two intruders following behind. Both Bordelli and Piras instinctively looked at his left hand, saw only four fingers, and exchanged a glance. After they had entered the house, Rivalta led them into a large room full of bookcases and carpets, a large fireplace in *pietra serena* and a fine eighteenth-century pendulum clock. Four identical sofas formed a square around a small round crystal table cluttered with useless but expensive objects.

'Please make yourselves comfortable,' Rivalta said calmly, sitting down. The inspector and Piras settled into the sofa across from him. A few seconds of silence passed. Bordelli and Rivalta looked each other in the eye like two animals trying to establish which is the stronger.

'Dr Rivalta, do you often go for walks in the Parco delle Casine?' Bordelli asked, still staring at him.

'Why, has it become a crime?' replied Rivalta with a smile.

Piras sighed with irritation. The man's manner was already getting on his nerves.

'It depends on what one goes there for,' said Bordelli.

'I go there to walk, not to kill little girls.'

'I see you're already abreast of the situation.'

'I read the newspapers,' said Rivalta, looking away for a second.

'At what time did you get to the park yesterday morning?'

'I have the vague impression you consider me a suspect, Inspector . . . Or am I mistaken?'

'Would you like to call a lawyer?'

'I don't need one, but if I'm suspected of something I'd like it to be clear.'

Bordelli nodded.

'Yesterday, you were at the scene of the crime shortly after the girl was killed, and I'm a policeman.'

'I'll forgive you for that, but nothing else,' said Rivalta, crossing his legs with an untroubled air.

'Thanks for being so understanding. Now answer my question.'

'I got there about nine o'clock and strolled for about an hour. But I didn't see or hear anything that might be relevant to your case,' Rivalta said wearily.

'What were you doing before that?'

Rivalta joined his hands behind his head and sighed as though bored.

'I woke up, took a shower, got dressed, went out in the car, bought the newspaper at the kiosk at Porta Romana, got back in my car and went and had breakfast like every other day. And then I went to the Parco delle Cascine . . . Would you like to know anything else?' he asked in the tone of an obedient child.

'What time did you leave the park?' Bordelli asked calmly, ignoring the provocation.

'As I said, about ten o'clock.'

'And what did you do after your walk?'

'I bought bread, some fruit, a steak, and then I went home. Thrilling, isn't it?'

Piras stared hard at the man, trying to figure out what he might be hiding behind his ironic, jaded expression.

'What do you do for a living, Dr Rivalta?' Bordelli continued.

'I live on a private income and study the Middle Ages.'

'Do you live alone?'

'"*If you are alone, you shall be all your own; if you are in company, you shall be half your own*," a certain Leonardo once said.'

Bordelli looked around; the place was sparkling clean.

'Who keeps house for you?' he asked.

'I do everything myself. I'm used to getting by alone.'

'Have you ever been married?'

'My wife is dead,' Rivalta said curtly, looking out the window.

'Do you have any children?' Bordelli asked. A wicked flash seemed to light up Rivalta's eyes.

'No,' he said, glaring at the inspector.

For a few seconds, no one spoke. In the silence, the rhythmical sound of the pendulum was clearly audible.

'How did you spend the afternoon of the ninth?' Bordelli resumed.

'How much longer is this charade going to last?' Rivalta asked, sighing calmly. He leaned forward and took a cigarette from a silver box lying on the crystal table without offering one to the others. Piras stared at him with hostility, clenching his jaw.

'You can answer my questions now, or, if you prefer, we could take a little trip down to the police station. What will it be?' said Bordelli.

Rivalta calmly lit his cigarette with a gigantic chrome lighter, then blew the smoke up towards the ceiling.

'Are you always so touchy, Inspector?' he asked with a friendly smile.

'Only when I'm hungry,' said Bordelli.

'The boy must be hungry, too,' said Rivalta, casting an amused glance at Piras.

The Sardinian kept on glaring at him with his nuragic face,[15] immobile as a rock.

'Answer the question: where were you on the afternoon of the ninth?' asked Bordelli, fed up with his antics.

'I was here at home. I spent the whole day rereading the poems of Hrotsvitha. They are magnificent,' Rivalta said, smiling.

'Is there anyone who can attest to that?'

'The woodworms in the rafters. Ask them,' said Rivalta, looking up towards the ceiling. Every so often his eyes contracted with disdain.

'I see you like to ingratiate yourself with others,' said Bordelli.

'Life is a rather nasty affair, and for consolation I try to amuse myself as best I can,' said Rivalta, snuffing out his half-smoked cigarette in a large red-glass ashtray.

'Have you ever been to the park of Villa Ventaglio?'

'I don't even know where it is.'

'Then I'll tell you: in Via Aldini.'

'I don't know that street.'

There was a creaking of mechanical gears, and at once the

pendulum clock began ringing the hour. All three of them remained silent, counting the chimes resounding in the room as in a church. It was eight o'clock.

'How did you lose your finger?' Bordelli asked as the last chime continued to resonate in the air.

'During the war. A piece of shrapnel,' said Rivalta, wiggling his four remaining fingers in the air.

'Why do you wear gloves in springtime?' asked Piras.

'Is that a serious question, Inspector?' said Rivalta, ignoring the young Sardinian.

'Fairly,' said Bordelli.

'Pretty soon you'll be asking me how many times I went to the loo last Sunday . . .'

'Possibly. In the meantime tell us why you wear gloves in springtime.'

'Bad circulation. I often have cold hands,' said Rivalta, half-closing his eyes as if bored.

Bordelli pulled out a cigarette and lit it. Piras couldn't stand all the smoke any longer.

'That'll be all for now, Dr Rivalta. But I would ask you not to leave the city until I say,' said the inspector.

'I hadn't planned to go anywhere.'

'I'm glad.' Bordelli gestured to Piras and they all stood up.

Rivalta accompanied them to the gate, walking in front of them without saying a word. As he opened it, he smiled coldly.

'Pleased to have met you,' he said in a clearly ironic tone.

'I'd wait before saying that,' said Bordelli, returning his smile.

'"*Never call a man happy until you've seen him dead . . .*" Who said that?' asked Rivalta, searching his memory.

'Seneca,' said Piras, looking him straight in the eye.

'Ah, well, I'm very impressed. It's not often one meets a cultured policeman,' said Rivalta, bowing slightly towards Piras.

'We'll be seeing you soon, Dr Rivalta,' said Bordelli, leaving the garden without turning round. Piras followed him in silence.

'It'll be a pleasure, Inspector. Perhaps we'll have a chance to talk about the Abbot Suger . . . or Mary of Aquitaine,' Rivalta said loudly from behind the bars. He then closed the gate and walked back towards the house, whistling the theme of Schubert's *Unfinished Symphony*.

Once they were in the car, Piras gave vent to his feelings.

'That prick really gets on my nerves,' he said, staring through the window as if he wanted to shatter it with his gaze.

'Don't get upset, Piras.'

Bordelli started up the car and they rolled at a snail's pace up to the corner of Via Metastasio. He looked around, then did a U-turn and went back. Driving slowly past Rivalta's gate, he took another good look at it. The garden lights were already out, and only one window on the first floor was illuminated.

'I want two fully equipped vans to keep watch over this villa, Piras: one here in front, which can also keep an eye on Via Prati, and another in Via Metastasio, as well as three unmarked cars in the general neighbourhood, in radio communication with the vans. We mustn't let Rivalta out of our sight for even a second, and when he goes out on foot he must be followed by continually different people. I want in-depth reports, down to the tiniest detail. And I want you to get down to work as soon as we get back to headquarters.'

'Okay,' said Piras, still pissed off, staring darkly at the street.

'Organise long shifts. I want very little movement. Rivalta must remain completely unaware,' said Bordelli, turning on to Via Senese.

'What about the telephone, Inspector?'

'Let's have it tapped . . . though I don't think it'll be of any help.'

'You look tired, monkey.'

'It's been a long day, Rosa.'

The fifty-year-old girl had finished giving him a back massage and filling him with tartines. It was almost midnight. Bordelli lay on the couch with his shoes off, a glass of cognac resting on his chest. From time to time he raised his head and took a sip. As usual, he asked about Gideon.

'He's out on the rooftops, the little Don Juan,' said Rosa, batting her eyelashes.

They started making small talk, about past loves, old friends they'd lost track of, the war. Bordelli told how, in September 1943, he'd seen the battleship *Roma* sink to the bottom of the sea. Two very modern, radio-controlled German bombs struck the ship a few minutes apart. Less than half an hour later, the dreadnought broke in two like a nutshell and sank with over a thousand men aboard. Had he not seen it with his own eyes, he would not have believed it. It really seemed like the end . . . but then, little by little, the Germans were thrown out of Italy.

Rosa, still working on her sweater for Bordelli, started talking about the time she used to ply her trade in little flophouses round the region. Sometimes funny things would happen, she said. Like the time a rich, fat Milanese gave her ten thousand lire just for massaging his ears.

'You have no idea how disgusting it was – his ears were full of hair,' she said, grimacing. Then there was that really skinny bloke with rabbit-teeth and sad eyes, who every Sunday at midnight would arrive at the house on his bicycle, just to bring her a bouquet of red roses. He wouldn't say a word, just handed her the flowers and ran away. Looking out the window, she would see him pedalling hard.

'You men are very strange sometimes,' said Rosa, sniggering.

'You women are too, I assure you.'

They kept on drinking and talking for a while, as Rosa knitted away. Round about one o'clock Bordelli started yawning. Finishing his cognac in a single gulp, he sat up and put on his shoes.

'I think I'll go home to bed,' he said.

'Ouf!' huffed Rosa.

She accompanied him to the door, and they stopped outside, on the landing. As usual, Bordelli kissed her hand. She seized him by the neck and starting kissing his face repeatedly.

'Sweet dreams, monkey,' she said.

''Bye, Rosa, thanks for everything.'

'My big sad bear . . . Come on, don't make that face.'

At that moment the other door on the landing opened slightly, and in the crack they could see an eye. Rosa huffed.

'Do you need something, Signorina Camilla?' she asked with an irritated smile. The door closed at once. Rosa detached herself crossly from Bordelli and went and knocked on Signorina Camilla's door, but it remained closed.

'Signorina Anichina, if you want to know what I'm up to, why don't you ask me? That way I could tell you to mind your own business!' said Rosa, knocking even harder. 'I know you're right there behind the door,' she continued, her anger growing.

At last the door opened, and Signorina Camilla Anichini appeared. She was about sixty, fat, and her forehead was covered with strange boils. She had the face of a power-hungry mother superior.

'I heard a little noise,' she said, looking offended. She was wearing a bonnet on her head and a light blue dressing gown covered with embroidery.

'Don't you ever sleep, Signorina Camilla?' said Rosa.

'I thought there might be burglars . . .'

'Well, what a relief to know you're standing guard for us!'

The old woman took offence, eyes narrowing with rage.

'Then make less noise when seeing your lovers off,' she said in disgust, casting a nasty glance at Bordelli.

'Oh, well, I'm sure you make less noise than I do, since you haven't got any men to see off . . .'

'Goodnight, Signorina Rosa!' the mother superior said between clenched teeth, slamming the door.

Rosa turned back towards Bordelli, shuddering.

'The old shrew!' she said. 'She spends her life with her ears glued to the walls . . . Why don't you have her arrested?'

'Forget about it . . . She's only a little curious.'

'One of these days I'm going to give her such a slap!' Rosa said in a loud voice, miming the gesture. Bordelli kissed her hands again to calm her down, then descended the stairs, followed, as usual, by a barrage of kisses.

The stars were out and it wasn't too cold. He realised he was agitated, and the thought of going home and getting into bed didn't appeal to him at all. For a moment he was tempted to go back up to Rosa's but decided against it, not wishing to trouble anyone with his bad mood. He got into his Beetle and drove off. Crossing the Arno, he passed by the church of Santo Spirito and, almost without realising it, found himself at Porta Romana. Like a robot he turned on to Via Senese and, after going a few hundred yards, turned right on to Via delle Campora. He drove slowly, head full of useless thoughts. He stuck an unlit cigarette in his mouth and turned round to look at VILLA SERENA. A number of windows on the first floor were lit up, and the inspector imagined Rivalta sitting in an armchair reading, or else cleaning the floors with a rag . . .

He sighed. There was no point in driving down this road. He knew it. It was only a way to relieve the anxiety he felt while waiting for something to happen. The phoney telephone-company van with the policemen inside was in place. Rivalta was under surveillance day and night.

When he got to the bottom of the street, he turned round. It was a very calm and quiet neighbourhood even during the day, and at night there wasn't a soul about. He drove past the villa again at a snail's pace and turned round once more to look at the lighted windows. Then he shook his head and accelerated. At the intersection with Via Senese he stopped and lit his cigarette. Turning left, he found himself at Porta Romana again, but instead of continuing straight down Via Romana on his way home, he turned right and took Viale di Poggio Imperiale. He simply didn't feel like going to bed, since he knew he would only toss and turn between the sheets, unable to fall asleep. He needed some distraction, to rest his mind a little. When he reached the top of the hill, he turned right for no particular reason. Driving with no destination in mind relaxed him, especially on the roads outside the city. He started going up towards Pozzolatico, trying not to think of anything, but his head was still percolating.

A few minutes later he was at Mezzomonte, where, he recalled, Dante Pedretti lived. Dante was a rather strange old man, a good six foot six inches tall, who spent his time fidgeting with inventions of his own that almost always proved useless. Bordelli had met him a year before, during his investigation into the murder of Pedretti's sister. He had liked the old inventor and invited him to his place for one of Botta's dinners. He hadn't heard from him for several months.

He stopped the car in a clearing and got out. It was past two o'clock, but he knew that Dante stayed up late. There was a bit of moonlight, and one could see fairly well. Heading down a grassy path, he passed through the gate, which was always open, crossed the untended garden, and went up to the large, turreted country house. The door, as usual, was not locked. He entered the house and went down the dark corridor, already smelling cigar smoke in the air. He descended the staircase leading down to Dante's laboratory, an enormous room that spanned the entire foundation of the house, with a flooring of wooden planks and a huge table cluttered with everything imaginable. He pushed the door open and looked inside. Dante was at the far end of the room, a giant in his smock, his head surrounded by a mass of white, unkempt hair. He was pacing in front of his workbench with his hands in his pockets, staring into the void with the inevitable cigar in his mouth, enveloped in a cloud of yellow smoke. His shadow moved over the surface of the walls, multiplied by the light of many candles, and he was mumbling to himself.

'May I?' asked Bordelli, opening the door wide.

'Greetings, Inspector,' said Dante in his booming voice, without turning round.

Bordelli came forward into the laboratory, walking past piles of old newspapers, broken chairs, bicycle wheels, big cardboard boxes with strange things sticking out. That chaos steeped in the past appealed to him, made him feel at home.

When he was at last in front of Dante, they shook hands.

'You recognised me at once,' said Bordelli, not too surprised.

'You have a beautiful voice, Inspector.'

'I hope I'm not disturbing you.'

'Not at all. I was just thinking aloud a little. Sometimes it's more effective than actually thinking . . . There are certain things that come out only when we speak, as if speech itself were a kind of corkscrew.'

'But the wine that comes out isn't always good,' said the inspector, smiling bitterly.

'Would you like a drop, Bordelli?'

'Of grappa?'

'Of grappa.'

'All right.'

'Now, where did I put it?' Dante started scanning the apocalyptic disarray of his workbench with his eyes. He began picking up one bottle after another, all of them without labels. He would look at them against the light and then set them back down.

'This must be it,' he said to himself. He opened a bottle, sniffed it, then shook his head, frowning. He put it back in the pile and picked up a big two-litre bottle. He uncorked it, brought it to his nose, and smiled.

'Found it,' he said.

Then he looked around again impatiently, puffing hard on his spent cigar. Now he had to find glasses. Bordelli meanwhile had gone and sat down on a dusty old sofa and lit a cigarette. Dante relit his cigar on a candle, and his face disappeared behind a dense cloud of smoke.

'Damn, I can't find the glasses . . . Would one of these do, Inspector?' he asked, fanning away the smoke with his hand and holding up a chemist's vial.

'That depends,' said Bordelli, looking worried.

'Don't worry, I wash them very carefully,' said Dante, and he filled two vials to the brim and passed one to his guest. Bordelli thanked him with a nod, then held the strange container up to the light. There were lines and numbers inscribed in the the glass: 10, 20, 30, and up to 50. Before drinking, he cautiously smelled the transparent liquid, which, until proved otherwise, could have been just about anything. He smiled. He would never have imagined that before he died he would drink grappa from a graduated vial. If he wanted, he could even keep track of how much alcohol he ingested.

Dante, as usual, remained standing. One rarely saw him seated. He needed to be always in motion. He took a big puff of his cigar, downed a sip of grappa, then opened his mouth to let the smoke out.

'You look tired, Bordelli,' he said.

'It must be the spring.'

'Ah, the spring,' said Dante, looking him in the eye. Then he shrugged and took another sip.

'How are the inventions coming along?' the inspector asked to change the subject. Dante smiled, shook the ash off his cigar, and emptied his vial in one gulp.

'I've finally understood something, Inspector. All my fussing about with these bloody gadgets has only one purpose, to allow my brain to look past certain thoughts that I would never get beyond if I wasn't concentrating on them. That's the sole purpose. And they're not even so special, these thoughts – actually, they're rather banal and desultory. Sometimes they're not really even thoughts. It's all just a path I must travel, otherwise I'd never get anywhere, and it gives me a sense of well-being. Nothing more.'

'Interesting,' said Bordelli.

'Perhaps, but only to me. More grappa?'

'Yes, please.'

Dante refilled the vials and stood in front of Bordelli.

'To return to the spring . . . I, too, read the newspapers, Inspector,' he said in a tone that made it clear what he was referring to. Bordelli half-closed his eyes in resignation, and downed his grappa in a single draught. It was nice and strong.

'I'd rather not talk about it,' he mumbled. 'Also because I wouldn't know what to say.' He lit another cigarette. At least Piras wasn't there to inhale all the smoke.

Dante kept looking at him with a mournful expression. He pulled hard on his cigar and kept spitting out large wads of tobacco. The inspector raised his receptacle in the air to request more fuel.

'This whole business of the little girls is driving me crazy,' he added, as Dante topped him up. He drank a long draught of grappa with gusto, following the burning sensation down his oesophagus. The inventor went over to his work table, stuck the remains of his cigar into a bottle already full of butts and immediately lit another with the flame of a candle.

'If a wretch kills little girls, I imagine there must be, at the source of his crime, an even greater wrong,' he said, emitting smoke from all his pores. Then he sat down slantwise on the bench, poking a finger through one of his smoke rings.

'I only want to stop him,' said Bordelli.

They remained silent for a few moments, smoking. The vials were already empty again. Dante refilled them once more to the brim and started walking about the great room. As the alcohol level in their blood increased, Bordelli sank ever deeper into the sofa, squashed by his thoughts. When he was in this kind of mood, alcohol did nothing to lift his spirits. On the contrary, it only made him feel heavier. He closed his eyes, trying not to think of anything, but his head kept spinning pointlessly round useless conjectures. Hearing Dante's steps come to a halt, he reopened his eyes. The giant was standing before him. His face had changed, and his eyes looked like red-hot glass. He brought the fingers of one hand together, wiggling and rubbing them against each other, as one does to remove dirt.

'We are insignificant beings, my dear Bordelli, fleas of the universe, and yet every one of us feels as if he makes the world go round. And perhaps we're right. Perhaps we're fleas that make the world go round . . . Have you ever read Pascal?'

'A very long time ago.'

Dante came even closer, till he was looming over the policeman, and then he raised his big hands in the air in a slow, solemn gesture, like some high priest from thousands of years ago.

'We are germs with the power to conceive of themselves and to imagine the existence of God,' he said, smiling with compassion. Then he burst into laughter and lowered his hands.

'Would you like to play a little game, Inspector?'

'All right,' said Bordelli, taking another sip that very nearly went down the wrong way.

'Now listen carefully. Close your eyes and try hard to imagine what I'm about to tell you. Ready?'

'Ready,' said Bordelli, curious. He was very tired and glad to close his eyes. The inventor circled round behind the sofa and after a few moments of silence started speaking softly, slowly, in the tone of someone telling a fairy tale to a child.

'Imagine you see the Earth from afar, and all the other little planets, circling round the sun, the same way you might look at a basket of oranges . . . Do you see them?'

'I see them,' said Bordelli.

'Good . . . Now try to step back, calmly, until our vast solar system becomes as small as a swarm of gnats . . . But don't stop there . . . Go even farther . . .'

Dante continued guiding Bordelli slowly through the galaxies, pushing him ever farther, sending him swimming through infinite space where time has no meaning . . . And he kept on babbling in this fashion for a good while. Bordelli obeyed without difficulty, with the grappa's help. He navigated with pleasure through the limitless void, floating amidst the planets, nearly forgetting he had a body and a memory. Passing through hundreds of star systems, he went very far, farther than he had ever gone before in his imagination, and still he kept forging on, farther and farther . . . At a certain point, Dante's booming voice made him reverse course and very slowly guided him back towards Earth. Bordelli passed through the Milky Way, past Jupiter, Saturn, Venus . . . then he descended, and before long he began to see the continents, as on a globe . . . then he saw the rivers and mountains, the Italian peninsula, the cities, the streets . . . until, after a long detour, he glided over a turreted farmhouse, isolated in the countryside . . .

'. . . Go inside and have a look, Inspector, you'll see two human beings talking and drinking grappa . . . two scraps of matter who in the face of infinity have about the same significance as the piss of a bacterium . . . two germs unable to see their own nothingness, but moved to passion by their greatness . . . That is why man is great . . . because, in spite of everything, he can stubbornly carry on living, believing in something, even the most inane things . . . Have you ever read Pascal, Inspector? Did I already ask you that?'

Bordelli didn't answer. After that voyage through the darkness, he opened his eyes slowly, bothered even by the light of the candles, and he seemed to feel more deeply the nothingness of the entire human race, made up of single particles even more useless, able only to eat, shit, make war and produce tons of DDT . . .

It took him a while to recover from his swim through the galaxies, struggling against the disturbing sense of being a germ abandoned in the universe, as alone as the last star at the far end of space.

Dante was still behind the sofa, and Bordelli could hear him puffing fiercely on his cigar. They remained silent a while longer, as if to allow the whole experience to dissolve by itself.

Bordelli slowly eased back into his customary existence, his banal life as a police inspector in a small Italian city. His mind reconstructed his customary small reality, which consisted of what his eyes could see, of convictions suited to everyday life, of his memory above all, so vague and yet so concrete, and vaster, perhaps, than the galaxies themselves.

Dante circled round the sofa and reappeared before him, an amused smile on his lips.

'Sometimes I go through the whole silly routine by myself, to help me fall asleep,' he said.

'And do you fall asleep?'

'Not always . . . Another grappa, Inspector?'

'The last forty centilitres, thanks,' Bordelli lied.

He left Dante's house at about 5 a.m., completely fuddled from a great many centilitres of grappa. But at least he felt a little less agitated than before. He drove back down the Imprunetana at twenty miles an hour with his head spinning. He felt as if he could still see galaxies and planets, as if the Beetle were a starship that had got lost in space.

Once at home he quickly undressed and got into bed, leaving the window ajar. In spite of everything, sleep didn't come easily. In the end he sat up and turned the light back on. He picked up a book, read one line, then set it down, open, on his legs. He lit a cigarette. The very last. Blowing the smoke up towards the ceiling, he started thinking about Milena – her mouth, her dark eyes full of life . . . She reminded him of a girl he once knew, Elena. He'd met her one evening in 1940, at a dinner at the house of friends, shortly before he embarked on a submarine. They spent a week together, staring into each other's eyes and making love, then parted with heavy hearts and without too many promises. All of Europe was a shambles, and hope seemed to cause more pain than anything else. When he returned from the war, Bordelli went looking for her, but Elena's house had been destroyed and nobody knew what had happened to her family.

He finished his cigarette, set the alarm for nine, and turned off the light. He lay down and turned on to his side, pulling the sheet up over his head. The grappa was still doing its part. Swimming in the darkness between stars, he slowly fell asleep.

At last, a day of sunshine. Crazed swallows darted in every direction against a clear blue sky, nosediving towards the rooftops and then veering away a split second before crashing. Bordelli went out at about half past nine. Except for a mild headache, he felt pretty good. He was about to get in his car when he changed his mind and headed towards the centre of town on foot, an unlit cigarette dangling from his lips. He realised with disgust that he'd smoked his last one only four hours before.

Crossing the Arno, he contemplated the bridges rebuilt after the war and suppressed the urge to light the cigarette. When he was in the Marches with his battalion, the Nazis had blown up all the bridges in Florence with mines, to slow down the Allied advance. To save the Ponte Vecchio the Germans had torn down the ancient palazzi of Por Santa Maria and Via Guicciardini, and the new buildings put up after the war had nothing whatsoever in common with those around them.

At the San Lorenzo market there was the usual confusion. The pedlars shouted loudly to get the attention of the women shopping. The youngest women wore low necklines because of the warm sunny day, and as he turned to look at them Bordelli wondered whether the gleams of joy he saw in their eyes were only the fruit of his fantasy, or if it was true that when the sun came out, women blossomed along with the flowers, as Diotivede always maintained.

He turned on to Via Rosina, matches in hand, but he managed to get to Via San Zenobi without lighting his cigarette. Ringing the buzzer for Professor Vannetti's flat, he pushed open the front door and went up the stairs. The professor was waiting for him in the doorway. He was short and rather plump, with the face of one who ate well and drank well. They shook hands and sat down in the professor's study, a smallish room with books lining the walls. In front of the window was a worm-eaten desk with a typewriter on top with a sheet of paper in it.

'What can I do for you, Inspector?'

'I'm looking for a Nazi.'

'You're not alone.' Vannetti laughed.

'It's a good thing . . .'

'Can you tell me anything else about this person?'

'He has a long black mark on his neck, from here to here,' said Bordelli.

Vannetti brought his hand to his chin and pressed his lips tightly together.

'That rings a bell, but I couldn't tell you right off who it is. You can look through my archive, if you like.'

'I ask nothing more.'

'It's rather incomplete, as you can imagine,' said Vannetti, throwing up his hands.

'It's just an attempt.' The inspector sighed.

'Come.'

Bordelli followed him into another room with large shelves full of file folders. The window gave on to an inner courtyard bathed in sunlight. Vannetti pulled out a folder bulging with papers and set it down on a Formica table.

'You can start with this one,' he said.

'I don't know how to thank you, Professor.'

'Not at all. I'll be in the next room. Don't hesitate to call me if you need anything.'

'May I smoke?'

'Of course.'

Vannetti withdrew into his study, and the inspector went straight to work. While the archive might well be incomplete, it was very well organised, with photographs accompanied by notes listing the crimes committed. Bordelli turned the pages slowly, feeling hurtled back in time at the sight of those faces. He saw his comrades again, heard their voices again. He'd seen many of them die, too many, blown up by those bloody German mines.

As he kept turning the pages he remembered Gerhardt Gütten, a former, not terribly important Nazi officer he'd met by chance at a hotel bar in Munich a few years after the war. A Nazi officer and a San Marco commander. It was hate at first sight. When it came out that Gütten had been at Cassino during the period when Bordelli was there, their mutual hatred increased. As they continued chatting, they looked each other icily in the eye. Each wanted to challenge the other, it was clear, and they were trying to find a way to do so. Each wanted to show the other that he, in the end, had come out on top.

They started drinking rum and Cokes, and slowly those glasses became an undeclared challenge.

'Will you have another drink?' Gütten would ask, a sneer on his lips.

'Another rum and Coke, thanks,' Bordelli would reply.

They drank, looking each other in the eye, and they kept on drinking. They were two dogs on chains not long enough to allow either of them to reach and maul the other. All they could do was drink and stare at each other, as if each sip were a gunshot. There was much more in those glasses than liquid: there was the contempt that had never left them . . . And there was a lot more rum than Coca-Cola.

'Will you have another drink?'

'Another rum and Coke, thanks.'

By midnight they were both very drunk, but the alcohol hadn't lessened their mutual scorn. The Italian 'traitor' and the Nazi tyrant carried on their war by means of drinks. The other people at the bar started watching them with interest. A struggle was under way, and everyone was waiting to see which of the two would collapse first. Before going to bed, Bordelli suggested they have another drink.

'What would you like?' Gütten asked.

'Rum and Coke, thanks,' Bordelli said, his vision blurred. Gütten signalled to the waiter to bring more drinks, inadvertently burping. The glasses arrived, and Bordelli proposed they down them Russian-style. They emptied their glasses in a single breath and both started to reel. Bordelli held his booze well, but that evening he had, in fact, gone too far. Gütten stood up to retire to his room, started to fall, but was held up by a friend.

'See you in the morning,' he said, staring at Bordelli with beady eyes drowning in his sweaty face.

'Goodnight,' said Bordelli. He stood up, trying not to stagger, and headed towards his room. The second he touched the bed, he fell asleep. And slept well. He woke up the next morning with a slight headache and could still taste the rum at the back of his throat. He took a hot shower, got dressed, and went down to the hotel dining room. Gütten arrived half an hour later. He looked a bit the worse for wear.

'Sleep well?' Bordelli asked.

'Superbly. I feel like a lion. And yourself?' said Gütten, red eyed.

'All systems go, thanks.'

'What'll you have for breakfast, Commander?' the Nazi asked mockingly.

Bordelli looked him straight in the eye and had trouble restraining a laugh.

'A rum and Coke, thanks,' he said.

'Oh no you don't! I can't!' said Gütten, raising his arms in disgust.

'You lose . . . same as at Cassino,' said Bordelli.

The Nazi dilated his nostrils and gave a forced laugh. He'd lost the battle, but he wanted to savour his defeat to the very end. He ordered the rum and Coke for Bordelli and personally handed it to him. Bordelli thanked him, downed the entire glass, and handed it back to Gütten with a smile. It was hard to swallow the stuff at ten in the morning, but the San Marco had won yet again. That was all that mattered.

The inspector finished thumbing through the first file and moved on to the second, then the third, then the fourth, and so on . . . Round about half past twelve he pulled down the umpteenth folder swollen with Nazis and patiently laid it on the table. He started turning the pages, increasingly nauseated by all the faces passing before his eyes. There was every kind of face, but all had the same avid, feckless gaze. By this point he was getting discouraged, but suddenly he came across a man with a broad face, blue eyes and a long black mark on his neck. He clenched his teeth hard. He'd found him at last: '*Karl Strüffen, Hamburg 1901, Nazi criminal, grey eminence of the Third Reich, condemned to death in absentia at the Nuremberg trials, located in Brazil in '49, in Argentina in '50, and in Switzerland in '53, after which he vanished without a trace.*'

Now he remembered. He'd seen him in Levi's archive, in '47. Casimiro had really been unlucky. He'd played cop with the wrong person.

He remembered the White Dove's dossier on Strüffen, which was detailed to the point of obsession. Their dossiers always ended with the same three words: *To be eliminated.*

The trattoria Da Cesare was always very crowded. One ate well there and spent no more than was necessary. The walls were covered with naif paintings, mostly rural landscapes, painted by the hundreds of artists who had swarmed in the wake of the Macchiaioli[16] like chickens in the furrows of the plough, endlessly copying and recopying, paying for their meals with pictures in order to survive.

Bordelli greeted the owner and slipped into the kitchen, where at that moment Totò, the cook, was busy with a basin full of spaghetti and mussels.

'Hello, Inspector.'

'Hello, Totò, will there be any of that left for me?'

'Of course.'

Totò finished filling the bowls, passed these on to the waiter, and handed Bordelli a generous serving of spaghetti.

'Wait till you taste this, Inspector. It's Totò's own recipe.'

Bordelli ate the first forkful and raised his eyebrows.

'Mmm,' he said, mouth full. The cook made an expression of satisfaction and put a bottle of white wine from the north in front of Bordelli before running back to the cooker to get more food for the waiters. That done, he finally had a moment to relax. He came back to the inspector and poured himself a glass of wine.

'You're a born cook, Totò,' said Bordelli, mopping up the sauce with bread.

'No, Inspector, I was born a labourer and only became a cook later on.'

'I didn't know that.'

'When I was still just a kid my parents sent me out to earn my keep, down in the village. Ten hours a day, mixing cement with a shovel and carrying pots of lime up ladders. For a beggar's pittance, Inspector. Evenings I'd come home so tired I wouldn't even eat . . . I remember one morning . . . I was twelve years old, maybe less . . . A fancy car with a chauffeur pulled up at the worksite, and a big fat guy with a beard and hat got out. You could see he was a bigwig. He walked with a cane, as if there was something wrong with his leg. He calls the engineer over and, with his hands in his pockets, tells him: "We're closing this place down tomorrow." The engineer says: "What do you mean, 'we're closing?' The engineer was from the north, a skinny bloke, always well dressed. "We're closing the place down tomorrow," the fat guy repeated. "And who the hell are you?" the engineer asked him, eyes popping out of his head. "And why should we close down?" The rest of us were all frozen, watching the scene. The fat guy didn't answer, but just turned and walked back to his car. Before getting in, he turned round and looked at the building under construction. The skeleton was already in place, as well as a few internal walls. "Nice building," he said, then, all sad, "Too bad it's so frail." Then he got in his car, made a signal to the chauffeur, and drove off. The engineer started cursing at him and then turned and looked at us. "Tomorrow's a workday," he said. "Nothing's changed. Tomorrow's a workday like any other." So the next day we were there working as usual, when the same big car pulls up round nine o'clock. The fat man steps out, taps his cane on the bricks to get our attention, has all of us gather in front of him, kids included. The engineer wasn't there. The fat guy looks at all of us and says: "How much do they pay you for a day's work? Actually, never mind, I don't even want to know. Whoever comes with me, I'll double his pay. But you've got to come straight away. In a minute it'll be too late. I'll count to three: one . . . two . . ." He never even got to three, because we were all ready to leave with him. When the engineer got there at half nine, there was nobody left. The worksite was shut down and he went back to Milan . . . That's the way things go in the south, Inspector.'

'And what about the fat guy? Did he give you work?'

'Of course, and he doubled our pay, just like he promised.'

'And what about the unfinished building? What happened to it?'

'It's still there, the same way we left it, Inspector . . . It's become a legend.'

'What've you got for a second course, Totò?'

'Grilled mullet or fried sea bass.'

'Let's have the mullet.'

Totò went and threw four mullets on the grill and came back to drink his wine.

'You know, I really ought to be going back home for a visit, Inspector. My grandmother's not doing so well . . . But how can I leave Cesare without a cook?'

'You've got a problem on your hands,' said Bordelli, who was already percolating a solution.

'I'd only need two or three days, just to put in an appearance.'

'Well, if you're interested, I've got a friend who could possibly fill in for you while you're away.'

'You really mean that?' said Totò, coming closer.

'Absolutely. He's a very good cook.'

'And who is he?'

'His name's Bottarini, but his friends call him Botta.'

'And has this man ever worked in a restaurant?'

'I don't think so, but I assure you he's very good.'

Totò gave a sneer of superiority.

'Cooking for three hundred people's not the same as cooking for three, Inspector.'

'He could manage, I'm sure of it.'

'If you say so,' said the cook with a sceptical expression, wiping his hands on his apron. He seemed a little jealous.

'I was just trying to do you a favour. If you don't feel like it, then . . .' said Bordelli.

The cook sighed with conceit and went to turn the mullets, brow furrowed. He let them cook for another minute, basting them with a sauce of mostly olive oil, then put them on a plate which he brought over to the inspector. He was acting somewhat strangely.

'Tell your friend to come and see me one of these days. I'd

like to ask him some questions first,' he said, looking very
serious.

'All right,' said Bordelli, amused by Totò's professorial
attitude.

The mullets were superb, and the wine went down like water.
The cook refilled his own glass to the brim and knocked it
back in one gulp before refilling it again.

'To change the subject . . . When the hell are you going to
catch this bloody killer, Inspector?' he said rather vehemently.

'Soon, Totò, I'll catch him soon,' said Bordelli, ignoring the
provocation. He had a fishbone stuck between the teeth at
the back of his mouth and couldn't manage to dislodge it.

At about half past two the inspector rang Levi's buzzer. He
wanted to have a little chat with him, but he also hoped to see
Milena again. The sun was high in the sky and there wasn't a
cloud to be seen. It was rather hot.

Levi greeted him with a smile, as if expecting this visit, and
saw him into the usual room. Through the open window one
could see diagonal bands of sunlight across the façade of the
building across the street.

'Did you like the little joke I played on you after my last
visit, Dr Levi?'

'Most amusing . . . Will you have a drink?'

'The usual, thanks.'

Levi filled two glasses with Hennessy, handed one to Bordelli
and left the other on the table.

'Dr Levi, why did you lie to me?'

'What do you mean?'

'I'm talking about Karl Strüffen.'

Levi closed his eyes and gave one of his smiles, but it was
clear that Bordelli's words had hit home. Despite the hour, he
picked up his glass from the table and calmly took a gulp of
cognac.

'My compliments, Bordelli. How did you arrive at that
conclusion?'

'With a bit of luck,' said the inspector, shrugging his shoulders in modesty.

'And what will you do now?' asked Levi, frowning slightly. He looked anything but serene.

'I want Strüffen,' said Bordelli.

'He's run away, you know.'

'I figured as much. That's why I'm here.'

Levi shook his head.

'Why do you want him? Karl Strüffen has already been convicted.'

'A friend of mine lost his life in this affair, and I have good reason to believe it was *your* Nazi who killed him . . . Do you know anything about this?'

'Inspector, we hardly spend all our time prowling around the villa, as some others do . . . We've known for some time that he's there. We need only find the right way to get inside the villa, without making any mistakes. But now you and your friend have got mixed up in this, and you've made some noise . . . And our man has flown away.'

'We've all been unlucky.'

'I'm sorry, Bordelli, but the Strüffen dossier is our prerogative.'

'And I know what that means, Dr Levi. But I want him alive. He must be tried for the murder of Casimiro Robetti.'

Levi looked him long in the eye, no hint of a smile on his lips any more.

'Let us do our work, Bordelli. We got here first. It was hard tracking down Strüffen. We succeeded only a short time ago, after years of searching . . . And now he's escaped again. He can't have gone very far, however. We'll find him again soon, and this time—'

At that moment a door opened, and Goldberg stuck his head inside. He said something to Levi in Hebrew, casting an untroubled glance at Bordelli.

'Excuse me just a moment, Inspector.'

'By all means.'

Levi left the room, closing the door behind him. Bordelli lit a cigarette and leaned back on the sofa. He was trying to think of how he might persuade Levi to turn Karl Strüffen over to him, though he didn't have much hope.

The door opened again and Milena came in. The mass of hair round her head looked like a cluster of snakes. She was beautiful, but that was not all. She had luminous eyes, and a gaze full of secrets.

'Hello, Inspector.'

Bordelli stood up with a smile and shook her slender, warm hand. He liked this woman very much, more than he could ever remember liking another. He knew Levi would be back before long, so he didn't want to let slip this opportunity. He took a deep breath, to summon the courage to speak.

'I'm sorry to ask you this way, Milena, but I don't think I have much time . . . What are you doing tomorrow evening?' he asked, blushing slightly. She looked at him in wonder.

'I'm dining with you, didn't you know?'

'Of course, how silly of me,' said Bordelli, beginning to breathe more easily.

'Nine o'clock, in front of the Giubbe Rosse, Inspector?'

'I'll be there,' said Bordelli, his cheeks hot.

They heard some footsteps, the door opened, and Levi returned. He looked at Milena.

'Could you let us have a moment alone?' he asked her.

'Of course . . . Come back soon, Inspector,' she said, walking away. When she was at the door, she turned and said to Levi:

'I'm dining out tomorrow evening.'

'You didn't tell me,' said Levi, almost resentfully.

'I just need a little peace and quiet. I work so hard all day.'

'A man?'

'Perhaps,' said Milena. She left the room, closing the door behind her. Bordelli coughed into his fist, embarrassed. Levi sighed and sat down, fixing his eyes on Bordelli.

'And what about Miss Olga?' the inspector enquired with apparent interest, to turn their attention away from Milena.

'Have you met the woman?' Levi asked with some surprise.

'It was love at first sight.'

'Fräulein Olga disappeared a few days after Karl Strüffen did. She stayed on a short while at the villa, probably on orders from her master, to see if she could understand what was going on.'

'Who is she?'

'A former mistress of Strüffen who has remained true to the old legend. She's of no interest to us.'

'Nor to me. I want Strüffen.'

'That's asking too much, Bordelli. You're well familiar with our principles and methods,' said Levi, pouring himself some more cognac. He seemed nervous.

'Strüffen must stand trial for murdering my friend . . .'

'Karl Strüffen was already sentenced at Nuremberg, Inspector. Why do you want him only to serve a life sentence?'

'I want him to bear the responsibility for this crime as well. Casimiro has as much right to justice as everyone else . . . Afterwards, you can do whatever you like with Strüffen,' said Bordelli.

'How can you be so sure it was our man who killed your friend?'

'Because I can put two and two together.'

'Care to tell me about it?'

'Why should I?'

'It could be useful to us . . . Don't you feel like it?'

'No, but I'll do it anyway.'

Bordelli calmly lit a cigarette and started telling the story in detail, as he had managed to reconstruct it by piecing together the facts available to him.

'One night Casimiro went walking through an olive grove at Fiesole, looking for some cabbage to steal. He saw a man lying on the ground and thought he was dead. He came running to get me, but when we went back together the man was gone . . . To your knowledge, does Strüffen have anyone living there with him in the villa, aside from Miss Olga?'

'He's called Rudolph, a former soldier of his,' said Levi, seeming quite interested.

Bordelli smiled and resumed his conjectures.

'In all likelihood, that evening Rudolph got tired of spending all his time shut up inside the villa like a prisoner, and so he grabbed a bottle of good cognac and went out for a walk in the olive grove . . . He drank a lot, fell to the ground, stinking drunk, split his lip and started bleeding. That was the state he was in when he was seen by Casimiro, who then came running to me. A short while later, our Rudolph wakes up – perhaps summoned by Strüffen – and goes back inside the villa, unaware that Casimiro has seen him. Then we arrive, and at a certain point a Doberman with a mouth like a shark comes out, headed straight for us, but luckily I'm able to get off a shot and kill it. I'm convinced the dog was Strüffen's.'

'Yes, it was his,' said Levi, refilling the glasses with cognac. Bordelli made a gesture of thanks and took a long sip before resuming his account.

'I'm also convinced that it was a stupid accident. Strüffen must live in perpetual fear of being discovered, and it certainly was not in his interest to draw any attention to that villa. The dog must have slipped out of an open gate, or through a hole in the wall . . .'

'I agree,' said Levi.

'Casimiro and I left a few minutes later. As we were descending towards town, for no particular reason, I turned the car round just before San Domenico and headed back up. When I got back there, the dog's carcass was already gone. Most likely Strüffen had heard the gunshot, come outside to check, seen the dead dog and decided to remove it, possibly thinking there might be trouble if anybody found it. As I was looking around, I suddenly heard a sound and hid. And, without being seen, I saw Strüffen look out over the stone balustrade in the garden, probably just to make sure there wasn't anyone prowling about below . . . But at that moment I didn't recognise him . . .'

'You hadn't told me that,' said Levi, seeming offended.

'I don't think the Dove has been any more talkative than I've been,' said Bordelli.

'You know very well how we work.'

'Well, the same goes for me.'

'And what happened next?' asked Levi, curious.

'I went and rang the bell at the gate and had the pleasure of meeting Miss Olga . . . But I don't think the valiant Karl Strüffen was too worried about my visit. To him I was only a pain-in-the-arse cop who had landed there by chance, and he was absolutely right. But I'm certain that in the days that followed, he kept the area around the house under strict surveillance, just to be sure . . . I myself would have done the same.'

'So would I,' said Levi.

'For everything that happened after that, I can only conjecture,' said Bordelli, throwing up his hands.

'Of course . . .' said Levi. 'Go on.'

'Well, as I imagine it, one evening Strüffen catches Casimiro prowling about the place and, pretending to be friendly, invites him to dine at the villa. He stuffs him with food and wine to get him to talk and, without too much trouble, even manages to make him say where he lives. Whatever Casimiro may have said, Strüffen surely realised that this had nothing to do with his Nazi past and was only a strange coincidence. But, given his situation, he couldn't afford to let a witness go. And so he killed the dwarf and got rid of his bicycle. He could have buried Casimiro's body in a field up there around Fiesole, and nobody would ever have found it. Instead he ordered Rudolph to wrap it up well and pack it into a suitcase and take this to Casimiro's own home . . . And that's what I can't understand . . .'

'Nor I, frankly . . . But I'm not too worried about it, since I can't understand why Strüffen tortured Jewish children, either,' said Levi, cold as ice. The inspector nodded.

'He must have had his reasons . . . Whatever the case, if Casimiro confessed that he was spying on the villa *for* the police, then, whether the body was found or not, Strüffen could have imagined that sooner or later someone would come and check on the villa. And so, just to be safe, after killing Casimiro he decided he needed a little change of scene for a while . . . and, without even realising it, he escaped just as the White Dove was about to put salt on his tail.'

'He won't get away next time,' said Levi.

'That depends,' said Bordelli.

'What do you mean?'

'Listen to me, Levi. Strüffen almost certainly fled only because he feared being discovered purely by chance, because of a Doberman and a silly dwarf who liked to play cop . . . And he probably just went for a long walk in the mountains or in some village not too far away from here. But if he knew that the White Dove was after him . . . well, I think he would get all the gods of the Third Reich moving and flee to the moon if he could, and he might even succeed in staying away for a very long time, if not for ever . . . What do you think?'

'What is your point?' Levi asked, staring at him.

Bordelli gave a roguish smile.

'If you don't let me have Strüffen, I will spread the news that the White Dove is on his tail, which should make a pretty fair mess of things for you.'

Levi's eyes flashed with fear, but he quickly recovered and returned the inspector's smile. He filled the glasses yet again, and took a sip of cognac.

'All right, then, you'll have your Strüffen . . . but on one condition,' he said.

'And what would that be?'

'Let us work in peace until we find him . . . It won't take long.'

'Do I have your word that you will turn him over to me?'

'You have my word.'

In his half-sleep the mutterings of the television sounded to him like the shouts of the SS during round-ups, and he started awake, looking for his machine gun. He was greeted by a western starring Gary Cooper and collapsed against the back of the sofa, head swimming with memories. Still groggy with sleep, he started thinking about the monstrosities he'd seen with his own eyes during the war. Old images passed before him like colour slides. They showed not only blood but humiliation and despair. He remembered the moment he'd heard the radio announce the Armistice; he felt the same sense of liberation in his breast he had back then. From the very start of the conflict, a hatred of his Nazi 'comrades' had grown within him, inescapably, and only after the 8 September armistice had he felt he was fighting a just and unavoidable war against a sort of disease.

A spectacle he'd witnessed in a southern village, a few months after the Armistice, came back to him. One morning he and his men had stopped at the top of a hill to spy on the town with their binoculars, and with their own eyes they saw women being raped, children massacred, houses burnt, entire rows of unarmed civilians executed. 'As soon as it gets dark, we're going down there,' Bordelli said to his men. There were ten of them, and they were all in agreement. Counting the hours and minutes, they began to make their way down towards the village the moment the sun set. They descended the slope in silence, faces smeared with mud, Bordelli at the head. His eyes were still full of the things he'd seen that morning, and his arms twitched with a desire to shoot. When they entered the village, they surrounded the elementary school in which the Germans were barricaded. An endless gun battle ensued, and a good number of hand grenades were thrown into the building. Eventually the San Marco squadron managed to enter the school and had to fight with daggers and bare fists to eliminate the last Nazis. When the battle was over, they realised there were no officers among the dead. And yet that morning they had clearly seen them ordering the massacres. They decided to inspect all the classrooms with the utmost caution. Kicking the doors in, one by one, they entered, machine-gun barrels first. At last they found them, huddling in the darkness of a broom closet. There were eight of them, in black uniforms with decorations gleaming. They immediately raised their hands, shading their eyes against the sudden blinding light. Muttering between their teeth, faces drawn from fear, they spoke in that accursed tongue of theirs, asking perhaps for fair treatment . . . Then one of them whispered in terror: '*Sammarko!*' The inspector could still see them all before him, eyes dilated and trained on him as if he were a beacon, Commander Bordelli, a San Marco officer with a machine gun in his hand and a bleeding ear. His sleepy memory lined them up for him again like so many Strüffens, all with white hair and a black mark on the neck. He remembered those moments well . . . The Nazis before him, innocuous as babies, hands on their heads and terror in their faces . . . He exchanged a look of understanding with his men and, after a few tension-packed moments, he nodded ever so slightly to say: Yes. They didn't even let them out of the closet. They merely took a step back and fired all at once on that mass of flesh in uniform, firing far more shots than was necessary, thinking of the babies tossed in the air and machine-gunned, looking straight in the faces of those smartly dressed men dancing disjointedly under the impact of the bullets. Blood very quickly covered the floor of the closet, spilled out over the threshold and started dripping down the stairs. The hardest thing was carrying the dead outside; not just the officers, but everyone else. They put them round the public fountain, forming a star. From the spout they hung a sign that said: A GIFT FROM THE SAN MARCO. They left the town at a slow pace, walking down the main street. Behind closed shutters burned the eyes of the few survivors. Peering out from under cover had become a habit for them. Bordelli tried to meet their glances between the slats of the blinds, hoping at least to hear a word. But not so much as a fly moved. At bottom only one thing mattered. The town was now free.

The western had ended some time ago, and the hum accompanying the test card rang as sad as a lament in his ears. It was only eleven o'clock. He'd collapsed on the couch without even having eaten. But he wasn't hungry. He lit a cigarette and poured himself a glass of wine. A couple of minutes later the signal went off and the snow appeared. The accompanying static got on his nerves. He got up to turn off the television, then sat there glassy eyed, staring at the shrinking little point of light on the picture tube until it disappeared. Mouth all pasty, he snuffed out the cigarette and shuffled to the bathroom to brush his teeth. But he couldn't find the toothbrush. He looked everywhere for it, then remembered that it had fallen into the toilet bowl that morning. He brought his face to the mirror to look at his wrinkles from up close. They seemed to increase with each passing day. He felt like a wreck. Rinsing his mouth out with water, he went and lay down in bed. He lit another cigarette, felt disgusted, and crushed it in the ashtray. As he was trying to fall asleep, Botta's face appeared to him, at the moment he'd suggested he go and work for a few days at Da Cesare in the place of a Pugliese called Totò.

He'd gone to see him around eight o'clock that evening at his lair in Via del Campuccio, and for a brief moment Botta had thought Bordelli's visit meant that he'd caught and arrested the child-killer.

'Not yet, Ennio, but I'll catch him soon,' the inspector had said. By this point he was always repeating the same phrase, to ward off bad luck.

'Stay for dinner, Inspector? I could whip up a *spaghetti alla carrettiera*, nice and spicy.'

'Thanks, Ennio, but I'm a wreck. I think I'll just go home.'

Looking around, Bordelli had noticed that the modest room seemed different from the last time he'd been there.

'Am I mistaken, Botta, or have you changed something in here?'

'The lights, Inspector. I bought a new light fixture.'

'That's new, too,' said Bordelli, pointing at a nice big cooker with six burners.

'Beautiful, eh?'

'I guess things went well for you in Greece.'

'I can't complain . . . And now I even know how to make moussaka.'

'So the clink's not your only cooking school.'

'Botta's never going back to jail, Inspector . . . Never.'

'Does that mean you're going to stop picking locks?' Bordelli asked, almost worried.

'No, Inspector, I'm just going to stop getting caught.'

'Listen, Ennio, I need to ask a favour of you . . .'

As Botta was putting the water for the pasta on the stove, the inspector told him about Totò and the trattoria Da Cesare.

'Of course I'm interested!' Botta replied, eyes popping.

'Then go and talk to Totò as soon as you can. I have the feeling he wants to give you some sort of test. But you'll understand each other, I'm sure of it.'

'As a lockpicking artist, I'm not so sure, Inspector, but as a cook, nobody can touch me.'

All cooks are the same, thought Bordelli. They always want to be the best.

'I have to go now, Botta. I can feel a nasty headache coming on.'

'Thanks, Inspector. Who knows? Maybe in my old age I'll open a trattoria with an international menu,' the thief said, shaking his hand firmly at the door.

'I'd give that some serious thought . . . Ciao, Ennio. Next time, if things are a little calmer, I want to hear about Greece.'

'G'night, Inspector.'

He spent the following morning rereading the reports of the murders, without results. He'd slept badly, as was nearly always the case of late. For lunch he ate a panino at the bar in Via di San Gallo and went immediately back to the office, which stank of cigarettes. He opened the window, and a gust of tepid air, heady with spring, wafted in, along with a few large flies. He thought about dinner with Milena, and despite everything that was happening, he felt a pang of emotion in his chest. It had been centuries since he had felt so intrigued by a woman. He looked at his watch: barely two o'clock. Seven more long hours before their appointment. He sat down and lit a cigarette. Casimiro's little skeleton was still in its place, hanging from the pen-holder. He tried to imagine the moment when the little dwarf drank the poisoned cognac. He clenched his teeth. The feeling of guilt was still gnawing at his stomach. He should have prevented Casimiro from playing spy.

But at least *that* murder seemed solved. He needed only to wait until the White Dove found Karl Strüffen. He hoped Levi would keep his word, even though this was far from a foregone conclusion. For the Nazi hunter, the White Dove came before anything else. At the moment, all the inspector could do was wait.

Three or four fat flies were flying a few centimetres below the ceiling, crashing into each other every so often. They made a terrible racket; it was impossible to concentrate. All he could do was watch them . . . Were there four or five? Suddenly one of them veered towards the window and went out, and the others followed like sheep. There must have been five of them. Or maybe not; just four. At any rate, they were gone, and Bordelli heaved a sigh of relief. He put out his fag-end and distractedly withdrew the last cigarette from the packet. He saw that it was broken, lit it anyway, but couldn't get any draw on it. He blew the smoke up towards the ceiling and started thinking about Davide Rivalta.

There was something fishy about the man. Something strange, and not just unpleasant. He was a cultured, intelligent man who wanted at all costs to be disagreeable . . . But there was more than this. There was something strange in his eyes, a destructive gleam, but at the same time a sort of wild joy. And he had been seen in the area of Sara Bini's corpse just minutes after the murder. It might be coincidence, of course, but . . .

Bordelli opened a bottle of beer, and as he was taking his first gulp, the phone rang. It was the commissioner.

'Good day, Bordelli. Any new developments in those murder cases?' Inzipone sounded nervous.

'I've made some progress on Casimiro Robetti,' said Bordelli.

'What kind of progress?'

'I'll tell you when it all becomes clear.'

'Tell me now.'

'I'd rather not.'

'And what have you got to tell me about the little girls?' Inzipone sighed, resigning himself to Bordelli's methods.

'Nothing serious yet, unfortunately.'

'And what about that man you've got under surveillance?'

'Davide Rivalta? We're still keeping an eye on him.'

'We've got to stop that killer, Bordelli, and we've got to do it soon . . . before anything else happens.'

'We'll catch him.'

'Well, keep me informed on this matter, at least. All right?'

'I'll get back to you soon, Dr Inzipone.'

The inspector hung up and leaned back in his chair. This case was turning into a nightmare. Every time the phone rang or there was a knock at the door, he expected the worst. He ran a hand through his hair, and it felt dirty. He felt beaten down, and didn't know which way to turn. He spent the afternoon in a state of shameful apathy.

It was already seven o'clock. He had to go home and get ready for dinner with Milena, and the thought made him shudder. He really needed to clear his head. Rushing out of the station, he waved goodbye to Mugnai.

After stopping first to buy a toothbrush, he went quickly home. He spent a long time cooking himself in a hot bathtub, eyes closed. He thought again about his journey through space, and it seemed almost like the memory of something he had actually done, which was, in a way, the truth. When he reopened his eyes, he realised it was already half past eight. He quickly got out of the water, dried his hair, and splashed on some aftershave lotion without having bothered to shave, just to smell nice. At ten minutes to nine, he got into the Beetle, stomach rumbling, and stepped on the accelerator so as not to be late. He felt as excited as a small child.

'I feel good with you,' said Milena, snuggling close to him. They were in Bordelli's bed, and had just finished making love for the second time. The room was in penumbra, lit only by the glow of a street lamp shining through the open window. Their clothes lay scattered helter-skelter on the floor. Bordelli kept his eyes closed, stroking Milena's back. He felt a sense of peace all through his body, only slightly disturbed by the usual obsessive thoughts.

They had gone to eat at a trattoria in the Sant'Ambrogio quarter, and had knocked back two bottles of wine. They had used the formal address through most of the meal, looking into each other's eyes like two teenagers. When Bordelli had asked her point-blank about the White Dove, Milena said she didn't feel like talking about work, and the subject didn't come up again. They had chatted about a great many things, jumping from one topic to another, as their desire to get to know each other kept growing. They had even joked and laughed a lot, enabling Bordelli to forget about all those murders for a while. When they left the restaurant, Milena said she felt like walking a bit. It was almost midnight. A few leftover scraps of cloud moved slowly across a star-filled sky. Along the river, Bordelli had lit a cigarette, feeling a strong urge to kiss the mouth of the woman walking beside him. Although it wasn't cold out, every so often a gust of wind ruffled their hair.

'Take me home with you,' she had said out of the blue.

'Yes, madam,' Bordelli had replied. And they had exchanged a smile of understanding and gone back to his car. On the drive home, they were both silent. Bordelli drove slowly, sniffing the air to pick up her scent. It was nice sitting in silence, listening to the sound of the Beetle. It was nice to see, out of the corner of his eye, Milena's leg swinging to and fro. It was also nice to look at the buildings' façades, the people passing by, to feel the steering wheel in his hands. It was all wonderful.

'This is where I live,' Bordelli had said, parking directly in front of the entrance.

'We know,' she'd said, in the tone of a spy.

They'd gone up the stairs without looking at each other. Once inside, she'd closed the door and kissed him on the lips, squeezing him tight and grabbing the hair on the nape of his neck.

'You move fast,' Bordelli had said, feeling Milena's hands fumble under his shirt.

'When I know what I want, I don't like to waste any time,' she had whispered, smiling. A minute later they were in bed . . .

Bordelli lay on his back, playing with Milena's hair, curling the locks round his fingers. But his sense of well-being was slowly beginning to feel contaminated . . . It was the murdered little girls, whose senseless deaths continued to gnaw at his brain. Milena had one leg over his belly, and every so often kissed him on the neck. It was nice to have her so close, to feel her hair on his shoulder, to smell the lovely scent of her skin and breath.

'I feel good too,' said Bordelli.

She began breathing more heavily, climbed on top of him, and they started all over again.

The little girl had gone out shortly after seven o'clock to buy milk just round the corner from home, as she did almost every evening. It usually took her only a few mintues, but today, after fifteen minutes, she still hadn't returned. She was nine years old and her name was Susanna. Her mother had gone out to look for her and asked the milkman, but he hadn't seen her. She'd asked the other shopkeepers as well, but they didn't know anything. That area of Gavinana wasn't very lit, and at that hour there was hardly anyone on the street. The woman became seriously scared and started looking for her daughter up and down the streets from Via di Villamagna to Piazza Elia dalla Costa, asking the few pedestrians she passed whether they'd seen a little girl with blonde hair wearing a yellow sweater. But nobody knew anything. In the end she collapsed, and around nine o'clock she called the police. Bordelli was informed and instinctively phoned Davide Rivalta. He let it ring a long time, counting the rings. At the twentieth ring, he hung up, then rushed to the radio communications room to speak with the officers who were watching Rivalta.

'What time did he go out?' he asked, squeezing the microphone.

'He's at home, Inspector. He got back at five and hasn't moved since. At the moment he's on the ground floor. I can see the lights on,' said the policeman.

Bordelli ended the communication and returned to his office feeling very disappointed. He tried ringing Rivalta again. He let the phone ring for a long time again, and just when he was about to hang up, he heard someone pick up.

'Who is this? Hello? Hello?! Who is this?' said Rivalta, half asleep. Bordelli hung up without saying a word.

There was a great deal of commotion at the police station. Hundreds of photos of the little girl were printed up in record time, to be distributed to the residents of the Gavinana quarter. The television news reports also broadcast a photo of Susanna, asking people to call the police if they had any information whatsoever, even the most insignificant. Meanwhile a veritable hunting party was organised, starting at the Parco dell'Anconella and going as far as the end of Via di Ripoli. They searched every garden, public and private, and checked every courtyard, as well as a broad stretch of open country around Ponte a Ema. The search lasted late into the night, but the girl was never found. Susanna Zanetti had vanished into thin air. Nobody had seen her talking to anyone, or getting into a car, or even walking down the street. How was it possible that no one at all had seen a little blonde girl in a yellow sweater? Bordelli's stomach was in knots. He hadn't slept much the night before, and the fatigue was muddling his brain.

'Are you thinking what I'm thinking, Piras?'

'Unfortunately, yes, Inspector, but I hope I'm wrong.'

'Fuck . . .' said Bordelli, lighting his thousandth cigarette of the day. During their search he had hoped the girl had simply, stupidly got lost, but several hours had now passed, and he no longer expected her to be found alive.

Round about four o'clock in the morning he felt on the verge of collapse and went home to rest for a while. He got into bed, turned off the light, and a few minutes later was already asleep, head full of memories of the war.

Shortly after dawn, a man phoned police headquarters, and Mugnai rang Bordelli at home.

'It's done, Inspector . . . They've found her.'

'Dead?' asked Bordelli, holding his breath.

'Dead,' said Mugnai. The inspector cursed and ran a hand over his sleepy face.

'Where?' he asked.

'In a wood between Bagno a Ripoli and l'Antella. The squads are already on their way there.'

'Ring Piras and tell him I'll be at his place in a few minutes . . . And inform Diotivede at once.'

The inspector dragged himself out of bed, got dressed in a hurry, and raced down the stairs. He was a wreck. As he got into the car, he felt a crushing sense of desolation. He had slept barely two hours, and his ears were ringing. Fatigue was altering his perceptions, and he kept thinking he saw a cat running under the Beetle's wheels. He swung by Via Gioberti to pick up Piras, who was already waiting in the doorway, bags under his eyes. They didn't even greet each other. The streets were almost empty, and they got to Bagno a Ripoli in a matter of minutes. Through the clouds shone a greenish light that did nothing to remedy the atmosphere of death. The air smelled strongly of rain.

They turned in the direction of Antella, and about half a mile later saw the flashing blue lights of several squad cars. Bordelli pulled up at the side of the road, and they both got out. Aside from the policemen, there was nobody there, not even journalists.

'Has the mother been informed?' Bordelli asked one of the uniformed cops.

'Scarpelli's taking care of that, Inspector.'

'Is he always the one to do that?'

'He's the best at that sort of thing, sir.'

'Where's the little girl?'

'Up that path . . . The man who found her is also there.'

'Come, Piras.'

They went up the trail, which ascended steeply through the woods, and past a bend they saw the silhouettes of two policemen standing motionless in the middle of the path. There was also an elderly man wearing a hat and holding a rather agitated hunting dog on a leash. When they reached the group, a very young policeman Bordelli didn't know came forward.

'She's over there, Inspector,' he said with the voice of a child, lighting the woods with a torch. Two bare little feet were sticking out from behind a tree trunk. Bordelli and Piras approached the body, followed by the child cop. The sun still hadn't fully come up, and hardly any light penetrated through the trees.

'Pass me the torch,' Bordelli said to the kid, taking it out of his hand. He shone it on the little girl.

'That was the gentleman who called us, Inspector,' the boy said under his breath, gesturing towards the man in the hat.

'Did he touch anything?' asked Bordelli.

'He didn't, but his dog may have when he found the body.'

'Go ahead and send him home.'

Piras had knelt down and was leaning forward to have a closer look at the little girl. The spectacle was more or less the same as in the other cases. Susanna was lying face up, beautiful, dark green eyes open. Her blonde, slightly undone braid stood out against the moss, and her yellow sweater was all soiled with dirt. Bordelli lifted it with one finger, knowing what he would find underneath. The teeth had sunk deep into the flesh, leaving a bluish imprint.

The wind was blowing, and great sinewy clouds passed overhead. An evil light filtered into the dense wood. A car was heard pulling up along the road, then a door slammed. A moment later Diotivede appeared on the path, black bag in hand. In the darkness of the wood, his bright white hair looked almost luminous. He made the faintest of gestures and without saying a word knelt beside the little girl and studied her for a few minutes. He checked the marks on her neck, the bite on her belly, the consistency of her flesh. It took him less time than the others. Then he stood up and, as always, started jotting down his first notes in his notebook.

'How long has she been dead?' Bordelli asked, without taking his eyes off the child.

'At a glance I'd say about twelve hours . . . and don't ask me if I'm sure,' the pathologist said under his breath, staring at him from behind his glasses with a look of disgust. He put his notebook in his pocket and headed back down the path without another word. Bordelli followed him with his eyes, rather stunned. All at once Diotivede stopped and turned round. He gestured to Bordelli to approach. Apparently he wanted to talk to him alone.

'Wait for me here,' the inspector said to Piras. He'd never seen Diotivede behave this way. Sticking a cigarette between his lips, he walked towards the doctor, wondering what he might have to say. When he was a few steps away from him, Diotivede resumed walking, but more slowly. Bordelli drew level with him, and they continued down the path side by side, without looking at each other. Waiting for Diotivede to talk, the inspector lit the cigarette. The wind was gusting through the trees, raising the hair on their heads, as it had the previous evening with Milena. The smoke he blew out of his mouth swirled in the air and vanished in a second. He suddenly realised the doctor was no longer beside him. Turning round, he saw that Diotivede had stopped a few steps behind him. They were standing face to face, in the darkness of that narrow path in the woods. Bordelli tried to glean something from Diotivede's eyes, but saw only his dark silhouette and white hair shining in the darkness.

The wind, the dawn, the twittering birds . . . Had the situation been different, it could have been a beautiful moment.

'Have I ever spoken to you about Aurora?' the doctor suddenly asked, his voice breaking.

'No,' said Bordelli, feeling a shudder down his spine.

'She was a niece of mine. Died in '39. Aged six.'

'What happened?'

'Crushed by a lorry.'

'You've never mentioned that to me.'

'When I saw her dead body, I felt in a way as if I myself had died. I shut myself up at home for many days. It was as if the world had stopped. I wanted it to stop. That seemed like the right thing to me. Then one morning I went out and saw people all around me, getting on with their lives as usual. I saw people walking, talking, queuing up for bread . . . Some were even laughing. Nothing at all had stopped. Only me. Then, slowly, I started to feel alive again, perhaps even more alive than before, as if Aurora's life had entered me . . .'

'Maybe these things really do happen,' said Bordelli.

'I don't know . . . But when I find myself looking at these dead little girls I feel just as powerfully as before that the world should stop.'

The doctor advanced a few steps and stopped in front of Bordelli. His eyes were now quite visible behind the lenses: two big eyes full of disgust.

'Find the killer, Bordelli,' he said. And then he went on his way down the little path without another word, medical bag dangling at his side. He looked like an old sorcerer returning exhausted to his underground burrow after a lost battle against the forces of Evil. Bordelli tossed his fag-end to the ground and squashed it with his shoe until it broke apart.

Midday. The strong wind made the antennae on the rooftops sway, even managing to knock a few of them down. Bordelli sat in his office, staring at the wall in front of him, in part because, aside from the yellowed plaster, there was nothing on it to look at. He thought distractedly that his office needed a good white-wash and started to feel dizzy. For neither of the past two nights had he managed to sleep more than three hours. Having forgotten an almost whole cigarette in the ashtray, he lit another. He smoked and stared at the wall; he stared at the wall and smoked. Every so often he ran a hand over his unshaven face, as if to wipe his soul clean of the mixture of horror and impotence wearing him down. He would have given anything to be truly floating in space through the Milky Way and other galaxies. He put out his cigarette, noticed the abandoned one, and smoked it as well. He took deep drags, angrily savouring the fist of smoke punching his throat. Then nausea came over him and he violently crushed the cigarette in the ashtray. He picked up the report on Susanna Zanetti again. Nine years old, blonde hair, found dead at dawn by a retiree's hunting dog in the countryside at Bagno a Ripoli. And nobody had seen anything.

Susanna's mother had been accompanied by the inevitable Scarpelli to Forensic Medicine to identify the body. When they raised the sheet she had bent over her daughter with a demented smile on her face. That child wasn't Susanna. She couldn't be Susanna. She might look like her, but she wasn't Susanna, she couldn't be. Susanna never kept her mouth open like that, Susanna never let her braid come undone, Susanna didn't have dead eyes like that, Susanna was alive, Susanna was at school, this little girl wasn't Susanna, Susanna didn't have dead eyes like that, this couldn't be her, Susanna never let her braid come undone . . .

Diotivede had already done the first tests and determined with certainty that Susanna Zanetti had been killed between seven and eight o'clock the previous evening. The means were the same, except for the traces of chloroform found in the child's respiratory tract. The murderer had put her to sleep so he could abduct and kill her at his convenience. She probably passed from sleep to death without even noticing.

Bordelli had nothing to sink his teeth into, and it was driving him crazy. Davide Rivalta's house had been closely watched, the surveillance reports were quite detailed. He reread them yet again, just so as not to be sitting there twiddling his thumbs. On the previous day Rivalta had left his house at 8.35 in the morning in his car. He had stopped at Porta Romana to buy the newspaper, then crossed the centre of town to go and eat breakfast at Castaldini's, one of the best pastry shops in Florence, in Via dei Mille. Around 9.30 he had gone for a walk in the Parco delle Cascine, and returned home at 11.00. He went out again at 4.30 p.m., on foot. He did a little shopping in the Due Strade and was back home at ten to five, after which time he remained at home for the rest of the day. At a quarter past seven the light on the first floor went out, and Rivalta went downstairs to the ground floor, almost certainly to have dinner. He went back up to the first floor at about ten o'clock. All the lights in the villa went out around one o'clock in the morning. He received no telephone calls all day.

This was more or less how it went every day, even if the hours weren't always the same. Rivalta never saw anyone, never got any phone calls, seldom went out, and almost always spent the afternoon on the first floor, probably in his study. He went to bed between 1 and 2 a.m.

Bordelli pressed his eyeballs hard with his fingertips. He was dead tired. He couldn't stop thinking about Rivalta, but didn't quite know why. Perhaps he was clinging to him because he had nothing else to hold on to, so that he could tell himself he wasn't running round in circles like a moron. He had to be very careful. If he let the strange Rivalta distract him too much, he risked missing important clues that might put him on the right track.

He opened a beer bottle and guzzled half of it. Then he picked up the phone and dialled Mugnai's internal number.

'Do me a favour, Mugnai, and call Piras for me at once.'

'I don't know where he is, Inspector.'

'Then go and look for him!'

'I'm already out the door, Inspector.'

A few minutes later Piras knocked, came in and sat down without saying a word. He looked even gloomier than usual.

'Piras, for Christ's sake! What the hell are we waiting for to catch this maniac?' said Bordelli, slamming his hand against the photos of the little girls. He had never felt so upset during an investigation. Normally he tried to keep from getting too emotionally involved, and he usually succeeded. But the three little girls weighed upon his stomach like a block of marble. The thought that the killer was still at large stirred an oppressive sense of restlessness in him that squashed him right there in his chair. He looked again at the photographs spread across the table: Valentina, Sara, Susanna . . .

'Say something to me, Piras, let's come up with an idea . . . I don't want to see another child murdered.'

The Sardinian stared at him with his coal-black eyes, which glistened as if he had a fever.

'I'd been hoping it was Rivalta, Inspector,' he said between clenched teeth.

'Me, too, damn it all, but it looks like we were wrong,' said Bordelli, stuffing another cigarette between his lips. By this point he'd decided to wait until the maniac was locked up in an asylum before kicking the idiotic habit.

'Why is he killing them, Piras? And why in that way?' he asked bitterly, blowing smoke into the Sardinian's face.

'We'll catch him, Inspector, I can feel it,' Piras said stiffly, waving the smoke away with his hand.

'I wish I knew when . . .'

'Soon.'

'How can you be so sure?'

'I can feel it.'

'Ah, you can feel it . . . blimey, what good news!' said the inspector. He put a hand on his forehead. It was hot. He'd woken up at dawn and still hadn't eaten anything.

'I'm sorry, Piras,' he said, holding up one hand and trying to calm down. The young man merely looked at him without a word. Bordelli got up from his chair and started pacing about the room, blowing smoke through his nostrils.

'I'm a little on edge, Piras. That son of a bitch is making fools of us all,' he said, forcefully crushing his cigarette butt in the already full ashtray. The internal phone rang, and the inspector picked up.

'Yes?'

'How many more little girls is that maniac going to kill, Bordelli? Why can't we manage to find him?'

It was Commissioner Inzipone again, and he sounded mightily pissed off. He was speaking, as always, in the plural.

'We'll catch him soon, Commissioner,' said Bordelli, not knowing what else to say.

'The minister of the interior just rang me, and asked me what the hell we were doing . . .'

'We'll catch him.'

'When?'

'Very soon.'

'What makes you think that?'

'Let's say I can feel it . . . We'll catch him soon.'

'Ah, you can feel it . . . Brilliant!' said Inzipone, who then unceremoniously hung up. Bordelli spat a few curses at the phone, finished his beer and hurled the bottle into the waste basket.

'Let's get a move on, Piras. Ring Signora Zanetti and find out when we can go and see her . . . Maybe something will come of it.'

'Shall I call her right now, Inspector?'

'Why the hell would you want to wait?'

'All right,' said Piras, as he jumped to his feet and dashed out of the office, looking offended.

Bordelli went and opened the window wide. He stood there looking outside: clear sky, courtyard full of cars, Mugnai outside the guardhouse, chatting with a colleague. He tried to think of other things. The night he'd just spent with Milena came back to him. It felt as if he'd dreamt the whole thing. She'd left just before dawn, kissing him between the eyes by way of goodbye. They hadn't said anything to each other in parting. There was no need. Bordelli had a clear sense of what was happening to him, and had the impression she felt the same way. But neither had the desire to put it into words. They knew where to find each other, but realised that it was a difficult time for both of them. She was hunting down a Nazi, he a killer of little girls.

Piras returned fifteen minutes later and said that Susanna's mother had agreed to see them straight away.

'What took so long?' Bordelli asked gruffly.

'She wouldn't stop talking, Inspector. She started telling me about her daughter and I felt like I couldn't . . .'

'All right, let's go.'

'Very nice,' the inspector said, looking at Susanna's drawings on the wall of her small bedroom. Piras nodded in agreement. They were large sheets of paper full of colour, on which people were black spots and animals had five legs to help them stand up straight.

Maria Zanetti was thirty-five years old, slender and rather pretty, with black, curly hair which she had sought to tame with a few hairpins. She smiled as she spoke, like a mother telling two friends how bright and beautiful her daughter is. The most disturbing thing was that she acted as if Susanna were still alive and about to come home from school.

'She keeps everything in order, all by herself . . . In this drawer are her stockings, here are her shoes, here are her blouses . . . And this is her homework table . . . pens, erasers . . .'

'Good girl,' said Piras, giving her rope.

'Oh, yes . . . And she helps me cook, wash the dishes, iron, do the shopping . . . In fact she always wants to go buy the milk herself . . . And there's no harm in that – the milk shop's just round the corner, after all . . .'

Bordelli and Piras exchanged a glance. They were waiting for the woman to break down at any moment and start crying.

'Signora Zanetti, are you married?' the inspector asked.

'I lost my husband two years ago, but I don't intend to remarry . . . no, no, I couldn't . . . I'd never find another man like Walter,' the woman said, shaking her head.

'Was he Susanna's father?'

'Yes . . . Susanna suffered a great deal when he died, but she's recovered nicely . . . Every evening she recites a little prayer for her father in heaven.'

'Is this him?' Bordelli asked, pointing at a framed photograph on the wall, in which a blond man held young Susanna in his arms.

'Yes,' the woman said, stopping in front of the picture, a sad smile on her face.

'He doesn't look Italian,' said Piras.

'He was German . . . from Hamburg,' she said, with admiration in her voice.

'Why didn't you and your daughter take his surname?' Bordelli asked.

The woman looked at him with mild astonishment.

'What do you mean? Walter's surname is Zanetti . . . His great-grandfather was Swiss Italian,' she said, as if this was somehow obvious.

'I'm sorry,' Bordelli said, not knowing what else to say. Maria Zanetti's eyes turned back to the photo, full of nostalgia.

'We met during the war, in a field hospital. I was working as a nurse for the Red Cross, and Walter was an officer in the Wehrmacht . . . He'd been seriously wounded in the shoulder. We fell in love immediately, but with all the confusion there was at the end, we fell out of touch. After the war I tried in every way possible to find him, but didn't have any luck. We finally met up again in '54 and got married almost at once. A year later, Susanna was born . . . Isn't he handsome?'

'Very,' said the inspector, to make her happy. Piras looked at the picture with suspicion, as if thinking of one of his father's war stories about the Germans.

'Even though we were separated by the war, I felt that sooner or later I would find him again,' Maria continued.

'Where did you meet up with him in '54? In Italy?' Bordelli asked, seeing that the woman felt like talking. She shook her head gently.

'No, in Munich. It was the will of God; there's no other way to explain it. He lived in Hamburg and had gone to Munich to visit some relatives, whereas I was there for my job. I worked as a seamstress for a dance company. And one morning, as I was walking down the street, there he was, standing right before me . . . It was God who decided, I'm sure of it.'

'Signora Zanetti, forgive me for asking . . . but do you have any enemies that you know of? Someone who might wish you harm, for any reason at all?' Bordelli asked.

'Oh, no. Why should I have any enemies?' she said calmly. She was folding Susanna's little clothes before putting them away in the wardrobe.

'Had you noticed anything unusual in the past few days? I don't know, someone following you . . .'

'Why would anyone want to follow me?'

'Had Susanna mentioned anything unusual to you? A stranger, perhaps, who had spoken to her, or something like that?'

'Susanna knows very well she's not supposed to talk to strangers. She's a very smart girl, you know . . . Would you like to read one of her essays? I'm convinced she's going to become a writer,' said the woman, opening a drawer.

'Yes, of course,' said Bordelli, resigned to the fact that he wasn't going to coax any information out of her. Signora Zanetti already had a notebook in her hand, a large notebook with drawings by Jacovitti on the cover. She started reading.

'Pinocchio was a wooden marionette and his father was an old man with white hair called Geppetto . . .'

'Come on, dear, don't get so discouraged. You're doing your best,' said Rosa, knitting slowly away, as usual. Bordelli was lying on the sofa. He'd been carrying around a headache since the morning, and it had worsened that evening. Even Rosa's massage had failed to make it go away. Maybe a storm was coming. He had the misfortune of being able to feel them coming well in advance.

'I would like to catch him before he kills anyone else,' Bordelli said bitterly, pressing his temples hard with his fingertips. He could no longer stand feeling so powerless. After his fruitless visit to Signora Zanetti he had phoned Dr Saggini to tell him the woman was not well, and the doctor had assured him he would go and pay a call on her at once. Aside from this, there were no new developments, and it wasn't very encouraging . . .

The cat came home from his rounds across the rooftops and started miaowing about the room, snapping his tail.

'Gideon's nervous, too,' said Rosa. At that moment a lightning bolt lit up the sky for a long second, and the lamps in the room started to flicker. Then, at once, a violent clap of thunder chased the cat under the sofa.

'Finally,' said Bordelli. 'It's coming.'

Usually his headache would begin to subside after the first flashes of lightning and eventually vanish altogether. There was another, louder burst of thunder, and the lights went off. The first raindrops started to fall, big and sparse, then ever more dense, until they became a downpour. Rosa lived on the top floor, and one could hear the water pounding the roof.

'What a wonderful storm!' said Rosa, moving in the dark. She lit a few candles and sat down in front of the window to watch the lightning. Bordelli sat up and poured himself more cognac.

'You know what, Rosa? I've been with a woman.'

'In what sense?'

'Well . . .'

'Oh, really?' she said, turning round to look at him.

'You don't seem happy about it.'

'That depends. I don't want you to end up in the hands of a witch.'

'Don't worry, she's not a witch,' said Bordelli.

'How old is she?'

'What's that got to do with anything?'

'Why won't you tell me?'

'About twenty-five, I'd say.'

Rosa burst out laughing.

'And what are you going to do with a child like that?' she said, hysterical.

'Rosa, what's got into you? You're acting like a jealous wife.'

'Jealous? Me? Of what? It'd take a lot of little girls to make a woman like me.'

'Don't get upset.'

Rosa came over and looked him in the eye as the thunderbolts cracked in quick succession, sounding like a bombing raid.

'You're all the same, you men. You let yourselves be taken for a ride for a little packet of fresh meat,' she said. The flashes of lightning filled the room, illuminating Rosa's offended face. The atmosphere was one of tragedy.

'Come on . . .' said Bordelli. He took one of her hands in his and kissed it. Rosa still pouted a bit, but seemed to be calming down.

'Is she really so beautiful, this infant?' she muttered in a childlike voice, lowering her eyes.

'What was that?' asked Bordelli, who, because of a thunderclap, hadn't understood.

'Is this child really so beautiful?'

'Extraordinarily beautiful.'

'Blonde?'

'Dark,' said Bordelli, squeezing her fingers.

'What about her feet? Are they pretty?'

'I've never seen such pretty feet.'

'Ah, there you go! So you've already slept with her!' she said, withdrawing her hand just as a lightning bolt lit up her eyes.

'What's the matter with you, Rosa?'

'Nothing's the matter with me.'

'Come on now, try to calm down.'

Rosa stood for a minute in silence, eyes wandering about the room. Then she stared at Bordelli again, looking unhappy.

'You won't forget about me, monkey?'

'What are you saying?'

'You won't forget about your Rosina?'

'What would I do without you?'

'Do you really mean that? You won't forget about your Rosina?'

'Never.'

Rosa sat down on the edge of the sofa and ran her hand through his hair.

'Shall I make you something to eat, monkey?' she said with a somewhat forced smile.

'You know what I'd like? A little plate of spaghetti, the way you do it so well, with a spicy tomato sauce.'

'Brown-noser!' she said, elbowing him.

'Seriously. Would you make me some?'

'You certainly can't say that girl cooks better than I do, 'cause I won't believe it.'

'Are you kidding? She can't even boil beans,' Bordelli lied.

Rosa looked at him with suspicion, then shrugged, grabbed a candle, and went into the kitchen humming a song by Celentano. The domestic squabble seemed to have been averted, but outside was sheer pandemonium. Bordelli took a gulp of cognac and lay back down. His headache was subsiding. He enjoyed lying there motionless, listening to the sounds of the rain and the crashing thunder, with Rosa bustling about in the kitchen, howling the tune to *Pregherò* off key. All that was missing was a warm fireplace. He closed his eyes and thought of Milena. Who knew where she was at that moment? . . .

Gideon recovered his courage and came out from under the sofa, jumped up on to Bordelli's paunch, lay down and started purring. It wasn't quite eleven o'clock. The air filled with an aroma of sautéd onions, carrots, celery . . .

'Put in a lot of hot pepper,' Bordelli said in a loud voice. Suddenly the lights came back on all around.

'Oh no, it was so lovely with the candles!' Rosa cried from the kitchen.

At midnight it was still raining buckets, and the sewers were at their limit. The lightning, however, had receded a bit into the distance. The Beetle was parked some thirty yards from Rosa's front door, near the corner of Via dei Leoni. In that narrow street the roar of the rainfall sounded like the sea during a storm, and in spite of everything, the spectacle had something fascinating about it. The inspector opened the tiny umbrella Rosa had lent him, pressed it down over his head, and made a run for it, but by the time he got inside the car, he was soaked to his underpants. Luckily it wasn't cold outside. He started up the car and drove off, the windscreen wipers struggling uselessly. His mouth still burned from the hot pepper.

He didn't feel like going directly home. He'd thought of something to do, though he wasn't sure it was a good idea. His headache was finally gone, and he didn't even feel very tired. He drove at a snail's pace to Piazza Antinori, still somewhat undecided as to whether he should do the thing or not. The rain kept coming down in torrents, and he couldn't see much, if anything, beyond the nose of the car. He slipped on to Via de' Giacomini with heart racing, and travelled its whole length, taking care not to scrape the tyres against the kerb. Then he turned right on to Via delle Belle Donne, and stopped a few yards down. Leaning forward to look at the windows of Levi's flat, through the sheets of rain he espied some lights and felt a shudder run down his arms. That was the effect the thought of Milena had on him. He was like an adolescent in love for the first time.

'Why are you leaving so early?' Rosa had asked him.

'I can't keep my eyes open.'

'You're not going to see *her*, are you? You seem so addled . . .'

'Oh, come on, I'm going straight home,' he'd said, running a hand over his face to simulate great fatigue.

He parked the Beetle with two wheels up on the pavement. The street was flooded; it looked like a torrent in spate. Holding Rosa's tiny umbrella just over his head, he ran and took shelter inside the great doorway of Levi's building. He was wetter than if he'd fallen into a bathtub. He knew that the best thing would have been to go home and take a nice hot shower, but he didn't always follow common sense. After a moment of indecision, he rang the buzzer and got an electrical shock in his finger. Bloody rain, he thought, looking over at the river of water that was beginning to flood over the kerb and inundate the pavements.

There was no reply. He began to feel like an ass. Protecting his finger with the sleeve of his jacket, he rang again, but the front door didn't open. He waited a while longer. It felt as if he'd been standing for ever in the downpour, like a fool . . . It was too ridiculous. As he turned away to leave, cursing the goddamned spring weather, the lock on the door clicked open. Immediately he regretted having rung . . . The stuff of mental retards . . . Milena wasn't going to like this little surprise one bit, he was sure of it. For a second he thought of running away, then summoned his courage and went inside. Leaning the tiny umbrella against the wall, he headed up the stairs, dripping water everywhere . . . Utter idiocy, he thought to himself.

'Who is it?' Levi's voice called from above.

'Bordelli.'

Levi waited for him in the doorway. He had a strange light in his eyes. One couldn't tell whether he was pleased or upset.

'I hadn't expected to see you, Inspector, in this weather . . . Any big news?' he said, shaking his hand.

'No, no news.'

'Ah, so you've come just to pay us a visit.'

'I guess I'm getting to like you,' said Bordelli, coming inside. Drenched to the bone, he sneezed. Walking through the apartment, he left a stream of water in his wake. Levi showed him into the usual room.

'I'll bring you something to dry yourself with,' he said, heading towards the door. Bordelli thanked him with another sneeze. He then took off his sodden jacket, tossed it aside, and collapsed into an armchair. His hair was still dripping and wetting everything around him. He really had been a bloody idiot to come here. Imagining that Milena was at home and had heard him come in, he felt as ashamed as a thief. On the other hand, the thought that she was there, only a few yards away from him, on the other side of those walls, brought butterflies to his stomach. Rosa was right. He was in a sorry state. He had best get the hell out of there and go home to bed. So he thought, at any rate. But he didn't budge.

Levi returned with a large, scented towel and handed it to the poor wayfarer lost on a stormy night . . . He looked at him with feigned compassion.

'Thanks,' said Bordelli. He rubbed his face and hair for a long time with the towel, to put off the moment of explanation.

'Cognac?' asked Levi.

'Just so you won't have to drink yours alone.'

'That's very kind of you.'

Levi went to get the cognac, filled two glasses, and set the bottle down on the coffee table. Bordelli raised his glass slightly, hinting at a toast, and knocked back a slug of cognac. He immediately felt better.

'Aside from your fondness for us, is there another reason for your visit?' Levi asked.

'Karl Strüffen,' said Bordelli, smiling.

'Ah, I see. You came here at this hour, through the Great Flood, to talk about Karl Strüffen . . .'

'I've been a bit anxious lately.'

'Don't be in too big a hurry, Bordelli. Our friend has hidden himself well, but we'll find him. It's only a matter of time,' said Levi, staring at him and smiling ironically.

'I'm well aware of that. I have a great deal of faith in the White Dove.'

'You need only have a little more patience.'

'I've got plenty of that, too,' said Bordelli. At that moment a telephone rang in another room, but only twice. A second later, Goldberg poked his head round the door. Levi excused himself to the inspector and went to answer the phone, glass in hand. Bordelli refilled his own. The rain was still coming down hard outside. He thought again of Milena and hoped she would come into the room, even though he knew he cut a pretty sorry figure. A fifty-four-year-old man behaving like a child . . . But he wanted to see her face, to hear her voice. He ran a hand over his stubbly face and sat there, staring at a crack in the ceiling with his glass in his hand. The only sound was the rain.

Levi was taking for ever, and the inspector lit a cigarette. Suddenly the door opened and Goldberg came in, took something from a drawer in the filing cabinet, greeted Bordelli with a nod, and went back out without so much as a smile. Maybe he was still sore at him.

Levi returned a few minutes later, excusing himself for having made him wait. He sat down across from him and refilled his glass.

'Milena's not here,' he said out of the blue.

'What's that?' said Bordelli, a little embarrassed.

'She's out of town . . . should be back in a couple of days.'

'Any news about Strüffen?'

Levi calmly took a sip of cognac without taking his eyes off his guest.

'Tell me something, Bordelli. Are you sleeping with her just to extract information?'

'No,' said the inspector, blushing.

'At any rate it'd be a waste of time. Milena will never know a thing about the organisation, even if you marry her . . . Another drop of cognac, Inspector?'

'The last.'

Bordelli left Levi's place at two o'clock, head spinning. It was still raining, though by this point he didn't care if he got wet. He forded the stream and got into his car. Letting the clutch out a bit too quickly, he fairly flew off the pavement. The streets were completely flooded, and the wheels raised great waves of water that crashed against the buildings' walls. While crossing the Ponte alla Carraia, he glanced out over the Arno. It was swollen with muddy water and coursing like a torrent in spate. It was frightening.

He got home, sneezing all the way, tore off his rain-soaked clothes, and threw himself down naked on the bed. He felt like vomiting. He embraced a pillow and dragged his mouth across it, his nostrils filling with the scent of Milena.

After an uneventful morning with no new developments and no hope, Bordelli headed out on foot to have a bite to eat at Da Cesare. He hadn't been back there for two or three days.

As he walked into Totò's kitchen, there was Botta, firing up a skillet.

'Ennio . . . how strange to see you here,' he said, going up to him.

'I passed the test, Inspector, as you can see. And I know all about your habits. Just take a seat and tell me what you want to eat.'

'You decide, Ennio. I trust you.' He patted him on the back and went and sat down on his stool.

As he resumed cooking, Botta appeared to be trying to think of something. He drained a pound of pasta, divided it into three bowls, poured some dense red sauce over each. He put all three on the sill of the serving hatch and called the waiter. After reading the next order, he dumped two packets of spaghetti into a pot of boiling water, stirred them for a second or two, then came over towards the inspector, wiping his greasy hands on his apron, exactly like Totò.

'How about some penne with asparagus, then pork chops made my own special way?'

'Perfect.'

Botta set a flask of red wine in front of him and immediately got down to work.

'And what about that killer, Inspector?'

'We can talk about it after I catch him, Ennio. For the time being I'd rather not hear any mention of it.'

'Shall I put a dash of hot pepper on the pasta?'

'You can even throw in a handful . . . But why don't you tell me a little about Greece in the meantime?'

Botta smiled and gestured as if to say that he could talk about Greece only in a low voice. Bordelli half-closed his eyes conspiratorially and sipped wine as he waited.

The penne with asparagus arrived, and Bordelli discovered he was famished.

'Good,' he said.

'The pork chops I make the way my father taught me: milk, tomato and fennel seeds.'

'Sounds a bit odd to me.'

'Just wait and taste it first, then tell me what you think.'

Botta went back to the cooker and appeared to be having a lot of fun. Every so often he came back to the inspector and whispered a few things about Greece. He'd gone there to give a hand to a Greek friend he'd met in jail some ten years earlier, at Salonika. He was supposed to help him sell fake archaeological artifacts to some rich Germans. Botta was a wizard at transforming counterfeit coins and little home-made vases into ancient objects. They'd worked together for a week in an Athenian basement under Botta's direction, then gone to Piraeus to please the German collectors. It had all come off quite well. The Krauts paid a fortune for a handful of phoney knick-knacks, and Botta pocketed thirty per cent. Returning to Italy, he passed through customs without any problem, hiding the cash in his underpants. After this deal, he could sit tight for a while and perhaps even devote himself to cooking.

'And you're telling these things to a policeman . . .' said Bordelli.

'You should have seen the joy in those Germans' eyes, Inspector . . . They were like children. I felt like their benefactor,' said Botta, pretending to be serious.

'Well, when you put it that way, there's not much I can say . . . And, after all, they *were* German.'

'Precisely,' said Botta, and then he went and put a generous amount of chopped onion in a skillet.

The pork chops arrived enveloped in a cloud of fennel essence. They had an unusual look about them, swimming as they were in a rather liquid, pink sauce. With some misgiving, Bordelli cut a little corner to taste them.

'Didn't you say you trusted me, Inspector?'

'Yes, but . . .' Bordelli said, not knowing what to say. He put the strange thing in his mouth, and before he had even swallowed, he sought out Botta's eyes.

'Damn, that's good,' he said.

'Never trust appearances, Inspector . . . It's just as true for meat as it is for people . . .'

'Listen, I want you to give Totò the recipe. I mean it.'

A few days later, late in the afternoon, Bordelli received a call at the station from Siena Central Police.

'Ciao, Bonechi,' the inspector said, happy to hear from him. But his face immediately changed expression. Piras, sitting in front of him, saw him squirm in his chair.

'Fuck!' said Bordelli, pulling the hair on the back of his neck.

'Another little girl?' Piras whispered. The inspector nodded. Bonechi's voice continued to rattle inside the receiver, as Bordelli stared at the top of his desk in rage.

'What time did it happen? . . . Shit, maybe we could have prevented it! . . . Why didn't you ring us sooner? . . . Of course, now there's no point in it . . . Wait for me there, I'm going to get in the car now and come . . . Meanwhile send someone to that area to ask around, see whether anyone saw anything . . . Where is it, exactly? Give me the phone number too . . .'

Bordelli wrote something down and hung up. Piras was already on his feet.

'Are we sure it was him, Inspector?'

'The girl had a human bite on her belly,' said Bordelli, trying to put on his jacket but continually getting the wrong sleeve.

They left the office in a hurry and raced down the stairs. It was past seven, and the sun had already set a while ago. It wasn't raining, but the sky was overcast and the streets still wet from the rainfall of a few hours earlier. The Beetle clattered like a tramcar, and Piras hung on to the passenger's strap, lacking the courage to protest. On Viale Aleardi, the inspector gripped the steering wheel with his knees and lit a cigarette.

'Don't say anything, Piras. You can open the window, if you like.'

The Sardinian rolled his window down halfway, still watching the street with concern. In Viale Petrarca, Bordelli passed a lorry rather unceremoniously, and the pissed-off driver blasted his horn.

'Did they tell you how it happened?' asked Piras, digging in his heels as if in a bumper car.

'The people live in a fairly isolated house in the country. The little girl had gone to the barn to feed the rabbits. When she didn't return, her mother went out to look for her. And it took her a while to find her . . . The body was behind a stack of wood about a hundred yards from the house.'

'How long ago did it happen?'

'By now it's been over an hour. Her mother didn't call immediately because she was too upset.'

'Fuck!' said Piras.

'We might have been able to catch him,' said Bordelli, biting his cigarette. He turned on to Via Senese and started going uphill. Some fifty yards before Via delle Campora he took his foot off the accelerator. He seemed undecided. He turned to his assistant.

'What do you say, Piras?'

'Let's give it a try . . .'

Bordelli downshifted and, instead of continuing straight towards Siena, he turned right. All of a sudden he wasn't in such a hurry any more. Driving slowly past Villa Serena, they noticed that the first-floor lights were on. The Lancia Flavia was in its place, parked slantwise in the garden. Bordelli drove on and passed by the surveillance van, an old wreck with one flat tyre, which used to belong to the telephone company and still had its name on the outside. When they reached the end of the street, he turned on to Via Metastasio and pulled up to the kerb.

'Wait for me here,' he said to Piras as he got out of the car, tossing his cigarette aside.

There was nobody on the street. There wasn't much lighting and it was hard to see. Bordelli walked calmly towards Rivalta's villa, stopping alongside the police van. He tapped lightly on the metal body four times, and the rear door opened slightly.

'Get in up front, Inspector,' a voice whispered.

Bordelli got in on the driver's side and leaned his neck back against the iron screen.

'Who are you guys?' he whispered.

'Rinaldi and Tapinassi.'

'You're everywhere, Rinaldi . . . Don't you ever rest?'

'I'm not the one who assigns the shifts, Inspector,' Rinaldi whispered back.

'How long has he been at home?' Bordelli asked, looking at the lighted windows of the house.

'Since half past one.'

'Does he often spend the whole afternoon at home?'

'I'd say so.'

'What did he do this morning?'

'He went out at half past nine, came home at eleven, went out again about midday, and came back home again at half one.'

'Did he do anything different from his usual routine?'

'No. We've been communicating with the unmarked cars . . . Has something happened, Inspector?'

'Another little girl, a short while ago.'

'Fuck,' Rinaldi and Tapinassi said in unison. At that moment the first-floor lights went out, and then a window lit up on the ground floor. One could see thick curtains behind the panes.

'Tell everyone else and then clear out, all of you. I'm going,' said Bordelli.

He got out of the van and went back to the Beetle. As soon as he'd closed the door, Piras looked at him with a questioning air. The inspector shook his head.

'I'm afraid we're going to have to forget about Rivalta, Piras.'

'Is he at home?'

'He returned at half past one and hasn't moved since.'

'Fucking hell,' the Sardinian said through clenched teeth.

Bordelli started up the car and made a U-turn. As they drove past Villa Serena they both turned round instinctively to look at the lighted windows. When they pulled up at the stop sign at the bottom of the street, they looked each other in the eye with a strange expression, as if they were both thinking the same thing.

'What do you say, Piras?'

'I'm game.'

'Good,' said Bordelli. He put the car in reverse and backed all the way up to Rivalta's villa. He pulled up beside the kerb, and they both got out. As they approached the gate, they both felt rather strange. Bonechi was waiting for them in Siena, and here they were wasting time, chasing their fantasies. But by this point they had made up their minds to see the thing through. Bordelli rang the bell and put a cigarette between his lips as they waited. He had time to light it and take a few puffs, and still the gate hadn't opened, nor had anyone come to a window. He rang again several times. Still no reply.

'Maybe he's asleep,' said Piras.

'Strange. A few minutes ago he came downstairs.'

'Maybe he's in the shower.'

'Perhaps,' Bordelli muttered.

Inside the house they heard the pendulum clock strike eight. The ground-floor windows were still lit up. They tried ringing the bell again, but still no sign of life. At that moment a light came on upstairs, on the first floor, then went out again a few moments later. Bordelli tossed his cigarette butt aside and attacked the bell, keeping it pressed for at least a minute. But nothing happened.

'Why won't he come to the door?' asked Piras.

'Let's go inside,' said Bordelli.

'How?'

'With the keys.' And the inspector pulled out his break-in device and opened the gate's lock without much difficulty.

'Damn, Inspector,' said Piras in admiration. They crossed the garden at a fast pace, looking all around. Passing the Lancia Flavia, they reached the front door. Bordelli immediately got down to work on that lock as well. He wasn't as skilled as Botta, and it took him a good couple of minutes before he managed to make it give way.

'There we are,' he said, and pushed the door open. The entrance was dark, but halfway down the hallway were two open doors with light shining through.

'Dr Rivalta!' Bordelli yelled.

'Dr Rivalta!' Piras yelled even louder. Nobody answered. Exchanging a glance, they drew their pistols and advanced as far as the first lighted room. It was a dining room. The table was set for one, and on the white tablecloth was a bottle of wine with a corkscrew beside it.

'Anybody home?' Bordelli said, entering the room. There was a strange atmosphere in the place. It was too quiet. Piras had gone ahead down the hall, still calling out Rivalta's name. The inspector went up to the table and glanced at the bottle of wine. Brunello di Montalcino, 1957. All at once he heard some hurried steps and Piras appeared in the doorway. His face was contorted.

'What the hell are you doing, Piras?'

'I went into the room next to this one . . . it was empty . . . there was nobody there . . .'

'So?'

'All of a sudden . . . the light went off.'

Bordelli opened his eyes wide, and his mouth opened by itself.

'What the hell are you saying, Piras?'

'I swear it, Inspector.'

'The bulb must have burnt out . . .' said Bordelli, hollow voiced.

'It's a chandelier with five bulbs, Inspector.'

'Jesus Christ!' said Bordelli, going up to the switch and flipping it. The light remained on.

'Shit, Inspector, that prick has fucked us all royally!'

'Son of a bitch,' said Bordelli. They rushed out of the room and started racing round the house like wolves drawn by blood. They went up to the first floor, where the lights in the darkened rooms didn't work. They lit their way with matches. When they entered a large room, the lights came on by themselves. Bordelli ran a hand over his head, muttering curses to himself. They went back downstairs and continued their search. A few mintues later they noticed a door partly camouflaged by the wallpaper. It was unlocked and led to a staircase. They descended the stairs to a cellar divided into a number of rooms. They began inspecting these and before long found what they were looking for: a complicated yet rudimentary device controlling all the lights in the villa. It was a great tangle of wires connected to a number of different clocks. On the wall was a big switch that almost certainly deactivated the mechanism. Bordelli threw the switch, then shook his head and punched the wall.

'Shit, Piras! What idiots we are!' he said angrily. His knuckles began to bleed.

'It wasn't so easy, Inspector,' Piras mumbled, in a daze.

They started searching the basement rooms for a secret passage leading out of the villa, but they didn't find anything. They went back upstairs. Now that the bloody device had been turned off, the lights functioned normally. Bordelli called up the telephone number Bonechi had given him, to inform him they wouldn't be coming just yet. He also asked him whether there were any new developments.

'No news at all,' said Bonechi.

'I'll call you back later,' said Bordelli, hanging up. He stood there staring into space for a few seconds, then shook his head.

'Let's get down to work, Piras.'

They continued to look everywhere for a secret door or anything at all that might serve as a way to leave the house unseen. Without success. In the end, they gave up. They went into the sitting room, served themselves two glasses of cognac filled to the brim, and sat down on the sofa to wait. They didn't have the courage to speak. All that could be heard in the silence was the sound of their breathing and, in the background, the ticking of the pendulum clock, which seemed to grow louder with each passing minute. Bordelli felt his scalp tingling from impatience. Time was slowing to a standstill.

Then the sudden chiming of the pendulum clock gave them both a start. They looked at each other without speaking, their eyes full of anger over having been had. The clock finished chiming nine o'clock. An air of suspense hung over the room.

A bit more time went by, and then, at a certain point, they heard a dull thud, as if from a closing door, and immediately some weary footsteps in the hallway. They leapt to their feet, hands on their pistols, holding their breath. The steps drew closer, stopped for a moment, then continued. They heard a yawn, and a second later Rivalta entered the room with an extinguished torch in his hand. Seeing the two policemen, he froze. He looked at them both for a few seconds, eyes full of contempt, then smiled haughtily, shrugged, and calmly went and sat down on the sofa. Setting the torch down on the coffee table, he picked up Piras's glass of cognac and took a sip.

'Well, what should we talk about? Cecco Angiolieri?'[17] he asked in a serious tone.

'Been out Siena way, Dr Rivalta?' Bordelli asked, staring at him, images of the little girls' dead bodies flashing through his mind.

'I've been wherever I please,' said Rivalta.

Piras clenched his jaw, eyes full of malice.

'Ingenious lighting system you've got,' said Bordelli.

'I enjoy working with my hands,' said Rivalta.

'How many more were you planning to kill?'

'I don't know what you're talking about,' Rivalta said calmly.

'You know perfectly well,' said Piras, face hard as a rock.

'Oh, do I?' said Rivalta. And as he reached for the cigarette case on the table, Piras pointed his gun at him.

'The boy's nervous, isn't he?' Rivalta said, smiling. He took a cigarette and lit it, blowing the smoke out through his nostrils.

Piras snatched the cigarette from his lips, threw it on the floor and crushed it with his shoe.

'Smoking gets on my nerves,' he said.

'I didn't know you were so impolite,' Rivalta said, amused.

'If it wasn't you, then why did you need to leave the house on the sly?' Bordelli asked with seeming calm, clenching his fists in his pockets.

'I like to play cops and robbers,' said Rivalta, taking another cigarette.

'Where is the secret passage?' asked Piras, increasingly upset.

'Well, if I tell you, then it's not a game any more.' Rivalta lit his cigarette and blew the smoke upwards, making a show of his desire not to bother the young Sardinian.

'Why did you kill them?' Bordelli asked again.

'I'm a bit tired, you'll have to excuse me. I really don't feel like talking just now,' Rivalta said calmly. From that moment on, he didn't say another word. He limited himself to looking the two policemen in the eye and smiling coldly.

In the end Bordelli got fed up, called for a car and turned Rivalta over to two officers, ordering them to take him to headquarters and to keep an eye on him at all times. Then, with Piras's help, he resumed looking for the secret passage. After half an hour of vain attempts, they discovered a hidden door in the tiled wall of the kitchen. They set about looking for the device to open it, and after a brief search Piras discovered a tile on the opposite wall that served as a push-button. The door opened inward with a groan, and behind it lay a passage.

'Shit!' said Piras.

Looking into the darkness through the doorway, Bordelli saw a staircase leading underground.

'Let's go,' he said.

He switched on Rivalta's torch and they began to descend. At the bottom of the stair was a tunnel carved out of the earth and reinforced with wooden framing, as in old mines. One could walk through it standing, and it seemed very long. They advanced slowly, for fear of booby-traps, and every so often saw the silhouettes of large rats scampering away.

'What direction do you think we're going in, Piras?'

'I think we're heading away from the front of the villa, which would be behind us.'

'Doesn't it seem like we're walking uphill?'

'Yes.'

A few minutes later they reached the end of the tunnel, where they encountered an iron door. Luckily it was open. They found themselves in a room with a floor of beaten earth and a vaulted brick ceiling. It looked like a wine cellar, but there were no bottles. At the opposite end was a staircase leading up, at the top of which they found themselves in front of a solid wooden door. It was locked, but there was a button on the wall to the right. The door opened slowly, again inwards, like the other. They went through, as Bordelli shone the torch about the space. It was an almost empty room whose floor was covered with dust. Piras went up to the far wall, turned on the switch, and the light came on.

'I want to see where we are,' said Bordelli. They went down a long corridor full of spider's webs half an inch thick and reached a large door. Opening this, they found themselves in a rather neglected garden. Next to the enclosure wall, under a canopy of sorghum, was a cream-coloured Fiat 600 Multipla, a rather ordinary car that wouldn't have attracted much notice.

They looked up to the house behind it, a small, two-storey villa from the early twentieth century, vaguely art nouveau. After crossing a half-yellowed lawn, they opened the gate and went out on to the street. They were in Via Sant'Ilario, another cross-street of Via Senese, about a hundred yards from Villa Serena. Bordelli shook his head.

'He came and went whenever he pleased.'

'But that doesn't prove that he's the killer,' said Piras, biting his lips.

'Let's go back inside.'

They went back into the house and started inspecting the rooms. There was little furniture, and everything was filthy. It was clear that, aside from the spiders, nobody lived there. In a first-floor room they found a few changes of clothes in a wardrobe. There were also several pairs of shoes, as well as some boots with fresh mud on them. Bordelli lifted one boot with two fingers.

'If the mud is the same as in Siena . . .'

'I'll bet my bollocks it is,' said Piras, smiling wickedly.

★ ★ ★

It was past two o'clock. Rivalta was seated in front of Bordelli's desk, a venomous smile on his lips, ignoring what was happening around him.

Piras sat motionless in front of the typewriter. His face looked tired, his eyes bloodshot. He'd gone to Siena alone to see Bonechi and returned around midnight with a few specimens of mud collected from the ground near the scene of the crime. The girl's name was Chiara Benini; she was seven years old.

The inspector paced back and forth across the room, slowly, a cigarette between his lips and his shirtsleeves rolled up past the elbows. He'd had De Marchi, a forensics technician, dragged out of bed and was expecting the results of the mud analysis at any moment. He'd also rung up Diotivede to inform him that he was almost certain they'd caught the killer and that he was waiting only for the final proof to declare the case officially closed. The pathologist had responded with one word alone, a word he almost never used: 'Fuck.'

'Why did you kill those little girls, Rivalta? And what's the meaning of that bite on the tummy?' Bordelli asked for the umpteenth time, without ceasing his pacing.

Rivalta didn't answer, didn't even look at him, but only spread the four-fingered hand over his thigh and started studying it. He acted as if he were the only person in the room.

'Why do you refuse to speak?' Bordelli asked.

Nothing. No answer, not even a raised eyebrow.

'Do you want a lawyer? It's your right, you know.'

Rivalta kept ignoring him, then began humming a song through his closed mouth. In the silent pauses, Piras dozed in a seated position, hypnotised by the sound of the inspector's steps. His head would bend slowly forward, then fall all at once, and he would wake up with a look of alarm. Bordelli kept on pacing back and forth, increasingly nervous. Suddenly the phone rang, and Piras leapt in his chair. Bordelli ran to pick up. As he'd been hoping, it was De Marchi.

'I've just finished now, Inspector. The mud matches up,' the technician said sleepily, with a furred tongue. Bordelli felt a shiver in his face.

'Go and get some sleep,' he said.

'I can't wait,' said De Marchi.

Bordelli hung up and shot a glance at Piras. Then he walked towards Rivalta and stopped behind his back.

'I'm afraid it's all over for you,' he said.

Rivalta had picked up a pen and was playing with it. He was clicking the tip in and out, and looked as if he was concentrating very hard.

'Why did you kill them?' the inspector asked again.

No reply. Rivalta's thoughts seemed somewhere else entirely. Bordelli put his cigarette out in the ashtray and ran a hand through his hair. He, too, was very tired. He circled round behind the desk and, without sitting down, leaned forward, resting his hands on the wooden desktop. He started staring at Rivalta.

'Tell me why you killed them,' he said yet again, restraining an urge to pummel the man's face. He wanted to know what had driven a man like Rivalta to strangle those little girls, and he realised he wanted to know at any cost. He could feel it becoming an obsession.

Rivalta seemed untroubled, though every so often a vertical furrow appeared on his brow, as if he were thinking of something. He put the pen back in its place, grabbed Casimiro's little skeleton, and couldn't hold back a smile. Bordelli stared hard at him and thought he glimpsed, behind those lively, violent eyes, a crippled soul.

'I'm asking you for the last time . . . Why did you kill those little girls?' he said harshly, practically yelling.

Piras woke up with a start and ran a hand over his face. Bordelli went up to Rivalta again, a strange expression in his eyes. He looked very pissed off, too pissed off, and Piras started to get worried. Rivalta, for his part, did nothing. He was shut up in a world all his own. Then the inspector raised the suspect's chin with one hand and raised the other hand as if about to punch him in the face. Piras shot to his feet and grabbed Bordelli's arm.

'Calm down, Inspector,' he said. Rivalta wasn't the least bit flustered.

'Take him away, Piras,' said Bordelli, lowering his fist, then running his hand through his hair. He went and sat down. Piras grabbed Rivalta by the shoulder.

'Let's go,' he said.

Rivalta calmly put the little skeleton back on the desk and stood up listlessly. He let the Sardinian handcuff him, and without a sound he left the room, towed by Piras.

Bordelli sat there staring at the wall, frowning darkly, an unlit cigarette between his fingers. He simply couldn't accept it. Why did Rivalta kill those children? How much hatred must he have inside him, and why? Dante Pedretti's words came back to him: 'If a wretch kills little girls, there must be, at the source of his crime, an even greater wrong . . .'

After a short spell he heard the sirens of a couple of squad cars leaving the courtyard of Via Zara with tyres screeching. He pressed his eyeballs hard with his fingers. The commissioner's words of congratulation came back to him, and those of the others as well, but none of it gave him any satisfaction.

MONSTER CAPTURED, said the poster for *La Nazione* in big block letters. Mugnai was having trouble holding back the journalists who wanted to talk to Bordelli.

'Calm down! . . . Please, calm down . . . The commissioner will tell you everything you want to know at eight o'clock this evening,' he kept saying, pushing back the herd. But nobody made any move to leave. They all wanted to talk to Inspector Bordelli, to get more details on the arrest, and they wanted to know why he wouldn't show his face.

Bordelli wanted only to be left in peace. The killer had been caught; he had nothing else to add . . . Especially since he didn't know much more than this himself, and it was eating away at him.

Early that morning Rivalta had been examined by a handful of psychiatrists, all of whom judged him to be in full possession of his faculties. For fear he might be killed by other inmates, he'd been put in a solitary confinement cell. Normally, those who attack children come to a bad end in jail. Bordelli still remembered a certain Bonanni, a man with an accountant's face who had raped a ten-year-old girl just after the war. They'd put him in a communal cell. That night, the three men sleeping in the same cell had cut his balls off and let him bleed to death. The guards had heard him screaming endlessly, but paid no attention. It was one of those rare occasions when inmates and warders were in agreement.

The inspector slipped out of the police station through the usual back door, without anyone noticing. There was a bright sun shining, and it felt pretty hot outside. He took off his jacket and unbuttoned his shirt collar. Feeling like taking a walk, he headed towards the trattoria Da Cesare on foot, and in no hurry. There were a great many flies about, and they buzzed round his ears as he walked.

Crossing the Viale Lavagnini, he entered the restaurant, which was packed, as usual. Almost everyone sitting at the tables was avidly reading the newspaper, letting the food on their plates get cold. Bordelli raised a hand in response to Cesare's and the waiters' greetings, which were warmer than usual and full of tacit understanding. Then he slipped into Totò's kitchen.

The moment he saw the inspector, the cook waved a copy of *La Nazione* in the air: MONSTER CAPTURED. He thumped his forefinger against the newspaper with obvious satisfaction.

'You finally caught him, Inspector . . . Lunch is on me today.'

'When did you get back, Totò?'

'Last night,' said the cook, hanging the newspaper from a hook as if it were a placard.

'Get rid of that, Totò, there's no reason to celebrate,' Bordelli said, sitting down.

'Out of the question, Inspector. In my kitchen I hang up whatever I like.'

'Then forget I said anything.'

The inspector noticed that Totò had dark circles under his

eyes, as if he hadn't slept for three straight days, and imagined the long, sleepless nights spent at his dying grandmother's bedside.

'How's your grandmother?' he asked with concern, expecting Totò to trace a cross in the air.

'Ah, the poor thing . . .' the cook said in a loud voice. Then, coming up to Bordelli, he whispered in his ear: 'Actually my grandmother's just fine, Inspector, she'll end up burying us all . . .'

'But wasn't she at death's door?' Bordelli whispered.

'She's never been better, Inspector. Eats like a horse and drinks like a fish. I was just feeling a little homesick, that's all . . . And there was also the feast of the patron saint. But I couldn't very well say that to Cesare . . .'

'So, did you have fun?'

'Hell, Inspector, you have no idea what holidays are like back home. You sing and dance till dawn, you drink like mad and just about anything can happen.'

'Sounds nice . . .' said Bordelli.

'Up here in the north you're all sulkers. You like making sport of others, but you really don't know how to have fun . . . It's like you're afraid of your own feelings, for Chrissakes.'

'Maybe one of these days I'll go down with you to see your grandmother,' said Bordelli.

Totò winked at him in agreement.

'A nice little *ribollita*,[18] Inspector?' he said loudly.

'*Ribollita* it is.'

Totò gave him a slap on the shoulder and went to fill a bowl. He added a drop of olive oil, one fresh hot pepper chopped fine, and a dusting of Parmesan cheese. Then he pulled out a large goblet, filled it with red wine, and put everything in front of Bordelli.

'Today I want you to be served properly, as you deserve,' he said.

'I could have caught him a lot sooner, Totò . . . Two little girls would still be alive. I was a complete bollock-brain,' said Bordelli, noticing two greasy fingerprints on the belly of the glass.

'What do you mean?' asked Totò, raising his eyebrows.

'I mean that the killer made a fool of me . . . He had a lighting system in his house that turned the lights on and off when he wasn't at home.'

'No!'

'The newspapers don't know this yet.'

'Totò never talks,' said the cook, proud to be let in on the secret.

'I let myself be fooled like a shitbrain . . .' Bordelli persisted.

'And why did he kill them, Inspector?'

'That's what I want to know! But I couldn't get him to tell me anything.'

'Who the hell knows what someone like that's got in his head . . .'

'Well, it seems nobody will ever know, Totò, and that's exactly what I'm having such a hard time swallowing.'

'The important thing is that you caught him, Inspector, the rest is just bollocks,' said the cook, shrugging. He went back to the cooker to do his job. He was particularly full of energy that day, perhaps because of the spring. He was handling the fish and steaks almost violently.

After the *ribollita* came the rabbit stew. Bordelli was nervous. He ate frantically and knocked back the wine as if it were water, watching the columns of smoke rising over the pots and pans on the stove. Totò cut a steak practically two inches thick, availing himself of the cleaver to cut through the bone, and threw it on to the red-hot grill. Then he returned to Bordelli and poured himself a glass of wine.

'You know what, Inspector? If I was a cop, I'd probably shoot certain people right between the eyes without a second thought.'

'It's a good thing you're a cook, Totò.'

'Have I ever told you about that guy back home who killed two twin girls in '55?'

'I think so . . .' said Bordelli, hoping he would drop it.

'He'd just escaped from the insane asylum and ran across the little girls playing in the woods . . . One was ten years old, the other was twelve . . .'

'Rather odd for twins, no?' said Bordelli. The cook froze for a moment, then waved his hand in the air.

'Never mind, Inspector . . . That madman raped them both, then chopped them into little pieces with an axe and dumped them in a river. He was found a few hours later, sitting in a field, drunk on grappa, his clothes soaked with blood. When they put the handcuffs on him he started crying like a baby . . . He said they should lock him up and throw away the key, and if they cut his head off, that would be even better. "If I get out again, I'll do it again, I can't help myself," he kept blubbering. So they locked him back up in the loony bin, and a few days later they found him dead with his head split open. He'd killed himself bashing his head against the wall . . . Bah! There's just one thing I wonder about all this: why the hell does the good Lord bother to create such people . . .?'

'A long time ago, some saint said that God always has his reasons, even if we can't understand them,' said Bordelli.

'So why doesn't He come and explain them to us? . . . Excuse me just a second, Inspector . . .' The steak was asking to be turned over. Totò stuck a fork in it and flipped it. Then he grabbed a handful of juniper berries and threw them on the hot coals. There was a crackling sound, and for a few seconds the steak was enveloped in dense smoke.

'Would you like a piece of this, Inspector?' Totò shouted, picking up the smoking steak.

'Another time, thanks.'

'A bit of pecorino?'

'I'm happy just as I am.'

Totò shrugged his shoulders, put the steak on a serving platter and summoned the waiter by slapping his hand against the wall. Immediately a hand poked through the serving hatch and carried away the three-pound slab of meat.

'How many people is that for?' Bordelli asked.

'Two,' said the cook.

'I would have thought at least four.'

'A little grappa, Inspector?'

'Just a drop.'

Totò filled the glass to the brim, as always, then raced to drain two pots of pasta. When he returned, he shot Bordelli a cocky, southern glance.

'To change the subject, Inspector . . . From what I'm told, that Bottarini didn't do such a bad job in the kitchen,' he said, trying to summon a magnanimous expression.

'I told you he knew what he was doing,' Bordelli ribbed him.

Totò tried to force a smile, but managed only to make an ugly face.

'Apparently Cesare wants to hire him for Saturdays and Sundays on a steady basis,' he said, feigning indifference.

'Great. That way the two of you can trade secrets.'

'Yes, yes . . . Very nice . . . But tell me something, what's this about the pork chops with milk and fennel?'

'There's tomato, too.'

'Tomato, too . . . Mmmm, my goodness!' said Totò, clearly pulling the inspector's leg.

'You really ought to try it, Totò.'

'Of course, Inspector! Milk and tomato sauce . . . it must be a masterpiece!' said the cook, coming towards the inspector with a malignant smile.

'Just taste it, Totò, then we can talk about it.'

'Some muck I won't even smell . . .'

'Listen, Botta even knows a lot of international recipes,' said Bordelli, who was amusing himself trying to provoke him. Totò opened his eyes wide.

'So what? A whole lot of people like to pretend they're American, too . . . They even made a song about it!¹⁹ But it certainly doesn't mean the Americans are better than we are . . .'

'What's the matter with you, Totò? Jealous?'

The cook poked himself in the chest.

'Me, jealous? Are you joking, Inspector? Why should I be jealous? Of what, anyway? Of a chop with tomato sauce and four bits of foreign slop on it?'

Bordelli finished his grappa and got up. He'd eaten and drunk like a pig, and his head was spinning.

'Don't get upset, Totò, you're still the best,' he said, seeing that his friend had taken childish offence.

'Now you're exaggerating,' said Totò, barely unable to restrain a grin of satisfaction.

'*Ciao, bello*, thanks for lunch.'

'It was my pleasure, Inspector. And be sure to come back tomorrow: I'm gonna make squid *in zimino*.'[20]

He sat up and stuffed a pillow behind his back. Then he lit a cigarette. The cool night air blew in through the open window. It must have been about 4 a.m. There was deep silence. Milena lay beside him, naked under the sheets, eyes still beaming with pleasure. She kept one hand on his belly and played around with all the hair.

'You braved the deluge just to see me . . .' she said, smiling faintly. Her hand climbed Bordelli's chest and lightly grazed a nipple.

'Oh, go on . . .' he said, seeming annoyed.

'What's wrong, Mr Inspector?' asked Milena, removing her hand.

'Nothing.'

'You seem strange.'

'I've got a bee in my bonnet.'

'Why won't you relax?'

'Because I've got a bee in my bonnet . . .'

'Give me a kiss,' said Milena, trying to pull him down, but he didn't move.

'Tell me what's wrong,' she said, shaking him gently. Bordelli had a tired face and deep wrinkles under his eyes.

'Why did he kill them?' he murmured, staring into space.

'Not that again . . . Isn't it enough that you caught him?' she said, poking his belly button.

'I want to understand,' said Bordelli, blowing smoke upwards. He could feel Milena's breast against his thigh, but not even her smooth, soft skin was able to distract him from his obsession. Milena tried to pull him towards her again, but he was as stiff as a broom. He couldn't stop thinking about Rivalta and the four little girls. He seemed trapped in a world all his own. At a certain point Milena lost patience, got out of bed and folded her arms across her breasts. She was naked but moved as if she wasn't.

'Look, Inspector . . . the killer is locked up in jail and will never kill again. What do you care about the rest?' she asked with great irritation.

'What's the matter with you, Milena?'

'I don't understand you,' she said, throwing her hands up. She seemed quite angry.

'Calm down,' said Bordelli, his eyes wandering down to Milena's naked breasts, which were as beautiful as those on a Greek statue.

'I just wonder why you're so fixated on this!' she said, more and more upset.

'And I wonder why you're getting so upset about it.'

'You're morbid.'

'I can't help it.'

'I really don't understand you,' she said, turning towards the window. She had a beautiful bottom, and two long legs that sprang up from the ground like gushing fountains. Bordelli fell silent for a moment, to admire all that beauty. Then he crushed his cigarette in the ashtray and pulled out another.

'I'm sorry, Milena, you're right. I'm a bit obsessed about this. But that man is not your typical madman; he's in full possession of his faculties. He knows exactly what he's doing, he lives a normal life among his fellow men, he's rich, he's intelligent, he wants for nothing . . . So why the hell does he decide one day to start killing little girls? I want to know. Does that seem so strange to you?'

'I'm going to take a shower,' she said, and she left the room without turning round. Bordelli thought again that he'd never seen a pair of legs like hers before. And he'd never met a woman like her, either, with eyes like hers or a head like hers. There was something special about Milena, she exuded life from every pore in her body, even when she was sad or cross.

Hearing the sound of the shower, he got up out of bed. He went into the bathroom naked and slipped into the shower alongside Milena. She started to rub the soap over his body and massage him.

'Are you going to relax?' she asked.

'I'm trying.'

'Let me help you . . .' And Milena got down on her knees in front of him and started to make love to him with her mouth. He caressed her wet head as he watched her, but the same questions kept popping up in his head: Why did Rivalta kill those little girls? Why did he bite them like that? What mechanism had ceased to function in his brain?

In the end Milena gave up, stood back up and resumed washing herself.

'Sorry,' said Bordelli.

'Never mind,' she said, cross again. She got out of the shower and started drying herself in front of the mirror. Along with everything else, she had a beautiful pair of feet, long and slender.

'We won't be able to see each other for a while,' she said, rubbing her head with the towel.

'How long is "a while"?'

'I don't know. I'll get in touch as soon as I can.'

'Is it to do with Strüffen?'

'Among other things.'

Bordelli put his head under the jet of warm water and closed his eyes.

'Are you going to stay a while or are you leaving now?' he asked.

'What would you prefer?'

'Can we sleep together?'

'I can't tonight,' she said, going out of the bathroom.

★ ★ ★

'Inspector, there's a woman asking for you,' said Mugnai, sticking his head into Bordelli's office.

'You mean *a lady*, Mugnai.'

'Isn't it the same thing?'

'Never mind . . . What's her name?'

'Giovanna Benini.'

'Bring her up,' said Bordelli, springing to his feet.

'I'll be right back,' said Mugnai, seeing the inspector's impatience.

Giovanna Benini was the mother of the girl killed in the Sienese countryside. Bordelli had never seen her before, and had seen her name only in passing in the reports, after Rivalta had already been arrested.

A few minutes later Mugnai knocked and opened the door without waiting. The woman walked slowly into the room, dripping rainwater from her overcoat. She was quite carelessly dressed, with a kerchief knotted tightly under her chin, and her face was etched with fatigue. She must have been at least thirty.

'Please sit down, Signora Benini,' said Bordelli, gesturing towards the chair.

'I prefer to remain standing,' the woman said in a whisper.

'I have no words to express . . .' Bordelli stammered, feeling inadequate. He had never been able to utter anything appropriate at moments like these.

'I've come to ask a favour of you, Inspector.'

'I'm happy to do whatever I can,' said Bordelli, pleased not to have to say any other rubbish. The woman was biting her lip, and her head was trembling slightly.

'I want to see the face of the man who killed my daughter,' she said in a single breath, staring at him with two small, bloodshot eyes. Bordelli shook his head and put a hand on her shoulder.

'Signora Benini . . . Why do you want to do a thing like that?' he said.

'I want . . . him . . . to see what a state I'm in,' she said, her voice breaking.

Bordelli sighed. 'I don't think it's a good idea.'

The woman started crying and covered her face with her hands.

'I can't believe it . . . I can't . . .'

'Do sit down, please . . . Would you like a glass of water?' asked the inspector, trying to lead her towards the chair. The woman embraced him, sobbing, her face pressed up against his shirt. She started whimpering something through her teeth, but it was incomprehensible. Bordelli didn't know what to say, and waited patiently for the woman to get it out of her system. Moments later, she raised her head, pulled out a handkerchief and wiped her eyes.

'I'm sorry . . .' she said.

'Don't you want to sit down?'

She shook her head and pressed the handkerchief to her mouth.

'If Friedrich was still here, this would never have happened . . . Never . . .' she said, shaken by another sob.

'Was he Chiara's father?' Bordelli asked, distracted by a thought that had begun buzzing in his brain like a great big fly.

'Yes . . . he died only a few months ago . . . We were supposed to get married in September,' the woman whined.

'He wasn't Italian, I take it?'

'He was German, from Cologne,' the woman mumbled, eyes full of despair.

'How did it happen?'

'An accident . . .'

'I'm sorry,' said Bordelli, looking thoughtful. The fly kept kept buzzing in his head, but he hadn't yet determined what species of fly it was. The woman grabbed one of his arms with both hands.

'Let me see that man; I want to see his face,' she said.

'I don't think that's possible,' said Bordelli.

'I beg you . . .'

'I can't.'

'I want to look him in the eye and ask him why he did it,' she whispered, rolling her eyes.

'What was that?' said Bordelli, staring into space. The fly had suddenly landed and turned into a suspicion that demanded to be clarified at once.

'Why did he kill my child? . . . I want him to look me in the eye and tell me,' the woman insisted, bursting into tears again.

'I'm sorry, Signora Benini, but I really don't think I can help you.'

'He killed my little girl . . . I want to look him in the eye and tell him—'

'I really can't, I'm sorry,' Bordelli interrupted her in a decisive tone.

Signora Benini took it badly, biting hard into her lip.

'I'm sorry to have disturbed you, Inspector,' she muttered, and without another word she flung open the door and went out. Bordelli let her go; he couldn't do anything for her. He went and stood in the doorway, waited for her to disappear down the stairs, then locked himself in his office. He sat down at his desk and scratched his head a long time, just like a monkey. Then he suddenly started rifling through the papers scattered across his desk and finally found what he was looking for. He picked up the telephone and dialled a number.

'Signora Bini, this is Inspector Bordelli.'

'Hello,' said Sara's mother in a thin little voice.

'Am I disturbing you?'

'Nothing can disturb me any more, Inspector.'

'You have to be strong,' said Bordelli, knowing how meaningless his words were.

'I'm glad you arrested him,' the woman muttered.

'If only we'd caught him sooner . . .'

'I feel sorry for the man,' she said without hatred.

'Signora Bini, I'd like to ask you something.'

'Go right ahead.'

'Was Sara's father German?' the inspector asked, holding his breath.

'Yes . . . Why do you ask?' she said.

Bordelli felt a shudder run down his neck.

'Nothing important . . . I'm sorry, signora, but why hadn't your daughter taken her father's surname?'

'At first she did . . . Up until a few months ago, Sara was called Isphording, but last year my husband and I decided to go to City Hall and try to have it changed to Bini.'

'And why is that?' asked the inspector, his mind already elsewhere.

'Sara still didn't know anything about her real father. She was going to start school in October, and we didn't want her to find out that way. We thought we would tell her everything in a few years, but wanted to wait for the right moment.'

'I understand.'

'We ran into some problems at the register office and began to think we weren't going to manage, or at least not in time for October. Then, with the help of a friend who works at City Hall, we finally managed . . . Though, as you can see, it turned out to be pointless . . .'

'I'm sorry,' Bordelli said, embarrassed to say something so banal.

'Why do you want to know these things, Inspector? Is there some new development in the case?' she asked, without any real interest.

'It would take too long to explain . . . Thank you so much, signora. That'll be all for now.'

Bordelli hurriedly said goodbye to the woman and hung up. He sat there for a few minutes staring at his hand on the receiver, then picked it up again. He rang Carla Panerai, Valentina's mother, and asked her the same question . . .

'Mugnai, send me Piras, would you?' said Bordelli, sounding rather agitated.

'Straight away, Inspector.'

While waiting he started pacing back and forth with an unlit cigarette between his lips. He'd slept very little the night before, because of Milena, and felt a bit groggy. His footsteps on the grit-tile floor echoed in his head like hammer-blows.

About ten minutes later the door opened and Piras came in.
'You were looking for me, Inspector?'

'Where the hell were you?'

'I was in Rinaldi's office, taking care of the—'

Bordelli cut him off with a wave of the hand.

'Piras . . . all four of those little girls had German fathers.'

'Holy shit!' said the Sardinian, jaw dropping.

Bordelli glanced at his watch. It was almost half past two.

'Let's go and see Rivalta,' he said.

They went out at once, got into the Beetle and headed straight for the Murate prison. It was still raining hard. Bordelli was nervous and continually moved his hands about the steering wheel. He couldn't wait to face Rivalta and tell him point blank what he had discovered. He was hoping to make him talk, to wrench something out of him as to the motive for those murders.

Entering the prison, they walked down the corridors in the company of a listless warder. Bordelli felt goosebumps along his arms, as he did whenever he thought he was getting close to a revelation. It seemed to take for ever to get to Rivalta's cell. The sound of their footsteps and the gates opening and closing echoed through the ancient vaults of the former convent. Water dripped on to the flooring from some unseen point in the vaults.

At last the warder stopped. He opened the cell door, took one step inside and yelled: '*Oh, fuck!*'

Rivalta was hanging from the bars over the window, a piece of metal wire looped round his neck. His eyes bulged out of their sockets and his mouth was hanging open. His tongue dangled all the way down to his chin, and was as black as spoilt meat. It was obviously not a suicide. His feet were more than a yard off the floor, and there was no sign of a chair or stool anywhere around him.

'Shit,' said Bordelli, looking at Rivalta's face.

'I guess that's the end of that,' said Piras, gesturing horizontally with his hand.

'Come, Piras.'

They asked the prison governor for a free room and got down

to work. In a little over an hour they interrogated all the guards on the cell block, one after another, and then the prisoners in charge of services. Not surprisingly, nothing of any use emerged. Nobody had seen or heard anything. Rivalta had been hanged by ghosts.

'What do you make of all this, Piras?' the inspector asked as they got into the car, his head aching. It was raining much less than before.

'I don't know what to say, Inspector. The first thing I thought was that he was killed by other inmates, obviously with the tacit approval of the guards . . . But what's strange is the way . . .'

'Normally in these cases there's a lot more blood,' said Bordelli, setting the car in motion.

'He wasn't even beaten,' Piras noted, curling his lips.

Bordelli dropped Piras off at the station and went to look for a quiet place to have a drink in peace. He wanted a moment alone to reflect. On top of all the things he hadn't yet managed to understand, now there was also the murder of Davide Rivalta: Why had he been eliminated? And by whom? He didn't understand a bloody thing any more.

After flinging open the door, the inspector went and sat down on a stool. Once he had a glass in front of him, he lit a cigarette. Only then did he notice that there was a guy beside him in jacket and tie, with a gaunt, bony face, who was staring at him. Bordelli glanced at him distractedly and immediately forgot about him. He wanted to be left alone so he could think.

'If I may . . .?' the man said, extending a white hand, thin as a blade, towards him. Bordelli looked at him without saying anything.

'The name's Mario Gallori, pleasure . . . I'm just passing through,' the man continued, hand still extended. He had a nasal voice and a strong northern accent.

Bordelli sighed and shook those cold fingers, smiling formally.

'Pleasure,' he said without a whit of pleasure.

'I sell washing machines . . . What do you do for a living?'

Mario Gallori had it written all over his face that he worked hard and wasn't the least bit satisfied.

'I'm sorry, but I want to be left alone,' said Bordelli.

'I didn't mean to bother you, sir, it was just to have a little chat . . . I'll just finish my beer and be on my way.'

The inspector's thoughts were utterly confused, and he continued to ignore the washing-machine man, who was tapping his fingers on the bar.

'You know how I feel? It's as if I were some kind of revolutionary . . . I'm one of those people who are helping this country to change,' he said in all seriousness.

'Of course you are,' said Bordelli, hoping it would end soon. He emptied his glass and then raised it in the air to order another grappa. Gallori pulled his stool closer.

'I can tell that you don't believe me . . . Do you realise what the invention of the washing machine means for Italian society?' he said, lightly squeezing the inspector's elbow.

'It means nobody will wash their clothes by hand any more,' said Bordelli, making a gesture of thanks to the bartender, who had refilled his glass. Gallori shook his head, waited for the bartender to leave, and then continued.

'That's the most visible change, but it certainly doesn't end there. With the invention of the washing machine, women will no longer have to spend their mornings slapping and wringing clothes at the wash-house or the sink, because that backbreaking work will have been taken care of . . . Do you realise what that could mean?'

Bordelli started cursing himself for coming into this bar. He had no desire to talk, especially about washing machines.

'Eh? Have you any idea, sir?' Gallori insisted.

'I don't know, I'd have to think about it.'

'No need to bother, I'll tell you myself. It's rather simple, after all, once you give it a little thought . . . I travel a great deal, I've got a Lancia Appia . . . it's parked right outside . . . But it's not mine, it belongs to the business . . . I could never afford a car like that . . . In short, I work like a dog and earn nothing . . . But never mind those things . . . What I really mean is . . . do you know how many kilometres I drive in a week?'

'How many?' Bordelli sighed, hoping to get rid of the guy in a hurry. The salesman held up two very long fingers.

'Two thousand. Sometimes even twenty-two hundred . . . With an average of ninety hours at the wheel per month. And do you know what I do when I'm driving?'

'What do you do?'

'It's quite simple . . . When I'm driving I think. And when somebody thinks, what happens? Because, sooner or later, *something* happens . . . What do *you* think happens?'

Bordelli stared at him, looking bored and hoping the man might suddenly understand the situation and stop talking. But the salesman gestured to the bartender to bring him another beer and then loosened his necktie.

'Anyway, I said to myself, the washing machine is a wonderful invention, that's what everyone says – you said it yourself, just now, I think . . . But with so much less work to do, and so much more time on their hands, women will have a lot more opportunity to set their little minds a-whirring, *to think*, that is . . .' he said with a snigger. But he hadn't finished yet.

'. . . and if women start thinking, what do you think that means?'

'It means something will happen,' said Bordelli, at the limit of his tolerance. The salesman grabbed the inspector's arm.

'Very good! I can see you're starting to get the idea . . . But do you know *what* will happen once women start thinking? Are you able to imagine it? Well, I'll tell you what will happen: overnight the country will change from *this* . . . to *this*,' he said, holding his hand palm down in the air and then flipping it over.

Bordelli stared at his glass of grappa with a wicked expression, determined not to say another word. Gallori regained his breath and snapped his fingers.

'Yes, that is precisely what will happen . . . And now you will ask me: will it be a change for the better or for the worse? What do *you* think? For the better or for the worse?'

The barman brought Gallori his beer, chuckling under his moustache. He could clearly see that Bordelli was at the end of his tether. The salesman took a sip and resumed talking.

'I've thought a great deal about this, you know . . . Ninety hours a month, watching the road roll under my tyres, you get the picture . . . And you know what I've realised? It will change for the worse, that's what. In fact, it'll be a disaster. And now you'll ask me why . . .'

Bordelli downed his glass in a single gulp, without the slightest enjoyment, then put his money on the bar and stood up.

'Signor Gallori, it's been a pleasure,' he said. Gallori stood up with him, shook his hand and clung to it as he kept on talking.

'The reason is quite simple . . . I don't read much because I annually spend forty-five per cent of my time sitting in my car . . . Which is hardly a drop in the ocean, you know, do the maths yourself . . . But in my youth, I studied a bit . . . not that it was my great passion, of course . . .'

The inspector managed to free his hand, made a last gesture of goodbye and, as the salesman kept rambling on, headed for the door. He stopped for a moment in the doorway to turn up the collar of his jacket, and before he went out, he heard Gallori's voice carrying on behind him.

'I didn't much like studying, but I did read some pretty good stuff in the end . . . Like everyone else, no? What do you think?' At this point the salesman was talking to the bartender.

Bordelli got into the Beetle feeling pretty cheesed off. It had stopped raining and the sky was clearing, but a light wind had risen. When he got home the sun hadn't yet set; the days were getting longer. He stripped off his damp clothing and took a hot shower to relax.

The bedroom stank of cigarette smoke. He went and opened

the window, then immediately lit a cigarette. The air outside was saturated with spring. The sky was clear, and the swifts were screeching. He leaned forward with his elbows on the windowsill and tried to put all the thoughts dancing in his head in order. But he was too tired. He finished his cigarette and dropped it into the street.

Having no desire to budge from his office, he had asked Mugnai to go down to the bar in Via San Gallo and fetch him two panini and a beer, and was now chewing and swallowing without paying much attention to the flavours. But he wasn't missing much. He'd slept little and poorly. He'd also dreamt about one of the dead little girls, who was walking along the edge of a chasm.

There was a knock at the door, and Piras came in and stood in front of the desk.

'What is it?' said Bordelli, noticing a strange twinkle in the young man's coal-black eyes.

'You won't poke fun at me, Inspector?'

'That depends.'

'Tonight I'm going out with Sonia.'

'Ah, so you've finally succeeded . . . But why are you telling me?'

'Because I'm pleased.'

'What about this business of Sardinians being so surly and reserved?'

'Bollocks.'

'Well, break a leg, Piras. Come back safe and sound.'

'I'll give it everything I've got, Inspector.'

Piras left with eyes sparkling, and Bordelli finished eating his panini. He opened the beer bottle with his house keys and lit a cigarette. Sonia and Piras. One could only imagine the sort of mischief a Sicilian and a Sardinian might cook up together.

Early that afternoon an envelope for Bordelli had been hand-delivered to the station by a very tall man who, based on Mugnai's description, seemed in every way to have been

Goldberg. Inside was a sheet of paper, unsigned, with a couple of typewritten lines on it: *Our friend is waiting for you in his villa at Fiesole. Don't keep him waiting.* And that was all. Bordelli put on his jacket, got into the Beetle and headed off to Fiesole without telling anyone.

He pulled up in front of Karl Strüffen's villa. As the gate giving on to the road was wide open, he drove into the garden and parked amidst the marble statuettes and flowerless earthenware pots. There was a bright sun overhead. A warm wind was blowing, laden with pollen, and a great many bumblebees buzzed in the air. As usual, the shutters were all closed.

As he approached the villa he noticed that the front door was ajar. Pushing it open, he went inside, pistol drawn. The lights were all on. He advanced slowly and, after passing through the vestibule, entered a rather long hallway. There was a nice smell of old furniture in the air. Farther ahead on the left was a great glass door thrown wide open. It led to a vast drawing room illuminated by two crystal chandeliers full of light bulbs. He went in without making a sound. There were a number of tiger skins on the floor, and suits of armour from various epochs lined up against one wall. It was all very grandiose. At the far end of the room was an armchair turned round to face a great stone fireplace, with a head of white hair sticking out, visible from the back. Bordelli approached, pistol cocked, holding his breath. He circled slowly round the armchair, but he'd already understood. He lowered his pistol and heaved a deep sigh. The man was Strüffen, of course, and he was obviously dead. His tongue was hanging out, his eyes half open, and there were rope marks round his neck. He'd been hanged, in keeping with the style of the White Dove. Between his contracted fingers was an envelope with two sheets of paper inside. One was handwritten: a confession to the murder of Casimiro Robetti, signed by Strüffen. It was quite detailed and described the whole affair pretty much the way Bordelli had imagined it. The second was typewritten and unsigned. It said:

Dear Inspector,
As you can see, I've kept my word. You've got what you wanted.
But no one condemned at Nuremberg can escape his sentence.

'The son of a bitch,' Bordelli said aloud. He couldn't help but smile. Pulling out his matches, he went and burned Levi's note in the fireplace. Then he returned to the villa's entrance hall and phoned the station to send for a squad car and ambulance, telling them there was no hurry.

He went out into the garden to smoke a cigarette and looked out over the balustrade that gave on to the olive grove. Another year and the ivy covering the buttresses would reach the top of the wall. Sighing, he looked up at the hills in the distance ahead, covered with forest . . . The Strüffen case had finally been solved.

It was just four o'clock, the sun still high in the sky. Only a buzz of insects marred the silence. Dropping his cigarette butt to the ground, he went back inside the villa and started wandering calmly from room to room.

In one room he found a billiard table. He grabbed a cue from the rack and took a couple of shots. In the absolute silence, he liked the crisp sound the balls made when striking one another. But he'd never played very well. Laying the cue down on the green felt, he resumed his wandering about the house.

The kitchen was vast and had a small door at one end that led to a large pantry full of wine bottles. He started reading the lables. It wasn't just any old wine . . . Saint-Julien, Margaux, Saint-Emilion, Clos Vougeot, Pouilly Fumé, Chambertin, Montrachet, Chateauneuf du Pape, Sauternes and, naturally, champagne. The goddamned French had created a heaven on earth, and not only at Cluny.

Continuing his little tour he found himself in front of a seventeenth-century glass-fronted cabinet full of liqueurs. As he opened it he smelled a lovely scent of old wood. The labels were from all the great houses, but he started looking for that cognac he hadn't yet had a chance to taste. He found several bottles of it and picked one up: *Cognac de Maricourt, 1913*. It had been made over fifty years before, when he was barely three years old. He held the bottle up against the light. The cognac had a magnificent colour. On a lower shelf he found a proper glass for it. Leaving the fine cabinet open, and holding the bottle by the neck, he returned to the room where Strüffen's dead body sat in the armchair. He dropped on to a rather uncomfortable sofa opposite the dead Nazi and wondered who all those bottles belonged to now . . . To the Italian government, the French government, or the White Dove?

He opened the bottle, poured some cognac respectfully into the glass, and took a sip. Diotivede was right. It was a master-piece. He raised the glass in the direction of Karl Strüffen.

'Regards to Adolf,' he said.

As he drank, the memory of a night in April of '44 came back to him. He was inside an old farmhouse with Tonino and Respighi a few hundred yards from the German lines. The moon was almost full and managed to light up the space enough so they could see one another's faces. Tonino was, as usual, talking about girls. In a moment of distraction, he took a drag of his cigarette just as he was passing in front of the window. The sharp, dry sound of a gunshot rang out in the distance and a split second later the windowpane exploded into splinters. Tonino felt the bullet graze the back of his neck and instinc-tively fell to the ground, dodging by an eyelash the second bullet, which smashed into the wall.

Then silence returned.

'Fuck!' said Tonino, crawling towards the wall. He ran a hand through his hair and saw that there was a little blood. He'd been damn lucky.

The sniper fired two more shots in rapid succession into the hole of the window, for no reason. It was a real nuisance.

'What should we do, Commander?' asked Tonino.

'Let me think . . .'

Moments later Bordelli told Respighi to stay in that room and to try in some way to draw the sniper's fire for a few minutes.

'I'm going upstairs . . . Just take care not to get yourself killed,' he said.

'Thanks for the advice, Commander. I hadn't thought of that,' said Respighi, sneering.

Bordelli went out and Respighi calmly tied a white rag round the end of a stick and started waving it in front of the window. The sniper took the bait, and the bullets came crashing into the room. It was fun.

Bordelli had gone upstairs, into a completely dark space. Kneeling down beside a window, he glanced outside from behind the wall. Every time the Kraut fired, he saw a white flash on the dark hillside opposite. He gently set his machine gun on the windowsill and, with the help of a chair, he managed, with patient diligence, to wedge it in place with the barrel pointing directly at those flashes of light. He left everything just like that, and then went to get some sleep with the others. The following morning he awoke at dawn. The other two were still asleep. He went upstairs and, crawling across the floor, went and crouched beside his machine gun. Taking care not to move it, and without even aiming, he made it fire a short burst. There was no return fire. He waited a few seconds, then tossed his beret in the air. A shot rang out in the valley, and a bullet splintered the window frame. He fired another burst, and a few seconds later two bullets slammed into the wall. It seemed there wasn't a bloody thing to be done. Perhaps the sniper was too far away. Bordelli fired another burst, then immediately another, longer one. Tonino and Respighi came up, flattening themselves against the wall.

'What's going on, Commander?'

'I was hoping to get him,' said Bordelli.

They waited a little while longer, but everything remained quiet. Bordelli tried tossing his beret into the air again, but the Kraut had nothing more to say about it. Maybe he'd been killed. After nearly an hour of silence, all three of them went outside to see what was happening. They had to be extremely careful. If the sniper was still at his post, it was like inviting him to take a little target practice. They started to climb up the hillside, hiding behind tree trunks, but no shots were fired. When they were halfway up the slope, they found the classic cement pillbox with the narrow slit for firing. The door was open, but all was silent. They didn't even hear a fly buzz. They approached with great care, ready to open fire, but there was no need. On the floor of the sentry box lay the lifeless bodies of three German soldiers, their faces disfigured. Bordelli slung his machine gun back over his shoulder and shook his head. Three shots, three bull's-eyes. At the country fairs he used to go to as a child, he would have won a piece of panforte.

That evening there was pandemonium at the station. A great many journalists had come from all over, even from Rome, all thirsting for details about the monster murdered in his jail cell and the ex-Nazi found dead in a villa in Fiesole. Mugnai was going crazy.

Concerning the Strüffen affair, the inspector – since he'd decided not to reveal to anyone that the old Nazi had been executed by the White Dove – pretended to be as stumped as everyone else by the incomprehensible murder.

Commissioner Inzipone was quite serene. True, Rivalta had been assassinated by unknowns, but in the final analysis he was only a murderer, and the case of the little girls had been solved, after all. As for the strange case of the hanged Nazi and the confession found in his hands . . . well, he really wasn't too worried about it. The important thing was that they had success-fully concluded their investigations. The rest was all detail.

Piras, on the other hand, was agitated. He was trying in every way possible to understand, not allowing himself a moment's rest. Seeing that Bordelli wasn't troubling himself with too many questions, he sensed that the inspector knew a great deal more than he was letting on, and he started giving him strange looks. He realised, however, that it wasn't time yet for explanations, and so he decided, for the moment, to leave him in peace. Round about nine o'clock he took leave of Bordelli, a smile on his lips, and dashed off to see the beautiful Sicilian girl.

Half an hour later, Bordelli slipped secretly out of the station and went to get his Beetle where he had left it, far from the journalists' reach, in a side street about a hundred yards from Via Zara. He drove placidly towards the centre of town, then parked in Piazza Antinori. Calmly getting out of the car, he lit a cigarette and slowly made his way to Via delle Belle Donne, all the way to Levi's front door. After a moment of indecision, he tossed aside his half-smoked cigarette and rang the buzzer. He was almost certain that nobody would reply, but the lock clicked open almost at once. He climbed the stairs in a rush and found Milena standing at the door.

'I was expecting you,' she said. She seemed strange, too serious.

'What's going on?' Bordelli asked. Milena didn't answer. She gestured to him to come in, then closed the door and walked down the hallway. The inspector followed her into the room in which he had always talked to Levi. It was empty. There wasn't even an ashtray.

'Has everyone left?' Bordelli asked.

'Yes.'

'What about you?'

'I'll be leaving soon. But I wanted to see you one more time.'

'Where are you going?' Bordelli asked, shuddering. Milena was about three feet away from him, her arms folded over her breasts, hair somehow held back behind her neck by a pen.

'I'm going wherever my work takes me,' she murmured.

'And who is it this time? Mengele? Or another mediocrity like Strüffen?' Bordelli asked. But his mind was elsewhere.

'I can't tell you,' she said with pain in her eyes. They sat for a few moments in silence, looking into each other's eyes. Bordelli pulled out a cigarette and lit it.

'Thanks for Strüffen, but I wanted him alive,' he said.

'You can't always have what you want,' she said.

'Is that why you wanted to see me? To tell me that?'

'I needed to tell you a story.'

'You're already with someone?'

'No, it's not about that.'

'Then what's it about?'

'Davide Rivalta,' said Milena, eyes flashing.

'What's Rivalta got to do with any of this?'

'His real name was Davide Rovigo . . . He was Jewish.'

'Did you know each other?' asked Bordelli, increasingly surprised.

'He was one of ours until a little while ago,' Milena said with a bitter smile.

Bordelli's eyes popped out.

'That's really something . . . And why did he stop being one of yours?' he asked, staring at her.

Milena sighed and leaned her back against the wall.

'He'd started doing things that were against our principles,' she said, lowering her eyes. She seemed very tense.

'For example?'

'Last year . . . when we were supposed to liquidate a Nazi in the Madrid area, Rovigo tried to eliminate his companion as well, a young Spanish woman who had nothing at all to do with the crimes of our target. We don't do that kind of thing. Our organisation is not interested in vengeance. We only execute the sentences passed at Nuremberg.'

'Of course.'

'After that episode, Rovigo was expelled from the Dove, and he took it very badly. When he left he threatened to throw a wrench into our plans and reveal everything he knew about the organisation, and we couldn't allow that. We spend a great deal of money and time locating a person, and we abhor waste. We cannot run the risk of getting any grains of sand in our engine. We'd been keeping an eye on him for some time, but he hadn't done anything unusual.'

'Were you aware the police had him under surveillance?'

'We realised it only a few days ago and were trying to find out why.'

'You could have asked me . . .'

'I decided against it,' she said. Bordelli nodded. He didn't know where to dump his ash, and in the end he let it fall to the floor.

'Did any of you know that Rovigo could leave his house without being seen?' he asked.

'Nobody knew about that passageway. It must have been made during the war. Rovigo seemed to have calmed down. We were becoming convinced he would never carry out his threats against us, and that he'd only been letting off steam. I never imagined—'

'Was it your organisation that killed him?' Bordelli interrupted her.

'Yes . . . because of the little girls,' she said, biting her lip. And she walked slowly to the window and started looking outside. Bordelli took a few steps towards her and stopped behind her. Even then, at such a moment, he could not help but admire her figure, whose beauty showed through her clothing. Milena kept on talking, without turning round.

'Rovigo spent seventeen months at Auschwitz. He suffered unbearable humiliation. He lost a finger there. It was torn off with pliers by camp guards. He managed to survive because he has a degree in chemistry, they'd put him to work in a laboratory. By the time the Russians arrived, he weighed sixty-five pounds. He lost almost all his family in the camps: father, mother, grandparents, cousins, brothers, his wife and . . . his daughter Rebecca, a little girl of eight whom he was madly in love with. He killed those children out of revenge, only because they had German fathers . . .'

'Jesus Christ,' Bordelli muttered.

'He'd become a monster, and we hadn't realised it . . .'

The inspector shook his head.

'He certainly was good at finding those children. In some cases it couldn't have been easy to know they were daughters of Germans,' he said.

'For someone who's worked with us it's easier than you think,' Milena whispered. They remained silent for a moment, not moving. She was still looking down at the street, as he looked at her.

'Why did he bite them on the belly?' Bordelli suddenly asked.

'Somebody'd told him that some drunken SS men had set a German shepherd on Rebecca just before they sent her to the gas chamber, and he probably wanted to avenge that as well. He took it out on little girls who were not to blame for anything, exactly as the Nazis had done. The organisation felt it had to treat him like one of them . . .'

'And so you had him hanged.'

Milena nodded, and then brushed a lock of hair away from her face.

'I took care of it myself,' she said.

'Why you, of all people?' Bordelli asked, sensing something. Milena turned round; her eyes were wet.

'Rovigo was my mother's second husband,' she said.

'Don't leave,' Bordelli said, staring at her.

'I can't do anything about it.'

'Bloody hell, don't leave,' he said again, hands pressing hard into his pockets.

Milena just looked at him stubbornly and said nothing. She was shaking, as if fighting an indomitable remorse, but her eyes were dry again. She drew near to Bordelli and kissed him violently on the mouth, thrusting her tongue forward as if wanting to reach the back of his throat. Then she suddenly pulled away, took his head in her hands and bit his lip, hard, practically making him bleed.

'I have to go now,' she said, staring into his eyes from very close up. Bordelli opened his mouth to say something, but she shook her head as if telling him not to, and then caressed his mouth.

'Did I hurt you?' she asked, taking his face in her hands again. Her fingers were cold. Bordelli didn't reply. He could feel the girl's heart beating chaotically against his chest. He wanted to kiss her, but did nothing. He merely removed Milena's hands calmly from his face and, without saying anything, headed for the door.

★   ★   ★

'What are you brooding about, monkey?'

'Nothing.'

'You seem sad.'

'I'm not.'

'You should be happy.'

'I *am* happy.'

'Liar. I know you too well.'

'I'd rather not talk about it.'

'All right, then, I'll leave you in peace . . . Would you like a little of that cognac you brought me?'

Bordelli nodded and flopped down horizontally on the sofa. He'd hardly slept a wink the previous night, tossing and turning the whole time with a stupid pillow in his arms, and now he was unable to relax. Feeling something poking into his side, he dug into his pocket and found Casimiro's little skeleton. He held it in his hand for a moment, sending a greeting in his mind to the poor little man.

Rosa sat down in front of him and poured some de Maricourt cognac into two snifters.

'To the best policeman I know,' she said.

'How many do you know?'

'Just you,' she said, laughing.

'What do you think of this cognac?'

'Oh, it's delicious,' said Rosa.

That morning Bordelli had gone back to Karl Strüffen's villa with Piras and, stripped down to their shirtsleeves, they had filled the Beetle with bottles. They didn't leave a single one behind. As they were driving back down to the city, Piras had started voicing a barrage of questions he had about the murders, but it was clear he was doing it to provoke Bordelli. There were a number of things he was unable to tie together, the young man said, and other details where he hadn't understood a bloody thing. It was as if he was missing a few important pieces to the puzzle . . .

'Have you finished reading Simone's story?' Bordelli had asked him, pretending not to notice his agitation.

'Of course.'

'Did you like it?'

'He writes well,' Piras limited himself to saying, without even mentioning the coincidence between the story and the case of little girls. It was obvious he was on tenterhooks. He was dying to know everything about the murders, including that of the Nazi.

They had sat for a while without talking, and Bordelli had started humming a song by Modugno.[21] In the end, Piras couldn't hold back any longer.

'I haven't understood a damn thing about any of this, Inspector . . . But I have the feeling that everything is perfectly clear for you,' he'd said decisively, seeing that Bordelli was still playing dumb. The inspector was unable to repress a mischievous smile, since he'd been expecting such a challenge for a long time. Someone like Piras couldn't accept not knowing.

'I'll explain everything, Piras, but first you must swear you'll never tell anyone.'

'Of course I swear,' said the Sardinian, drooling with curiosity.

Bordelli felt he could trust him. He'd lit a cigarette and, driving slowly along, told him everything he knew, leaving nothing out. He'd even told him about the White Dove, but without naming any names. Piras had listened to the whole story and hadn't even complained about the smoke. When it was over, he'd shaken his head.

'Shit, Inspector!'

'It wasn't easy . . .'

'And the upshot is two killers who can't be brought to trial.'

'Well, not quite.'

'Why not?'

'I believe that a beautiful Sicilian girl has come out of this, too . . .'

'What's Sonia got to do with this?' Piras said with a cocky grin on his lips.

'If you ask me, you two have already had sex,' Bordelli ventured in a rather wicked tone. He was bitter over Milena's departure and felt like needling someone better off than him. Piras had given him a dirty look, a single, nasty stare, and shut himself up in the most nuragic of silences for the rest of the drive.

'Come on, Piras, I was just kidding,' Bordelli had said, trying to make up. But Piras needed time to work it off, and kept on wearing a long face. His silence was stony and arid, like his native land.

When at last they got to the station, the inspector had a couple of officers unload the bottles confiscated from the Third Reich, and they'd divvied them up, with everyone getting something or other. Bordelli immediately thought of bringing his share to Rosa's, since it was a lot nicer drinking with her than sitting in front of the telly at home and filling his glass alone. Piras had disappeared for the rest of the day. No doubt he'd gone out again with Sonia, and Bordelli thought of him with a tinge of envy. A Sicilian and a Sardinian, an unpredictable combination . . .

Gideon was asleep, curled up in an armchair, sated with food and travel across the rooftops. Rosa was knitting away. That evening she, too, was rather quiet. She was still working on Bordelli's sweater. She'd made a lot of progress, and every so often would measure it against his person.

Bordelli was thinking of Milena and felt his stomach tighten. He ought not to think of her, didn't want to think of her. Closing his eyes, he let more distant memories carry him away . . . He found himself near Colle Isarco in April of '45, just after the war had ended. He and what remained of his men had stopped a train on its way back to Germany, loaded with stolen goods. One wagon was chock-full of French cognac, and it had taken them several hours to unload it. There were forty of them, and they decided that each man was entitled to three cups of cognac a day: one in the morning for breakfast, one after lunch and the third in the evening. They finished all the bottles in a couple of weeks. It was one of Bordelli's better memories of the war years.

'You still haven't told me your girlfriend's name,' Rosa said suddenly, still working her knitting needles.

'She's not my girlfriend any more,' said Bordelli.

'Poor boy . . . So she's already dumped you?'

'Would you give me a little more cognac?'

As Rosa refilled his glass, Gideon suddenly raised his head, as if he'd heard something. He jumped down from the armchair and went out on to the terrace, tail straight up in the air. It was the night of the new moon, a night as dark as Bordelli's mood . . . Milena had come into his life like a pimple on his skin and had vanished as quickly. But in the end it was better this way. Much better. Thirty years' difference. It was too ridiculous. On the street, people would have taken him for her father, maybe even her grandfather . . . And anyway, it would never have lasted. She was too young, and so beautiful, so dark, with the eyes of a creature of the forest . . . What the hell was she doing with someone like him? Who knew what had initially attracted her? . . . He was just one of many, no doubt, between one White Dove assignment and the next. She'd come into town, slept with a police inspector, and left. What the hell could a girl of twenty-five know about things such as love? . . . But, when you came right down to it, he didn't really believe in it all that much himself – in love, that is. He knocked back a mouthful of cognac and felt it burn in his stomach. Love didn't really exist, he thought. It was only one way, like so many others, to hope that something would never end. An all-too-human delusion, he thought, but not a very intelligent one. Nobody truly loves, nobody really knows what the hell he's talking about when he pronounces the bloody word. Much less a girl of twenty-five as beautiful as her, with coal-black eyes and raven hair, and a slightly roguish mouth that curled up ever so faintly on one side when she spoke . . . Come on, Inspector, thirty years' difference! You're already old and want to play the schoolboy . . . You're ridiculous . . . No, it's much better this way, better it should end immediately . . . Otherwise, one ends up dreaming . . . And he didn't feel like dreaming any more. It was enough to have made love with that dream five or six times . . . He didn't want anything else from her . . . It made no sense to love and dream . . . What the hell was the use? In the end you just die anyway, and nothing is left, not a goddam thing . . .

'What did you say, Rosa?'

'I didn't say a thing, darling.'

'I thought . . .'

'What is it, love? Are you hearing voices?' she said, giggling.

'I think I'll go home to bed. I'm a wreck.'

'Aw, just wait a bit longer, I've almost finished the sweater. Look how lovely . . . Want to try it on?' said Rosa, flourishing it in the air.

'Another time,' said Bordelli, getting up.

'Bah . . . There are a lot of women in this world, Mr Sourpuss.'

'I'm just a bit tired.'

'Bah!'

They said goodbye at the door, and Bordelli lazily descended the stairs. He felt strange. He felt pissed off. Not only because of Milena, but because of everything. He got into his car and drove off. It was past three, and there was nobody about.

Instead of going home, he went to the police station. Only after he was already back in his office did he realise that someone had greeted him on the stairs, and he hadn't replied. He leaned way back in the chair, whose springs were getting weaker by the day, and noticed that the wheels squeaked slightly. He would have to oil them. He lit a cigarette, knowing it wouldn't be the last.

One way or another, the two murders had been solved. Another Nazi had been executed, a child-killer was underground, forever buried with his madness. It was all over. Over . . . At least until the mental balance of someone else started to tip.

As he crushed the fag-end in the ashtray, a big, sluggish fly landed on his wrist. It was fat and black, with hairy legs. The inspector held his hand still, so it wouldn't fly away, and so he wouldn't feel alone.

Acknowledgements

I thank my father, again. When I was a child, he used to tell us war stories after dinner, some of them amusing, some of them horrifying. But he always had a twinkle in his eye that made me think that it must be wonderful to fight in a war. I was so convinced of this that, whenever anyone asked me as a child what I wanted to do when I grew up, I would say: 'Make war.' I later understood that the gleam in my father's eye was only from the joy of storytelling, of being still alive to tell of things that would otherwise have died with him. And perhaps the desire to write is nothing more than this. Even Botta's recipe for pork chops with milk, fennel seeds and tomato sauce came from my father. Here it is:

Botta's Pork Chops
Put the pork chops (preferably not too thick) in a frying pan with a bit of water and cook them well on both sides until the water has almost entirely evaporated. Add a cup of chopped tomatoes and turn the chops several times. Then add a cup of milk and a handful of fennel seeds, and when the sauce begins to boil, turn the heat down and leave uncovered to reduce the liquid until the sauce has reached the proper point of density. Then remove the pan from the burner, cover it and leave it in peace for a couple of minutes.

Thanks also to Véronique for having invented Inspector Bordelli's name.

To Carlo Lucarelli for having saved me at the outline stage.

To Francesca and Enzo for their passionate medical advice.

To my editor Daniela, for having put up with me during proofs.

To Francesco for having pointed out to me a number of passages in need of revision and for having suggested the beautiful Sonia's surname to me.

NOTES

by Stephen Sartarelli

1 – The *Legge Merlin*, a law named after Socialist MP Lina Merlin, was passed in 1959, outlawing organised prostitution, including brothels, while keeping prostitution – that is, the exchange of sexual services for money – technically legal. The effective upshot was to drive most prostitutes into the streets.

2 – See page 33 of the text.

3 – The Torre di Arnolfo is the crenellated spire of the Palazzo Vecchio (also called Palazzo della Signoria) in the central square of Florence. Traditionally attributed to Arnolfo di Cambio (*c.* 1240–*c.* 1300–10), it was built in 1299.

4 – 'Marshal' is a rank specific to the carabinieri in Italy.

5 – Rosolio is a cordial of spirits and sugar often flavoured with rose petals and/or orange blossoms and a variety of spices.

6 – Alkermes (also written *Alchermes* in Italian, from the Arabic *al-qirmiz*, for 'cochineal') is a sweet red liqueur flavoured with herbs and spices and now used principally in the preparation of pastries and for other cooking purposes.

7 – On 8 September 1943, the Armistice was signed between Italy and the Allied forces after the latter had successfully captured the southern half of the peninsula. This was followed by a German invasion and occupation of the north and the resuscitation of Mussolini and his lapsed regime in the puppet government called the Republic of Salò, head-quartered in the small northern town of the same name.

8 – Sweet fried ricecakes typical of Tuscany.

9 – A suburban district of Florence.

10 – Celentano: 'Stay away from me' (1962), a cover, with Italian lyrics, of the Gene McDaniels song 'Tower of Strength'.

11 – A tributary of the Arno on the outskirts of Florence.

12 – Actually, the Normans did more than 'pass through' Sicily. They ruled it from the late eleventh century through the twelfth, and settled there in considerable numbers. The Kingdom of Sicily founded by them lasted, in various forms and sizes, until the early nineteenth century and was the oldest kingdom in Italy before the Unification.

13 – The Viali are the broad, late-nineteenth- and early-twentieth-century boulevards that encircle the ancient centre of Florence.

14 – An Italian sweet flavoured with hazelnuts and almonds and other essences.

15 – Nuragic: Of or pertaining to the *nuraghe*, the conical megaliths in central Sardinia, which have come to symbolise the island. 'Nuragic' thus can also mean, simply, 'Sardinian'.

16 – A school of Italian painters active in Tuscany in the second half of the nineteenth century. Pre-dating the French Impressionists by a decade or two, they painted outdoors and broke up colour into little spots or *macchie*, hence the name *macchiaioli*.

17 – Cecco Angiolieri (1260–1312) was a medieval Italian poet from Siena.

18 – *Ribollita* is a classic Tuscan peasant soup consising, with some possibility of variation, of leftover bread, cannellini beans, carrots, onions, cabbage and chard.

19 – '*Tu vuo' fa' l'americano*' ('You like to pretend you're American') is a popular song from 1956 by Neapolitan singer Renato Carosone (1920–2001). It was sung by Sophia Loren in the 1960 film *It Started in Naples*, with Clark Gable looking on, and was more recently featured in the film *The Talented Mr Ripley*, sung by Fiorello.

20 – *in zimino*: A Tuscan sauce for fish and seafood made of leafy green vegetables, such as spinach or chard, garlic, onion, tomato, white wine and aromatic herbs.

21 – Domenico Modugno (1928–94) was a popular Italian singer, best known for his international hit song '*Volare*'.